BLOODY MAGIC

"Santeros aren't all a bunch of uneducated savages," Kroll said. "They've got all kinds of followers: doctors, lawyers, college professors. People who believe they can attain any goal they want, as long as they have the right magic."

"Doctors and lawyers didn't do *this*," Vince said.

"No Christian ever told them to rip the guts out of a helpless animal," Tommy added.

"I wouldn't be worried about the animals if I were you," Kroll said. "A human being makes the magic even stronger."

And the sight of Cherry Dressor's dismembered, mutilated body flashed before Vince's eyes. . . .

The Killing Moon

Bill Kelly, NYPD
and
Dolph Le Moult

AN ONYX BOOK

NEW AMERICAN LIBRARY

A DIVISION OF PENGUIN BOOKS USA INC.

PUBLISHER'S NOTE

This book is a work of fiction. Names, characters, places, and
incidents either are the product of the author's imagination or are
used fictitiously, and any resemblance to actual persons, living or
dead, events, or locales is entirely coincidental.

Prologue

THE MAYOMBERO SNIFFED THE PREGNANT AIR WITH broad black nostrils like glistening caldrons. He listened carefully to the noises of the trees, insects and frogs, night birds with pale plumage, fluttering bat's wings: the spirit of Oke, the mountain god. Above him a yellow waxing moon hung in the treetops: hiding behind black clouds, reappearing to dance seductively with her daughters, the Irawo stars, never stopping in one place long enough to wane and lose her magic, to fall into the oceans.

The Mayombero squinted into the blackness, his face creased beneath an overlay of ceremonial white paint, ocher dyes taken from hillside clay, maroons ground from berries, patterned into a multicolored girdle of Ochumare, goddess of the rainbow. Unblinking, his hunter's eyes penetrated the black, empty expanse of forest, alert for alien sounds and movements. Finally he saw the thin, flickering trail of lanterns approaching from the east, from the nation of the dead. He turned and went inside, spread a ritual straw mat on the floor, and sat cross-legged in the candlelit room.

One by one, the young men extinguished their lanterns and entered the room. Their naked black bodies gleamed with sweat from their labors, and their faces were smeared with soot and soil. The last to enter approached the Mayombero, placed a black cloth bundle on the straw mat, and unwrapped it. Carefully he separated its contents onto the open cloth and stepped backward.

The Mayombero inspected each part of the *kiyumba,* the dead body. "This is the *mundele*?" he asked them, examining the amputated fingers and toes, the collapsing lump of heart muscle, its pale, severed arteries still oozing blood, and the mound of wrinkled human brain gleaming in the flickering half-light.

"The *mundele,*" they replied in chorus, assuring him that the digits and organs had been taken from the grave of the murderer Farantino, a white man who had been hung on the grounds of the penitentiary and buried only that afternoon.

The Mayombero prostrated himself on the floor beside the array while an assistant covered him in a black sheet and lit five candles, placing one each at the Mayombero's head, feet, and shoulders. He could feel himself tense as his assistant sprinkled the body parts of the *mundele* on top of him. His eyes rolled into the back of his head. The muscles of his jaw tightened reflexively behind a froth of spittle. His legs and arms began to convulse as the spirit of the *kiyumba* entered his body. He was in a place apart now, a place where the gods and spirits of the sacrifice dwelled. Chango, god of fire, thunder, and lightning; Oya, his concubine, writhing sinuously to the rhythm of *bata* drums. Her head was enshrouded in a beaded veil of pearls, and her open satin gown cascaded in her wake. Her firm black breasts peaked to erect nipples, spewing the mother's milk of the galaxy across the sky. Her naked hips writhed, taunting, tempting her beloved to come lie with her and fill the night with stars . . .

The spell ended. The Mayombero stood as his assistant scooped the body parts into a blackened iron pot. He watched as the assembled initiates added wax and ashes to the mixture, then rum and lime, the carcass of a small black dog, the still-shuddering head torn from a live chicken, sand and seawater, the testicles of a bull, herbs and tree bark, and a few drops of holy water from the nearby Cathedral de la Madona del Norte. *"Chango mani cote, Chango mani cote olle masa . . ."* Their blended voices chanted the incantation as the mixture was mashed together with a wooden pestle. *"Chango arabari cote ode mata icote soni sori . . ."*

A portion of the brew was removed from the pot with a tin ladle and given to the Mayombero. He blessed it, sprinkled some on the straw mat in the form of a cross, and waited while his assistant placed seven small piles of gunpowder on the blade of a sharp *fula* knife. He closed his eyes in prayer, allowed a drop of the mixture to fall from the pot onto the knife, and blinked involuntarily as the heaps of gunpowder ignited spontaneously. He grinned with satisfaction, knowing that the magic would be strong. The soul of the murderer was now fused with his soul, existing only to do his bidding. He raised the tin ladle to the night sky, saluted his companions, and drank it down.

The Mayombero sniffed the pregnant air with broad, black nostrils like glistening caldrons. The killing moon hid behind the clouds.

1

Yetta Mink halted at the entrance of the Gateway Shopping Plaza in The Bronx and rearranged the overflowing bags of aluminum cans in her red toy wagon. They were the bounty of an entire night's work rummaging in local trash bins and garbage cans. Two hundred and seven cans: she had counted them twice to make sure. The lazy snot-noses the supermarkets hired these days tossed the cans into their separate bins so fast it was impossible for them to get an accurate count. She had caught them more than once attempting to shortchange her. A few cents here or there meant to them nothing, but to Yetta it was life and death. Two hundred and seven cans translated into ten dollars and thirty five cents in her pocket. She could eat for a week on that kind of money.

Thomas Falcone dug a morsel of bran muffin from his molar with a wooden toothpick and paid his check at the cash register of Patsy's Coffee And in the shopping plaza.

"Whatta you say, Tommy?" Patsy DiStefano asked as he rang Falcone up and handed him change for a twenty-dollar bill. "Gonna be a scorcher out there today, eh, *paisan*?"

Falcone nodded and took a green candy mint from a glass by the cash register. He had been eating breakfast at Patsy's for the past eight years, and every time he finished, Patsy would complain about the weather.

9

"Freeze your nuts out there today, Tommy," he would say in winter; or "Fuckin' drown out there, *paisan*," on a rainy spring day. Falcone left a penny on the counter for the mint and stepped outside into the heat.

Gaetano Bruno saw Falcone headed toward him as he unlocked the metal grating in front of his shoe-repair shop next door to the supermarket. It was just after eight. "Your shoes are ready," he said, ushering Falcone inside, where the air was hot and stale, smelling of leather and polishing wax. "Just give me a minute to shine 'em for you."

Falcone stared idly out the window while Bruno shined his shoes, and saw Yetta Mink winding her way through the parked cars in the lot. She was stooped and grimy, her ulcerated legs oozing yellow between layers of wrapped gauze. He had seen her here before and always felt sorry for her. It was impossible to tell her age behind the soot, but he guessed she was his mother's age, had she lived. He took the brown paper bag containing his shoes from Bruno, paid the bill, and walked outside as she approached.

"Can I give you a hand with your wagon?" he asked courteously as she passed.

She squinted at him suspiciously. "Do I know you?"

"I was here last Wednesday. I helped you carry your cans into the supermarket, remember?"

Yetta did not remember. "Go away," she said angrily, lurching forward into the path of an oncoming bakery truck.

A screech of brakes. The truck missed her by inches. "What the hell do you think you're doing?" the driver yelled out the window at her.

"Stick it where the sun don't shine!" Yetta extended her middle finger and resentfully tugged her wagon away.

Inside the truck, Oxbridge Pell dragged nervously on his cigarette as they resumed driving toward the supermarket at the far end of the shopping plaza. At 8:10, a time he would normally be crawling out of bed and pouring his first cup of coffee, he'd already been on the road for an hour. Worse still, he had at least another four hours to go: six more stops at six more supermarkets, thirty-two more cases of bread and rolls and pastries to be off-loaded before they would head for home and he could climb into the air-conditioned comfort of his BMW.

He stretched in the passenger seat as the driver pulled the truck into a loading zone. Tedium, he thought, noting the exact hour, minute, and second of their arrival on his time sheet, the grinding tedium of the route salesman. In the five years he had been employed in the accounting offices of IBF Industries, he'd come to view their acquisitions, products, and personnel as statistics on a ledger sheet. They were anonymous items of commerce that could be manipulated on his computer screen to improve the profit picture. Now the illuminated figures had acquired new meaning for him. "Transportation expenditures" had become Lulu, a 1978 model green-and-white Dodge truck with a sputtering air conditioner and leaking transmission. "Product" was now seedless rolls and croissants, prune danish and raisin pumpernickel. "Personnel" was a fifty-six-year-old family man with bunions and a bad ticker named Otto Kellerman.

Otto Kellerman was no longer an abstraction, a social-security number and performance-evaluation chart stuffed into a personnel folder. Otto was a man he had shared the last several weeks with, a man who at first viewed him with suspicion because he was from management and management was the enemy. Otto had worked for IBF since his graduation from high school, and he couldn't remember a single moment in all that time when management had done anything for him or his family. Otto was a union man and he was convinced that without the union his family would be living in tatters. He would be retiring in a few months on the small pension his union had won for him. He planned to take his wife, Donna, down south to Cape

Coral, where they could fish and trap crabs and kiss the New York winters good-bye forever.

Oxbridge Pell was doomed to spend the next fifteen years mired in the obscurity of middle management, writing statistical time studies that were even more boring to him than they were to the people who had to read them. He ground his cigarette to powder in the nearly full ashtray on the dashboard and scowled.

The man in the alley next to the supermarket stepped away from the wall to escape the surge of superheated air coming from the air-conditioner outlet. He shielded his eyes from the fireball sun and stared out over the parking lot at the gathering press of vehicles: at an armored Brink's truck parked in front of The Bronx Savings bank. A gray-uniformed guard was casually smoking a cigarette alongside. It would be delivering the weekend receipts from Yonkers Raceway, he knew, perhaps as much as six million in cold, hard cash, sitting there in a sardine can with wheels, waiting for someone to pry it open and help himself. He grinned reflexively as he fingered the small talisman resting next to remote-control unit in his jacket pocket.

He could see Yetta Mink coming toward him, wagon and cans in tow. She was bundled in layers of shirts and shawls and sweaters hanging dark and sooty on her skeletal body. Over all of it a torn black wool coat draped almost to her ankles. He tugged his soaking shirt collar, wondering how she could stand that many clothes on a day like this.

He checked his watch: 8:13. He lifted the remote-control mechanism partially out of his pocket and carefully released the safety switch, noting with satisfaction that the red warning signal at the top lit up as it was supposed to. If today was the same as every other day, it would be only a matter of minutes to the detonation. Schedules were important when you were dealing with something as unstable as high explosives, he knew. Fortunately, his target was on a tight schedule. He poised his thumb carefully above the activating button and scanned the lot.

The gray-uniformed guard standing by the armored car was joined by another, and together they walked to the rear of the vehicle, shouting a prearranged code to the guard inside. He released the locks and opened the doors. Squinting through the haze at the vehicles and pedestrians in the lot, he paused briefly, determined that nothing was amiss, and climbed from the back of the truck with his revolver drawn.

Beyond the Brink's truck, Thomas Falcone made his way across the lot to his blue Volvo sedan, placed the package containing his shoes on the roof, and rummaged through his pocket for his keys. He unlocked the door on the driver's side and was engulfed in a rush of torrid air as he climbed inside. He reached across the seat and opened the window on the passenger's side, angry at himself for leaving the windows sealed in the first place. Suddenly he remembered he had left his package on the roof and stepped back outside onto the steamy pavement.

The explosion tore the sky apart.

Inside the coffee shop, Patsy DiStefano found himself sprawled beneath the counter as the blast blew his store window inward, showering the breakfasters with shattered glass. He was stiff, afraid to move a muscle, afraid to even free himself from the piles of debris that covered him. There was a moment of deathly silence, a moment when the air turned inside out and all he could hear was the ringing in his ears, the exaggerated pumping of his heart. Then a low moan came from the back, and another—a flurry of excited screams. When he finally extracted his left hand and brought it tentatively to his face, his fingers brushed bare cheekbone beneath the blanket of his torn flesh.

The blast hit Gaetano Bruno like a runaway freight train and propelled him backward through the length of the shoe-repair shop, pinning him behind a wall of overturned machinery, splintered wood. He blacked out momentarily, and awoke to the unfamiliar smells of nitroglycerine and cordite. Slowly he realized that his life's work had disintegrated before him. A hot, incessant blast of air, rushed through the open store front, and white cardboard shoe tags and yellow paper receipts fluttered in midair over piles of torn and battered footwear. Then he relaxed, thankful that his life had been spared. He was as yet unaware that his spinal cord had been severed by a blast-propelled length of steel pipe.

Inside the supermarket, Otto Kellerman froze against the bakery shelves as the force of the explosion blew the place apart. An unenunciated shriek of terror swelled inside his throat, paralyzing him, blocking out the sound. He felt his bowels and bladder go, and a tug of wrenching pain as fear gripped his damaged heart and held it in a vise. Then he collapsed onto the debris-strewn floor as it burst and ceased to beat.

Yetta Mink howled in pain as a chunk of ricocheting plaster tore into her ankle. The concussion cleared the forward shelves of merchandise. Soup cans and dish detergent bottles became lethal projectiles, sending patrons and employees scurrying for cover. The seventeen-year-old clerk counting Yetta's treasure dived beneath the counter, upending her wagon and sending the cans flying. She frantically attempted to scoop them up before her entire night's efforts vanished in the smoke and chaos. Then she realized the task was hopeless, and she cried.

2

TAKE-IT-TO-ME, TAKE-IT-TO-ME, TAKE-IT-TO-ME . . . THE blades of the antique floor fan wheezed with every labored rotation, moving the stagnant air, sustaining the illusion of a breeze inside the Three-Seven detective squad room. It was too hot to work in the Homicide room; too hot to put a dent in the piles of paperwork littering the chipped metal desks, to lift the telephone and feel the sucking wet kiss of the receiver on your ear. Too hot to collaborate; to make an effort to communicate with one another, to refill the crusted coffee machine with water, to make bad jokes and groan at them, or laugh at them or even think about them. Too hot to move around, to work up enough energy to go to the crapper. Too hot to fart, almost.

The sultry air hung against them like the press of mortal sin, weighing them down with torpor, immobilizing them in stages of undress that reflected their sex, body condition, and length of service. Detective Third Grade Leila Turner sat near the unoccupied holding pen, legs spread, skirt drawn almost to her waist, fanning herself lethargically with a yellow legal notepad. Detective Third Grade Hector Vargas, who was called Street Crime at the Three-Seven, stood near the open window in his undershirt, his muscles glistening brown with sweat in the reflected morning sunlight. Detective Second Grade Walt Cuzak had unbuttoned his shirt almost to his waist, revealing a sprawl of matted chest hair sprouting from his middle-aged paunch. Vince Crowley, senior detective in the squad, sat motionless at his desk with his shirt sleeves rolled above the elbow, tie removed, collar open at the neck.

It was the thirteenth straight day of 90-degree heat, the hottest July since they started keeping records of such things in The Bronx. The streets of the precinct were almost empty, abandoned by a drained and surly population for the sanctuary of airless apartments: portable fans stirring the torrid atmosphere, fire escapes suspended in dark crevasses between buildings, rusting metal tubs filled to the top with cold water, naked bodies sprawled on clinging sheets, untouching, the sporadic whine and sputter of an air conditioner, but only here and there. Air conditioners were for downtown, where the money was.

Technically, the Three-Seven squad was supposed to be air-conditioned, but that was a joke. The central unit that had been installed when the precinct house was built in 1979 worked about as well as everything else in the gray concrete building that had come to be known as the Führer Bunker. Occasionally it would clatter and gasp, cough up a gust of tepid air that buoyed them momentarily, then descend again into brooding silence.

Car air conditioners worked a little better. As often as they could, the detectives would abandon the squad room for a cruise around the neighborhood to try to uncover something happening on the blistering streets that would look good on the DD-5s, but the heat had discouraged even the criminals. Normally they could count on a sharp rise in crime during the summer months, particularly violent crimes like murder and assault, as the hot weather strained at ties and tempers, but this summer was different. The unrelenting heat and humidity had gone beyond the point of being an irritant and had become a scourge to criminals and police alike.

Spiritless drug dealers put aside their streetwise arrogance for the refuge of boarded-up crack houses and shooting galleries. Veteran hookers in sweat-soaked halter tops and clinging leather hot pants abandoned their favorite street corners for windowless cubicles in welfare hotels. Dreadlocked Rastafarians carrying glistening silver Magnums and black 45s surrendered hard-won street turf to the relentless sun and descended into the dark labyrinths of abandoned tenements. Swaggering Puerto Rican youths wearing satin jackets in defiance of the heat muscled vagrants and junkies out of urine-soaked hallways and basements crawling with vermin. Muggers, rapists, purse-snatchers, shoplifters, pickpockets, had all fled the suffocating streets. Crime was way down in The Bronx, and cop business was bad. It was dull as hell.

The job had become an effort for the detectives of the Thirty-Seventh precinct. Even the matter of who was to be their new commanding officer now that Captain McLarnen had retired was hardly discussed anymore. Nothing much was happening anyway, and they didn't need a C.O. to tell them how to hang around the station house feeling miserable.

Walt Cuzak sat in front of the teletype machine watching the incoming reports through half-open eyes. "Get a load of this," he reported to nobody in particular. "Someone dug up a grave out at Woodlawn Cemetery last night and removed the body. Guy had just been buried yesterday morning."

"Ghouls!" Leila Turner shivered.

"Who'd have the energy in weather like this?" Vince Crowley unbuttoned another shirt button and wiped his sweat-soaked neck with a handkerchief. "Graverobbing's hard work."

"Probably necrophiliacs." Detective Tommy Ippollito suggested as he entered the squad room.

"Necro-*who*?" Street Crime eyed him suspiciously.

"Necrophiliacs. Guys who fuck dead bodies."

"Your mama!" Street Crime scowled.

"Look it up if you don't believe me." Tommy walked

smugly to his desk and began sorting through his paperwork.

"Just goes to show how much you know, humphead," Walt Cuzak said, reading the remainder of the teletype report. "That body wasn't fucked. They just cut off the fingers and toes and took out some entrails."

"Jeez, that's sick. What kind of entrails?" Vince Crowley asked.

Cuzak scanned the report. "Doesn't say. Just entrails."

"What difference does it make?" Leila Turner protested. "This whole conversation is disgusting!"

"Who says the body wasn't fucked, anyway?" Tommy challenged. "What'd they do, take a vaginal smear from a corpse?"

"It was a guy, you jerk," Cuzak shot back. "You can't take a vaginal smear from a guy."

"Probably buggered him," Tommy said. "Necrophiliacs do that sometimes."

"The word is 'necrophile,' not 'necrophiliac,'" Leila Turner said irritably. "And I'd really appreciate it if you all could find something more elevating to talk about than buggering. It's uncomfortable enough in here without that."

The telephone rang and Vince answered it. "Thirty-seven squad, Crowley."

"You can stop being acting C.O., bro." It was the desk sergeant, Augie Piro. "Captain Michael Sweeney will be here to take over before the day is out."

"Sweeney? Where'd you hear that?" Vince asked.

"Just got a call from an unimpeachable source downtown."

"Did your unimpeachable source tell you anything about this guy, like where's he from, for instance?"

"Just his name."

"You ever hear of him before?"

"There was a Sweeney in Safe and Loft in Brooklyn . . . back around '75–76, I think," Piro said.

"Think it's the same guy?"

"Who the hell knows?"

"Thanks, Augie." Vince hung up. "Any of you ever hear of a Captain Michael Sweeney?" he asked the squad.

"Sweeney . . . Sounds familiar." Walt Cuzak searched the ceiling.

"Safe and Loft guy," Vince said.

"Nah, that was Jimmy Sweeney," Walt corrected him. "He retired on a medical disability a couple of years ago. Ulcers, bleeding piles . . . something like that."

Vince walked next door to Robbery, where Steve Appelbaum and Snuffy Quade were sharing a cold pizza and a six-pack of Bud. "Either of you ever hear of a Captain Michael Sweeney?"

"Wasn't there a Sweeney back at the academy?" Snuffy asked.

"Jeez, he'd be a hundred and eight by now," Steve said. "My wife's maiden name was Sweeney."

"No shit, you married a *shiksa*?" Snuffy asked.

"Captain Michael Sweeney," Vince repeated. "I don't think he's any relative of your wife's."

"Not unless he's an alcoholic ignoramus like the rest of them," Steve said. "Come to think of it, he probably is. Why else would they send him up to this cesspool?"

Steve had a point. Whoever he was, Michael Sweeney would be their fourth C.O. in less than three years. Commanding the Thirty-seventh Detective Squad at the Führer Bunker was not considered a prize posting in the hierarchy of the police department, where maintaining a high profile was the prime requisite for advancement. Crime victims in the precinct were powerless and unimportant. They were robbed and beaten and butchered with abandon every day of the week, and nobody downtown gave a rat's ass because it didn't figure in their career plans. Solving crimes done to poor people in poor neighborhoods didn't rate a whole lot of TV time, and TV exposure was the juice of promotions. There were no celebrities at the Three-Seven.

Vince returned to his desk and dialed Squeeze Grady at the 106 precinct in Queens. Squeeze was an old partner from Vince's vice-squad days at the Seven-Three in Brownsville, Brooklyn. He'd gotten his nickname from an uncanny ability to squeeze a fortune of lucrative overtime out of the most routine cases the department had to offer. Squeeze was a legend in the detective division. His methods were so slick and imaginative they had become an underground primer for officers on the way up. O.T. was, after all, the only way most of them could make ends meet.

"Hey, brother, it's Crowley here," Vince said when Squeeze came on the line. "What's happening out there?"

"Vince, you old son of a bitch!" Squeeze seemed genuinely glad to hear from him. "Nothing's happening out here. Nothing ever happens out here. They get two DWI's and a domestic dispute in one week and they think they got a regular crime wave on their hands. I'm lucky if I can glom five or six hours of O.T. a month offa this rinky-dink outfit. What can I do for you, pal?"

"You know everybody who's worth knowing in the department. The name Captain Michael Sweeney mean anything to you?"

"Sweeney . . ." Squeeze rolled it around. "Old guy? Got a gimpy right leg?"

"Probably not," Vince said. "You know how things are today. All the old guys took the money and got out while the getting was good."

"Don't remind me," Squeeze said sourly. "Most of these young punk officers coming up today wouldn't know a homicide from a horse race. Six months outa the academy and they make them lieutenants in charge of community sings or ethnic sensitivities or some crap like that—"

"Captain Michael—"

"Afraid I can't help you, bro. He can't have too much on the ball if they're sending him to the Führer

Bunker. From what I hear, you guys ain't getting the department's shooting stars up there this year."

Vince laughed. "Yeah. Our last three C.O.s sure went out in a blaze of anonymity—" Street Crime signaled Vince from his desk. "Gotta go, Squeeze, talk to you later." He hung up the phone and walked to the front of the squad room.

"Got a report from the Gateway Shopping Plaza." Street Crime handed him a torn sheet of paper. "There's been an explosion. They say it looks like World War Three out there . . . bodies all over the place."

Vince checked the sheet and hastily jotted the time and manner of notification in his notebook. "Okay, ladies and gentlemen, let's lock and load and get our asses in gear." He grabbed his jacket and put it on. "It's time to go out there and start earning those big bucks the city pays us."

The room erupted in a flurry of activity as they dressed, checked their weapons, and headed out the door. The heat was suddenly forgotten in the heady flush of anticipation they all felt. Somewhere out there was death and destruction and human misery: citizens in desperate trouble, outlaws storming the barricades of their frail endurance. And they were a part of it all, the cavalry galloping to the rescue, bugles blaring the charge, repeating rifles and sabers and campaign head-gear pressed flat against their foreheads, cotton ker-chiefs masking the dust from a thousand horses' hooves.

Damn! It was good to be a cop again.

3

NYPD FORM UF61   August 24, 1989
INITIAL REPORT OF CRIME
Det. V. Crowley   COMPLAINT # 8081
INVESTIGATION OF DOA   VISIT TO SCENE

1. At 0921 hours this date, notified by patrol supervisor of an explosion at the Gateway Shopping Plaza, Dyre Ave. at 223 St. (Sector Charlie).

2. At 0951 hours, accompanied by Dets. Ippollito, Vargas, and Cuzak of 37 PDU, arrived at above location and observed an area of extensive damage in the parking lot resulting from the explosion.

3. First officers on the scene, Ptl. Chang and Doolittle, reported two male DOAs and an undetermined number of serious injuries resulting from the explosion.

4. Preliminary questioning of eyewitnesses was inconclusive, and as of this report, the cause of the explosion is yet undetermined.

The Gateway parking lot was a smoking, terrifying montage of twisted metal and broken bodies, haphazardly parked police and emergency vehicles. An inad-

equate cordon of blue-uniformed patrolmen struggled
to contain the gathering press of reporters and bystanders behind yellow plastic barricades. Everywhere
were torn and burned victims, some propped uncomprehendingly against the wheels of automobiles, others screaming out in pain, staggering aimlessly among
the parked cars, numb with shock. Paramedics admin-
istered to the wounded, applying bandages and salves,
carrying them to waiting ambulances on stretchers and
gurneys, administering life-sustaining fluids dripped from
plastic bottles they carried overhead.

Officer Walter Chang lifted the thin strand of yellow
ribbon separating the victims and their rescuers from
the mob of curiosity-seekers and admitted Vince and
Tommy.

"You first on the scene?" Vince asked Chang.

"Me and Johnny Doolittle," Chang replied, leading
them through the litter of broken metal and glass
covering the asphalt surface of the parking lot. "We
were cruising about six blocks away, over on 229th
Street. Sounded like the blast was inside our glove
compartment. The ground shook underneath us,
man—"

"They got any idea what kind of bomb it was?"

Chang shrugged. "Whatever it was, it blew out windows a half-mile away. My guess'd be dynamite, about
six sticks."

Thirty yards away, bomb-unit personnel moved awkwardly through the impact area in bulky web suits:
thirty-five pounds of brown steel mesh protected their
chest and crotch, and thick metal helmets covered
their faces. They walked clumsily, like spacemen in an
alien atmosphere, sifting through the smoldering debris piece by piece, searching for undetonated de-
vices, parts of the mechanism that had set off the
explosion.

Vince and Tommy approached cautiously and were
halted by a member of the squad. "Nobody's allowed

in there until they've checked the area for unexploded bombs."

They backed off and moved around the periphery, past Crime Scene and Emergency Services vehicles rimming the explosion site, past members of the D.A.'s investigative unit recording the scene with hand-held videotape cameras, to the front of the supermarket, where paramedics were positioning a sealed body bag in the rear of the coroner's van. Shem Weisen, Bronx Chief Medical Examiner, emerged from the supermarket looking haggard. "This is a bitch," he mumbled to Vince as he approached.

"How many killed?" Vince asked him.

"Just two so far," Weisen said. "Whoever was in the car that exploded and this guy—" He indicated the body being placed in the van. "Poor son of a bitch had a coronary when the bomb went off."

"Any idea who the guy in the car was?"

Weisen shook his head. "I haven't even gotten to examine him yet—or what's left of him. Those bomb-squad bozos won't let anybody in until they're finished." He wiped his sweat-soaked brow with a paper towel. "I wouldn't be surprised to see some more corpses before this thing is over. There's a lot of debris that hasn't been cleared away yet, and some of the wounded are hurt pretty bad."

Vince continued on down the sidewalk to where Street Crime and Cuzak were questioning a group of bystanders who were all talking at once. "Whatta you got so far?" he asked Walt.

"Not much. Everybody ducked when the thing went off so nobody saw a lot."

"It was horrible!" a woman in the crowd yelled. "There was a fireball that went up in the sky!"

"Anyone suspicious seen in the area?" Vince asked.

"We're checking it out," Walt said.

Vince scanned the street beyond the parking lot.

"Let's make a sweep of those buildings. If it was remote, it could've been detonated from out there."

"Check." Walt signaled Street Crime to start the search.

Tommy Ippollito had begun questioning a short, nervous man standing near an empty bakery truck. "This is Mr. Oxbridge, Pell," he told Vince as he approached. "Mr. Pell was in the bakery truck when the bomb went off. He says he got a pretty good look at the explosion."

"Do you work for the bakery?" Vince asked.

"I'm an auditor for IBF Industries," Pell replied shakily. "The bakery is one of our acquisitions."

"And just how did you happen to be in the truck, sir?"

"I was doing a time study . . ." Pell took a deep breath to calm himself. "Can you imagine? My first time out in the field, and something like this happens."

"You must've been pretty frightened," Vince said.

Pell shrugged. "Sure, who wouldn't be? But I saw it all. I'll never forget what I saw."

Vince shot a sidelong glance at Tommy. "Okay, Mr. Pell, if you'll just give your statement to Detective Ippollito here, it'll be a big help to us—"

"I know what you're thinking, Officer," Pell interrupted him. "You're probably saying to yourself, 'How could this little jerk see anything when he was cowering on the floor of a bakery truck, afraid for his life?' Let me tell you something. I've been with IBF almost five years. I'm what the corporate world calls a 'bean counter.' That's basically a detail man, somebody who gets paid a lot of money to keep track of a lot of stuff nobody else wants to be bothered with. I get paid to notice things other people wouldn't ordinarily notice, things that could affect efficiency, productivity. I may not be the bravest guy in the world, but I saw what happened whether I wanted to or not. I guess it's my training."

Vince smiled. "And what did you see, Mr. Pell?"

Pell steadied himself. "There was a man, middle-aged, wearing a brown suit with stripes. He left the coffee shop, went into the shoe-repair shop, and stayed in there a few minutes, then came out carrying a package, walked across the parking lot, and got into a blue sedan. That was the car that exploded. It blew him up across the lot like he was a rag doll." He shivered.

Tommy wrote the information in his notebook. "Anything else you remember?" he asked. "Did you see anyone suspicious in the lot prior to the explosion?"

"I'm afraid that's all," Pell apologized.

Tommy closed his notebook. "Thanks, Mr. Pell. This information will be very useful to us. I'd appreciate it if you'd stay available in case we need to talk to you some more. Can you be reached at your office?"

Pell closed his eyes and sighed. "No, I don't think so. Not for a while, at least. I think I'll go home and spend some time with my family. IBF will get along fine without another bean counter for a couple of days, know what I mean?"

For the first time, Vince noticed that Pell was standing in his stocking feet. "How did that happen?" he asked.

Pell looked down. "I dunno. I must've taken my shoes off while all this was going on."

"Was there a reason for that, sir?"

Pell shrugged. "Beats me . . . Funny what you find yourself doing at a time like that."

Media vehicles had begun to arrive: cameramen with searching minicams, network stringers with microphones cornering anyone who was willing to talk to them. They assembled a picture of what happened from on-lookers, shopkeepers, emergency medical personnel, scribbled notes, as the cameras swept the scene of destruction, spoke solemnly into the camera of outrage and loss. Technology being what it was, an abundance of misinformation would be splashed across television screens in a matter of minutes, but there was little the police could do about it. The explosion was a media event, and an unspoken departmental taboo prohibited anyone on the scene from making a statement to the press. One of the glamour boys from downtown would be along shortly to preen for the cameras. It was too glittering a photo opportunity for them to pass up.

A member of the bomb squad informed Shem Weisen that the impact area had been cleared. Vince and Tommy followed him through the maze of random devastation in the parking lot to the bloodied, broken heap of what had once been a man. Weisen checked mechanically for the remnants of a pulse, then began examining shreds of the victim's clothing.

"Any I.D.?" Vince asked him.

Weisen shook his head negatively.

"The bomb guys found parts of a wallet all over the place," a nearby patrolman volunteered. "I think they gave it to somebody from CSU."

"It was probably blown from the body flagrante delicto," Tommy volunteered.

"What the fuck are you talking about, Ippollito?" Weisen groaned.

"Flagrante delicto, while the crime was being committed," Tommy responded. "It's a criminology term."

"Tommy's taking a night-school course in criminology," Vince explained to Weisen.

"Don't you ever stop taking those goddamn courses?" Weisen grumped, probing the victim's legs and groin. "Last time I saw you it was business law. Before that it was creative writing or some crap like that. What the hell's with you anyway? Can't you just be a cop like everybody else at the Three-Seven?"

Tommy rolled his eyes. "I might've expected that from some of the dopes back at the precinct, Shem, but I figured you for having a bigger vision than that. You're supposed to be a scientist, for chrissake."

Weisen eyed him malignantly. "Get this straight, Ippollito. I can't get through an afternoon on this stinking job without downing a quart of sour mash bourbon. Does that sound like science to you?"

"It sounds to me like you better track down someone from CSU and see what you can find out about that wallet they found, Tommy," Vince broke in. "Let's see if the I.D. matches up with what we got here."

"Knowledge is freedom," Tommy protested to Weisen as he departed.

"Your ass sucks grass," Weisen shot back.

"Don't mind Tommy," Vince said after he was gone. "He's just restless, you know how young guys are."

"Let him be restless someplace else," Weisen muttered resentfully. "This job's hard enough without having to translate his bullshit. Flagrante delicto . . ." He shook his head. "If that don't beat all . . ."

He was probing the victim's chest, inserting his rubber-gloved fingers into angry wounds torn open by the blast. "This guy's too intact to have been in that car," he said flatly. "If he'd been sitting in the driver's seat, his whole lower torso would've been blown away, judging from the force of the blast. His chest wall is caved in, skull and upper body sustained typical blunt-force injuries, but he's too damn clean to have been inside. My guess is he was someplace near the vehicle, but not in it."

Vince penciled the comment in his notebook. "That could rule out an ignition-detonated device, couldn't it?"

Weisen looked up at him irritably. "I'm a coroner, for chrissakes, not an explosives expert."

Vince ignored the outburst. "Too powerful to have been a grenade. Most likely a time mechanism or remote," he said, to himself.

Tommy made his way through the gathering throng

of emergency police and fire personnel crowding into the now-cleared impact site. "I.D. in the wallet they found was for a Thomas Falcone—" He checked his hastily scribbled notes. "3180 McLean Avenue, Yonkers."

"Age, height, weight?" Weisen asked impatiently.

"Birth date, September 15, 1949. Five foot, nine and a half inches. One seventy pounds," Tommy read from the notebook. "Eyes brown, hair brown."

Weisen examined the blood- and soot-covered face. "That'd be about right. Probably the same guy."

"Falcone. You ever hear that name before?" Vince asked Tommy.

Tommy searched the sky. "Not really."

"Not a mob guy . . . a politician maybe? Solid citizens don't go getting themselves blown up in parking lots."

Tommy shrugged. "Maybe it was an accident."

Vince eyed the devastation in the parking lot. "Yeah, like Hiroshima was an accident."

Weisen stood, motioned for his assistants to remove the body to the waiting M.E.'s van. "If you want my opinion, you're damn lucky it happened when it did. A little later in the afternoon and you would've had dozens of bodies out here. Whatever went off in that car was a blockbuster. I was a medic in Korea and I saw artillery explosions that didn't do this much damage."

"What's the count so far?" Tommy asked.

"Just the two dead. Ten or twelve wounded." Weisen began walking toward the van. "A lot of trauma injuries. I got a shoemaker who'll probably never walk again."

Tommy shook his head. "I don't get it. A guy wants to ice someone, why not stick a knife in his ribs or shoot him in an alley someplace like any decent killer would do? What's the point in blowing away innocent bystanders? It just doesn't make any sense at all."

"Who said this business was supposed to make

sense?" Vince commented, accompanying Weisen to the door of the van. "We're just supposed to catch 'em, cuff 'em, and read them their rights, not make sense outa them. We're cops, remember? Not shrinks."

"You guys want to join me inside for a quick pop of eighteen-year-old hooch?" Weisen asked, entering the van.

Vince checked his watch. "Maybe later, Shem, when we got a little more time."

Weisen shrugged. "So I'll drink with my clients inside. They got all the time in the world."

"Speaking of your clients, what am I if I'm humping dead bodies, a necrophile or a necrophiliac?" Tommy asked him.

Weisen scowled. "Jesus, Ippollito. Don't you have enough going on in your life without getting into that shit?"

4

NYSDMV FORM G-7   PAGE 01
DMV COMPUTER REC. TERMINAL P36
RESPONSE TO YOUR INQUIRY: THOS. IPPOLLITO, DET.
37PDU.
TIME: 10:36. DATE 08/24/89

QUERY SENT TO NCIC AND NLETS***
NO NY STOLEN/WANTED INFORMATION FOR PLATE #
WD1388
MVD INFO*** REGISTRATION INFO***
   REG WY6751 STATE N.Y. EXP DT. 05/90 TYP REG 01
   VEHICLE YR. 88 MAKE VOLVO MODEL 2806 STYLE 4DR
   COLOR BLUE VEH. ID # 196390573650063 TAX TN 13520
REGISTERED TO: ANDREA I. FALCONE
3180 MCLEAN AVE., YONKERS, N.Y.

Andrea Falcone parted her curtains and watched the two strangers climbing her front steps. There was something about them that she didn't like, something grim in their plodding ascent that told her they meant nothing but trouble. She closed the curtains, pressed the wrinkles from her apron with open palms, and waited for the knock on her front door.

"Mrs. Andrea Falcone?" Vince Crowley asked as she opened the door.

"Yes?"

"Is your husband Thomas Falcone?"

"Yes . . ."

"Mrs. Falcone, I'm Detective Crowley from the Thirty-seventh Precinct in The Bronx. This is Detective Ippollito. I wonder if we might have a few words with you inside?"

She became alarmed. "What is it? Is something wrong?"

"If we could just come inside, Mrs. Falcone," Vince urged her.

"Something's wrong, isn't it?" Her eyes had become wide, pleading.

"I'm afraid so, ma'am. Maybe we should go inside where you can sit down."

"Oh, my God, it's Thomas. Something happened to Thomas!" She backed away from the door. Her trembling hands covered her open mouth. "What is it?"

Vince placed a hand on her shoulder and steered her toward an overstuffed sofa in the front parlor. "I'm afraid your husband has been in a serious accident—"

"What kind of accident? Where is he? I want you to take me to him."

Vince steadied her as they walked. "I'm very sorry, Mrs. Falcone."

"Thomas isn't dead, is he?"

"I wish there was something I could do, Mrs. Falcone."

Vince and Tommy both grabbed her as she sagged onto the sofa, gasping, her face contorted in disbelief. She pushed them away angrily, stared into the empty hallway, where a man's raincoat and hat hung limply from a wooden peg by the door. "You've made some mistake. It couldn't have been Thomas. He was just here."

Vince stood awkwardly before her as she collapsed into a sobbing, birdlike mound. "It was very quick. Your husband was in no pain." It was a bumbling, predictable thing to say. As many times as he'd had to do this over the years, the canned reassurances always sounded hollow and inadequate.

"How did it happen?" she asked weakly.

"There was an explosion, ma'am . . . his automobile. Is there someone I can call for you—a relative, a neighbor maybe?"

She shook her head. "I don't understand. Was he in a crash?"

Vince shot a quick glance at Tommy. "Maybe your priest or minister?"

"Thomas is a very good driver."

Vince looked around the small, cozy living room filled with comfortable clutter. His eyes stopped at a framed photograph on the wall, a portrait of a younger Andrea holding an infant in her lap. "I don't think you should be alone at a time like this, Mrs. Falcone. Do you have a son or daughter I could call?"

She stared at Vince with red-rimmed eyes. "You're not answering my question! How did it happen? I have a right to know!"

"There was an explosion. We believe an explosive device was detonated in or near his car."

"He was murdered?"

"We have no way of knowing that yet, Mrs. Falcone."

"Everybody loved Thomas!" She choked. "He was a wonderful husband, a wonderful father . . ." She began sobbing again. "He didn't have an enemy in the world."

Vince and Tommy drove silently, shaken by the encounter.

"How do you see it?" Tommy asked finally as he pulled into one of the designated parking places in front of the precinct. "By me, this guy was no big shot. Nobody worth blowing away, if you know what I mean. I got furniture that's better than what I saw in that living room."

"Hard to tell at this point. A guy doesn't have to be

rich to have enemies." Vince stopped at the front desk to return th short-wave radio he'd checked out earlier.

"Bad one out there, huh?" Augie Piro asked him.

"World War Three, bro," Vince said. "Any sign of that Sweeney guy while we were gone?"

"Ain't seen hide nor hair, but he might've slipped by while I was in the back with Doyle and Novack. They were the sector car that took that Woodlawn Cemetery call this morning. Really crazy shit, man. They cut out the heart and liver—ritualistic shit like that."

"Doyle and Novack cut out the heart and liver?" Tommy asked.

Piro eyed Tommy malevolently. "Get yourself a partner who don't have shit for brains, Crowley."

Vince walked back to the turnout room, where officers Bobby Doyle and Stosh Novack were lounging in front of the TV set, intently watching a soap opera. "Hear you guys pulled a weird one this morning."

"Fuckin' awful," Doyle responded, his eyes glued to the set. "I never seen nothing like it."

Vince switched off the set. "Wanta tell me about it?"

"What'd you go and do that for?" Novack moaned. "It was just starting to get good."

"The cemetery," Vince reminded them. "What happened?"

"Somebody dug up a body . . ." Doyle checked his notebook. "Guy named Farantino, just buried yesterday. They hacked the body up, took out the heart and liver and God knows what else, cut off the poor stiff's cock and his fingers, burned some candles, and sprinkled chicken feathers all over the place."

"Chicken feathers?"

"Looked like chicken," Doyle said. "Maybe it was a pigeon. Who the fuck knows?"

"Was the body buggered?" Tommy asked.

"Buggered?" Doyle looked questioningly at Novack and shrugged. "Coulda been, I guess."

"Necrophiliacs," Tommy said, nodding knowingly.

"There were markings scratched in the ground alongside the corpse. Circles and swirls, shit like that," Novack added.

"You get any pictures?" Vince asked.

"Guys from the D.A.'s office were out there. They took shots of everything," Doyle said.

Vince shot a puzzled look at Tommy. "The D.A.'s guys were out there? What the hell for?"

Doyle shrugged. "Hey, man, ours is not to reason why . . . Know what I mean?"

"Check." Vince flipped the dial and the TV screen came alive with the soap opera: *God, Ginny, you're going to have to face it once and for all. Your father is a latent homosexual . . .*"

"Why do you think the D.A.'s so interested in a grave robbing?" Tommy asked as they climbed the stairs to the squad room.

"Beats me. Maybe the stiff was a relative." Passing the C.O.'s office, Vince looked inside. "No sign of our new leader?" he asked Leila Turner.

She tore a sheet of paper from the notepad on her desk. "Not on my tour, but there was some swinging young bimbo up here asking for you. I dunno, Crowley. There must be something about you that I'm just missing." Turner grinned and wiggled her hips provocatively as she handed it to him.

"Bimbo?" Vince scanned the handwritten note. "Whatta you mean, bimbo? This is my daughter Katie, for chrissake."

"Your daughter?"

"Yeah. Something wrong with that?" Vince walked to his desk and began to dial the number on the note.

Turner shrugged. "Nothing wrong. I'm just surprised you have a daughter so . . . sophisticated."

"Katie, it's Daddy," Vince said when she answered the phone.

"Daddy. I'm sorry I missed you at your office."

"Where are you?" Vince asked.

"In Brooklyn. Didn't Mother tell you?"

Vince was embarrassed to admit he hadn't spoken with his ex-wife, Jessy, in months. "Not really. What's up?"

There was a pause. "Maybe we ought to get together, Daddy. Are you free tonight?"

"I have plans for tonight, but I could break them—"

"It's really not all that important," she interrupted him. "Tomorrow's okay. Actually any time is fine."

"You going to be there for a while?"

Another pause. "I'm living here now."

"Living there . . . in *Brooklyn*?"

"I'll tell you all about it when I see you."

"Why not tell me about it now?"

"Talk to Mother, then call me back and we'll have lunch"

"What's going on, Katie? You're not living out there by yourself, are you?" Vince asked.

"God, Daddy, I'm not a child anymore," she wailed.

"You're seventeen."

"I was eighteen last month." Katie hung up.

"What's that all about, partner?" Tommy asked as Vince replaced the receiver.

"Katie, my daughter. She's living in Brooklyn."

"What's wrong with Brooklyn?" Detective Steve Appelbaum asked from the doorway of the Robbery room.

"Katie's just a kid."

"So? Brooklyn's fulla kids."

"Not my kids." Vince dialed Jessy in Connecticut.

"Katie just called," he sputtered when she came on the line. "What's going on anyway?"

"Nice to hear from you, Vince." Jessy's voice was cool.

"Hi, Jess. How's everything up in Marion? How're you feeling? Still going to the AA meetings? How're Kelly and her new boyfriend? Your old man? Let's see, what else? Oh, yeah, what the hell is going on with Katie?"

Silence. "Sarcasm doesn't become you, Vince," Jessy said finally. "It never did."

He grimaced. "Okay. I should've called before this. I'm sorry. Would you mind telling me what's with our youngest daughter . . . please?"

"I imagine you know as much about it as I do," Jessy said. "Katie's decided to live in Brooklyn and become an artist."

"Can't she be an artist in Connecticut?"

"Katie couldn't be an artist anywhere," Jessy said acidly. "She couldn't draw a straight line if her life depended on it."

"So what's with Brooklyn?"

Jessie paused, breathed heavily into the receiver. "She's living with a man . . . a Pakistani she met in Paris last summer."

"A what?"

"His name is Senji Rula. He's some kind of swami or something."

The air went out of him. His mind raced for a picture of a Pakistani. Had he known any? Worked with any? Arrested any? None that he could remember. They were short and swarthy and sinister, he decided; evil, bearded images hidden behind layers of greasy cotton robes, curved scimitars hanging at their waists, herding innocent, young American girls into the bowels of creaking ships that would transport them into a life of white slavery. "How the hell could you let a thing like this happen?" he demanded.

"I didn't let anything happen," Jessy answered. "I heard about it the same way you did. She just called me last week and told me about it."

There was a flurry of activity in the outside hallway. Vince saw an unfamiliar figure enter the C.O.'s office. "I can't talk about it now, Jess. I think our new commander just walked in. I'll talk to Katie tomorrow and straighten this whole thing out."

"And just what is it you're planning to do?" Jessy asked.

"Talk to her, for chrissake. Somebody in this family's got to set her straight."

"I see." Jessy's voice had become icy. "All of a sudden you're planning on becoming a father?"

He rolled his eyes. "Hey, that's unfair. You know I've always been there when Katie needed me."

"Like you were there for her birthday last month?" The phone went dead.

5

"IT WAS A SCENE REMINISCENT OF STRIFE-TORN LEB-anon or the north of Ireland: shattered storefronts, smoking heaps of twisted metal, everywhere the cries of the wounded, the dying . . ."

Vince watched the morning report of the Gateway Plaza explosion as he dressed. The sonorous voice of a male reporter muscled in above the pictures of death and destruction: ". . . Police speculate that an explosive device was placed in a parked automobile, possibly detonated by a timer mechanism . . ." The screen became a close-up of a fully uniformed, gold-braided police inspector looking somber and concerned.

Vince switched off the set with the remote control. "I thought I'd see you out there yesterday," he said to Connie, who was still curled in a tight ball beneath the sheets on the bed.

Connie Talbot rolled and stretched. "Um, what time did you get in last night?" she asked sleepily.

"Late. You were sound asleep."

"The story of our lives." She struggled to a sitting position. "Is that coffee I smell?"

"Hot and strong." Vince took a sip from the mug on his nightstand. "Gimme a second and I'll get you some."

Connie watched him as he continued dressing. "This is getting to be a routine with us, Crowley. You know?"

"What's that?" he yelled behind as he walked to the kitchen.

"I get home and you're out on a case. You get home and I'm out covering a story for the network. One way or the other we both end up going to bed alone."

Vince returned to the bedroom and handed her a cup of steaming black coffee. "It's our jobs. Cops and TV reporters don't get to live normal lives, you know that."

"I know it, but I don't have to like it." She drank some of the coffee and made a face. "God, Crowley, you did it again. This coffee is strong enough to develop primitive life-forms. Did you use water or just melt the beans down on the stove?"

Vince grinned. "Precinct coffee. The only way I know how to make it."

"Any sign of your new C.O. yet?" Connie asked.

"I dunno. There was a guy nosing around in the office yesterday that might've been him, but he just checked things out and left without saying anything to anybody."

"Why didn't you go up and introduce yourself to him?" she asked innocently.

Vince rolled his eyes. "You got a lot to learn about the police department." He drained his mug. "So how come you weren't out there covering the Gateway blast yesterday? You could've done a better job that that putz your station sent."

"Don't ask." She sank back into the pillows. "For some reason the powers-that-be have decided I should start covering the political beat. Instead of chasing the really juicy stories, they have me trying to worm straight answers out of birdbrains who wouldn't recognize the truth if it hit them over the head."

"Hey, I thought you were tired of standing out in the rain and catching cheeseburgers on the run. At least your politicians stay mostly inside, and they eat pretty good."

Connie stared at the ceiling and moaned. "I wish I was a secretary or a computer programmer, something really dull and predictable like that. God, I hate all these intrigues."

Vince sat on the side of the bed and ran his fingers through the tangle of her hair. "Don't give me that, Connie Talbot. You love being famous, and you know it. You'd go nuts if you went out to dinner and weren't recognized by at least one person in the restaurant." He buried his face in the crevasse of her neck and allowed his hand to slip inside her nightgown and caress her warm breasts. "Two weeks away from the network and you'd be a complete basket case."

"I'd be willing to try if you would," she said, resolutely ignoring his advances.

"Try what?"

"Something different." Connie sat upright on the bed. "How long have we been roomies, Vince, six, seven months?"

"Something like that."

"And in all that time, how many evenings have we spent together?"

"Jeez, you're beginning to sound like Jessy." Vince stood and resumed dressing. "I'm a cop, Connie. You knew all about that when we started."

"I guess." She extricated herself from the bed, made her way to the window, and looked out at the morning crush of delivery trucks clogging the street below, the cacophony of their horns and engines lost in the hum of the air conditioner. "Dinner tonight?"

"I promised to meet Katie. I could bring her over if you'd like."

Connie thought about it. "Better not. One of us probably isn't ready for that yet." She walked him to the door and kissed him lightly on the cheek. "See you one of these days, cop."

"Yeah, newsperson, one of these days."

Tommy was waiting for him when he arrived at the squad.

"Got some follow-up on Thomas Falcone." He opened a thin manila envelope with the victim's name written across the front in ballpoint pen. "Seems he was a salesman for a manufacturing company here in The Bronx." Tommy checked the folder. "Contech, out in Throgg's Neck by the projects. They manufacture small gasoline motors and machine parts, it says here."

Vince checked his phone messages. "Anything else?"

"Shem Weisen sent a copy of his report." Tommy handed it to Vince. "Nothing surprising. Falcone died of severe blunt force injuries to the brain. Lotsa broken bones, caved-in chest wall, massive loss of blood. About what you'd expect from an explosion like that."

Vince scanned the coroner's report and the accompanying color photographs of the body: eight close-up Polaroids of individual wounds on the head, limbs, and torso. "How about our eyewitnesses? Anything new there?"

Tommy shrugged. "Nothing we can take to the bank. Everybody was too busy covering up to see what was going on."

"Anything from Forensics yet?"

"Not yet. Want me to give them a goose?" Tommy asked.

"Too hot to cause trouble." Vince unbuttoned his shirt collar. "Let's travel out to Throgg's Neck and see if we can find out why a manufacturing salesman was important enough to get himself blown away."

They drove leisurely, relishing the cool blast of the car's air conditioner, found the plant in an almost-deserted section near the bay and circled it several times before Tommy pulled up to the padlocked gate.

"Can I help you gentlemen?" A tall black man dressed in the uniform of a security guard approached them from a shed near the gate.

"Police." Tommy flashed his shield. "We'd like to speak with someone in charge."

The guard checked Tommy's I.D. carefully, returned to the shed, and obtained permission on the telephone for them to enter. "You'll want to see Mr. David Benítez, the plant manager." He pointed to a door near the side of the brown one-story structure, unlocked the gate, and let them pass.

Inside, they were met by a male Hispanic thirty to thirty-five years of age, average height and weight, bearing no outward scars or contusions. Vince and Tommy produced their identification and followed him through a maze of small cubicles to his office at the rear of the plant.

"Now, what can I do for you gentlemen?" Benítez asked when they were seated.

"I presume you've heard about Thomas Falcone," Vince began.

Benítez shook his head sadly. "Terrible thing. Tom was one of this organization's most-valued employees. I can't understand how a thing like this could happen."

"We'd appreciate it if you could fill us in on his association with your company. How long he worked for Contech, what his job was, his friends, possibly any enemies—stuff like that." Vince said.

"Let's see." Benítez searched the ceiling. "Tom Falcone was here when I began working for Contech eight years ago. I'd have to pull his personnel file to give you the exact date he started with us. His job description was account supervisor, but that's just a fancy way of saying he was a salesman. As far as friends, I don't think there was anyone here who didn't like Tom. He certainly didn't have any enemies that I was aware of. Tom Falcone was a decent, upstanding family man, Detective. I don't think you'll find anyone in this company who'll tell you otherwise."

"Can you tell us what it was he sold for your company and who he sold it to?"

Benítez smiled faintly. "That's a harder question than it sounds. It'd be safer for me to answer it if I told you a little bit about the company itself. Contech started as a small, minority-owned machine tool shop in the mid-seventies fabricating industrial parts for local industry. In 1984 the company received its first federal contract under guidelines mandating that a percentage of government business be awarded to minority enterprises. All that means is that we finally were given a slice of the pie. We could bid in areas where we were formerly shut out by huge, monopolistic interests, and be given equal or in some cases better-than-equal status when it came to the awarding of government contracts."

Vince nodded. "Equal opportunity, makes sense to me. And what was Thomas Falcone's part in all of this?"

"Well, among other things, he represented our interests in Washington. Tom spent a great deal of time there. If you check his personnel files, you'll see he wasn't here more than a couple of days every week."

"So he was a lobbyist," Vince said.

"If you want to call it that. To be fair, though, Tom was more than just that. He started here as an apprentice machinist and he knew every facet of the operation from the ground up. I guess you could say he was a field engineer, a super salesman, and an ambassador of good will for us, all wrapped up in one."

"When he was here, did he have an office?" Vince asked.

"Sure, what there was of it." Benítez led them to a one of the cubicles down the hall, unfurnished except for a plain metal desk, an electronic typewriter, a neglected house plant in the corner. "Tom never used this much. He preferred working in the field, even made most of his phone calls from public booths."

Vince and Tommy looked around the cubicle. Its stark field gray walls were unadorned except for a small calendar bearing the emblem of a local Bronx savings bank. Vince flipped through the pages of the calendar, then turned his attention to the desk. There was a photograph of Andrea Falcone in a plain silver frame, resting near the telephone. Vince lifted it and read the handwritten inscription: "More than yesterday, less than tomorrow, Andrea." He replaced it on the desk and began sorting through the drawers.

"Not much here," he commented as he opened the almost-empty drawers. "Looks like he hardly ever used this place."

"Like I said, he was pretty much on the go all the time," Benítez said from the doorway.

Vince gathered a few scraps of paper from the top drawer. "Okay if I take these with me?"

"Sure. Take anything you think will be of help," Benítez agreed.

Vince found a sheet of blank paper, inserted it in the typewriter, and activated the memory button. Dutifully, the machine printed out its last message, a short note addressed to someone named Julio: "Had a wonderful time with our mutual friend and companions. Hope to see you soon. Best, Tom." Vince showed the note to Benítez. "Any idea who this Julio might be?"

Benítez shrugged. "We're a minority-operated enterprise, Julio's a fairly common Hispanic name."

Vince folded the note and put in his pocket. "You have any idea when Falcone might've typed this?"

"Not a clue," Benítez answered. "I can find out when he was last in the office, but I can't tell you whether he used the typewriter. As a matter of fact, Tom rarely used it as I recall. He wasn't much for modern technological gadgets. I think deep down inside he was really a seat-of-the-pants machinist up to the end."

"Okay." Vince gathered up his meager acquisitions. "I'm going to need to talk to anyone here who did business with him on a regular basis, Mr. Benítez. I'd appreciate it if you could make up a list of those persons and get it to me in the next day or so. Also, I'd like a copy of your telephone records for the past six months to a year, particularly those calls made from this office. Is that going to be a problem for you?"

Benítez hesitated. "I don't think so. I'll have to check with the owners before I can get them to you."

Vince took a last look around the tiny office. "Why don't you have the owners bring the material with them when they come in to see me? I'm assuming they'll be on that list you make up."

"Of course. I'm sure they'll want to cooperate with you in any way possible. Tom Falcone was a valued employee and a valued friend. A big chunk of our operation was invested in him."

"Hard man to replace, I guess," Vince observed.

"Impossible," Benítez concurred.

"Any idea why someone would want to put a bomb in his automobile?"

Benítez shook his head. "It's the craziest thing I ever heard. The only thing I can say is it must have been a case of mistaken identity. Tom Falcone didn't have an enemy in the world."

Outside in the parking lot, Vince rested against the side of the car, waiting for the furnacelike air inside to escape through the open door. "I dunno, Tommy. Something just doesn't add up here."

"What's that?" Tommy asked.

"Falcone's desk had been cleared out. Somebody's been through it in the last twenty-four hours, rifled through the drawers and wiped everything clean."

"How can you be sure of that?"

"No dust."

"So maybe they have a cleaning lady?" Tommy suggested.

"There was dust on everything else in the room. Did you see that plant in the corner? It was dead as a doornail, hadn't been watered in months. Cleaning ladies are real careful to take care of things like that. The leaves of the plant were covered with dust and so were the keys of the typewriter. Whoever cleaned that place was strictly interested in what was on or in that desk. Like I said, it just doesn't add up."

Tommy climbed into the driver's seat and started the car. "So whatta you make of it?"

"I dunno . . ." Vince felt the cold breeze from the air conditioner on his sweating face and eased back into the vinyl upholstery. "I dunno, partner, but I'm gonna find out."

6

WALT CUZAK, SNUFFY QUADE, AND STREET CRIME were gathered in front of the television set in the squad room when Vince and Tommy returned.

"You just missed your girlfriend interviewing our illustrious district attorney," Walt said.

"Tom Quinlan? What about?" Vince asked.

"Seems he's thrown his hat in the ring. He's going for Guido Derosa's old congressional seat in the nineteenth district."

"I'll be dipped." Vince deposited the papers he had taken from Contech on his desk. "What makes him think he's got a chance of taking that seat away from Santiago?"

"Beats me." Walt shrugged. "Ask him yourself. All he said on camera was the usual political shit about getting The Bronx moving again."

Guffaws all around.

Quinlan's announcement was not a big surprise to Vince. The energetic Bronx D.A. had been on a career fast track for as long as Vince had known him, keeping his name in the news while he was scanning the horizons, poised for his shot at the political big time. The untimely death of eight-time congressman Guido Derosa must have seemed like that shot to Quinlan, Vince thought, shuffling through the random scraps of paper on the desk. Julian Santiago, the man named to complete Derosa's unexpired term, was having trouble filling the old man's shoes. There were rumors of scandal, disappointment at his political naïveté. By the uncompromising standards of Bronx politics, Santiago was considered a lightweight.

"He may be overreaching here. Santiago may be a dope, but he's a Latino dope," Tommy observed. "That district's gotta be fifty percent Puerto Rican."

"You think Latinos just vote for other Latinos?" Street Crime challenged him. "What the Hispanics in this city want is decent jobs and housing, man; a chance for their kids to walk down the street without being assaulted by some crack junkie. Not some semiilliterate figurehead who's only qualification for the job is that he was born south of the border."

"Hey, calm down, man." Tommy threw his hands helplessly in the air. "I wasn't making no racial remark there. Don't get your balls in an uproar."

"*Congressman* Tom Quinlan . . ." Vince shook his head. "If that don't beat all." He lifted the phone and dialed the D.A.'s office. "What's this crap about you running for Congress?" he asked when Quinlan came on the line.

"Ask Connie. We had a coffee after the press conference and I filled her in on everything," Quinlan said.

"Think you have a chance?"

"My people tell me all I gotta do is keep from making a complete asshole of myself and I'll win by thirty points."

"That may not be so easy for a guy like you," Vince joked. "By the way, while I got you on the phone, what were your guys doing out at Woodlawn the other day?"

"That cemetery desecration thing? That was our new anticult unit at work. They check out anything that smacks of Satanism, voodoo, shit like that."

"Cult cops? How come I never heard about them?" Vince asked.

"It's not something we want a lot of publicity about," Quinlan said. "Cults are a tricky matter. You nail

them for doing something illegal and they start screaming that they're a religion and you're trampling all
over their first-amendment rights."

"Sounds like a crock to me."

"It is, but I'm not about to make any waves right
now," Quinlan said. "A lot of my soon-to-be constituents are into that Latin American voodoo shit and I
wouldn't want to alienate them."

"Why not campaign with a dead chicken tied around
your neck?" Vince suggested.

"Very fucking funny. Are you finished here? Can I
get back to work, or do you have something even
dumber you want to get off your chest?"

"Let me know if there's anything I can do to help,
Tom."

"You know I will, buddy. Thanks for offering."
Quinlan hung up.

It was almost six, no time for Vince to go home and
change for his dinner date with Katie. He cleared his
desk, chalked himself out, and drove downtown to
Colinini's Restaurant in the shadow of Manhattan's
Criminal Courts Building.

"Good to see you, Crowley." Sal, the bartender
remembered him and greeted him warmly. "Don't see
you around these parts much anymore." He poured a
Scotch on the rocks and placed it on the bar.

Vince saluted him with the drink. "I'm taking my
daughter out to dinner, so I figured I'd try to impress
her."

"You got a daughter, no shit?" Sal looked surprised.

"What's so strange about that?"

"I dunno. I guess I never had you pegged as a
family man," Sal said. "You got any other kids?"

"Another daughter, a couple of years older than
this one. Both of them live with their mother in
Connecticut."

"Divorced, huh? Me too." Sal shook his head sadly.
"Guys like us always get the shit end of the stick when
it comes to marriage, know what I mean?"

"Guys like us?"

"You know, guys with balls. I usta tell my old lady I needed some time with my friends. You know, bowling, cards, maybe a little strange pussy every now and then—nothing serious, just enough to keep the old juices flowing. There wasn't no way I was just going to just curl up and die of old age. Women don't understand shit like that. It pisses them off that a guy will tell his buddies things he would never tell his wife. Wives know a lot about a lot of stuff, but they don't know shit about friendship."

It hit closer to home than Vince wanted to admit. With him it had been his job, but that made little difference to Jessy. What she had wanted was a full-time husband, and she resented the department as if it was another woman competing for his attentions. She especially saw the bond between him and his partner as a threat. In that, Sal was right. There was just no way of explaining the devotion partners feel for one another to a woman. There was no way they could understand that the bond a policeman shared with his partner went beyond simple friendship, beyond trust, beyond love. The bond was forged in need and desperation, in the absolute, unwavering knowledge that their lives were only as good as their commitment to protect one another. Jessy had wanted to share a life. A partner had to be willing to surrender his.

Vince checked his watch: 6:54. Still no Katie, but that was no surprise. Being late was Katie's heritage, the consequence of being her mother's daughter. Jessy Sloan Crowley had never been on time for anything in her life, and she had passed it on to Katie and her sister, Kelly. Like their mother, they considered being on time a bother.

Vince hailed Sal and ordered another Scotch.

Katie showed up at seven, resplendent beneath a clinging black sheath dress and much too much makeup: a blend of Hollywood starlet and Tremont Avenue hooker. Vince swallowed hard and walked to the door to meet her.

"Hi, Daddy!" Her greeting was too enthusiastic to be sincere. "It's been ages." The mascara fluttered.

"Hi, baby." Vince kissed her and almost gagged on the penetrating smell of her perfume. "What's that stuff you're wearing, *Evening in Newark?*"

"Daddy!" She glared at him.

"Sorry." He shrugged helplessly and escorted her inside to their table. "It's just hard getting used to you this way."

"What way is that?" she challenged him.

"You know . . . I guess I'm used to my little girl. I mean, do you always wear that much makeup?"

"You sound just like Mommy," Katie groaned. "I'm eighteen. What do you want me to wear, Doctor Denton's?"

"Sorry again. I guess I'm really putting my foot in it tonight." Vince buried his face in the menu. "Everything is great here. If you're really hungry, I'd suggest the scalloppine. Best in the city."

"I understand how you feel," Katie persisted. "I really do. You and Mommy have this idea about how I'm supposed to turn out, and so do I. Right now our ideas are a little different, but I have to do what I think is right for me. I know that's hard for you to understand."

Vince watched her across the table, a little girl hiding behind inexpert layers of cosmetics. "I want to understand, Katie. Why don't you tell me about it?"

The question seemed to take her by surprise. "There's not much to tell. I want to study art and I've enrolled in Pratt Institute. I have an apartment near the school and I start classes in September. I know it's not what Mommy wanted for me, but it's what I want for myself."

"How about this Senji Rula character?" Vince asked.

Katie rolled her eyes. "*Oh, God!* What did Mommy tell you about him?"

"She said you were living together."

She shook her head angrily. "That's not true, and Mommy knows it. Senji is a good friend, that's all."

"So what is the relationship here?" Vince asked carefully.

"There is no relationship," she protested. "At least not the kind you're thinking about. Senji showed me around Paris last summer. He also helped me find an apartment when there weren't any to be found."

"An apartment of your own?" Vince broke in.

"Yes, Daddy. I'm living alone, virtuous and abstinent."

The waiter came and saved him from having to comment. "I'll have the scampi," Vince said, relieved. "How about you, baby?"

Katie eyed the menu absently. "Some kind of salad, I guess. And bring me a sidecar."

A sidecar! Vince felt his stomach tighten. It was the first time Katie had ever ordered a drink in front of him. "So this Senji Rula guy and you are nothing but buddies?" he asked when the waiter left.

"Senji is a kindred spirit. He understands my needs."

"Oh, jeez," Vince muttered.

"My artistic needs," she groaned. "I'm taking a class from him, nothing more."

"How are you managing to pay for all this?" he asked.

"I have some money. If you remember, Grandpa Sloan put some money in a trust for Kelly and me. I got mine when I turned eighteen last month."

He cringed. "I'm sorry about missing your birthday. That was dumb of me."

"Forget it." She brushed it off. "The fact is that I'm sort of independent now, and I'm trying to find my own way. Senji is my friend and he's helping me do that."

Vince shook his head uncomprehendingly.

"Senji is an instructor at Pratt," Katie explained. "He's forty if he's a day, and I'm not interested in him sexually, if that's what you're getting at."

"Maybe you're not interested, but how about him?" Vince found himself asking. "The way you look—"

She cut him off. "You're just going to have to let go, Daddy. I'm not your little girl anymore."

That hurt. "You'll always be my little girl, Katie," Vince said weakly.

"You know what I mean." She took the sidecar from the waiter and slugged it down.

Dinner was a cheerless affair. Both of them ate without appetites, making safe, trifling comments about the food, the weather, anything but what was really on their minds. Vince paid the check and walked outside with Katie, ignoring the envious stares of male patrons as they passed. "Am I going to see you soon?" he asked as she climbed into a taxi at the curb.

"I hope so, Daddy." She brushed his cheek with her lips. "I'll call you when I have my place in some kind of order. Maybe you can come over to dinner."

"I'd like that." He waved as the cab pulled away.

There was a telephone booth at the corner. Vince inserted a quarter in the slot and dialed the precinct.

"Thirty-seventh Squad. Vargas here." Street Crime was still on duty.

"Hi, Hector. I want you to run somebody down for me, a Pakistani named Senji Rula." Vince spelled it out. "Find out if there's any paper on him, any outstanding warrants, unpaid parking tickets, any goddamn thing at all. I want to know if he was ever busted for anything . . . if he was ever caught picking his nose on the sidewalk or scratching his ass in public. I wanta know if this creep ever had a bad thought, capish? And when you're finished with that, run him through Immigration and see if he's got a green card. Think you can handle that?"

"Can't you wait until tomorrow and do it yourself?" Street Crime complained.

"Tomorrow's my day off. Just do it, okay, pal?"

So much for letting go.

7

VINCE SIPPED HIS COFFEE AND DISCOVERED THAT IT was heavily laced with anisette. "I hope you don't mind . . ." Andrea Falcone eyed Vince and Tommy nervously. "That was the way Thomas always liked it."

"A man after my own heart," Tommy replied, smiling.

"Thomas always liked anisette after dinner," she went on. "It was the only time he ever drank, and then only a little in his cappuccino. Thomas wasn't what you would call a drinking man."

"I'm sure, Mrs. Falcone." Vince shifted his weight uncomfortably on the sofa. "I'm sorry to bother you so soon after your husband's death, but there are questions I have to ask, and I'm afraid you're the only one who can answer them."

She nodded. "I know, Detective Crowley, you're just doing your job. Thomas would have appreciated that. He was a hard worker himself."

"I understand that his job took him away from home a lot, Mrs. Falcone. Would you mind telling me if you were in touch during those times? Did you know his whereabouts when he was in . . . say, Washington? Were you aware of who he was doing business with, who he might have been seeing down there?"

"Not really." Andrea shrugged. "Thomas kept his business to himself. I never asked him about it. He always left a telephone number in Washington where he could be reached in case of emergency, but I can't think of a single time I ever had to use it."

"Any chance you might still have that number?" Vince asked.

She retrieved a white index card with the number printed on it from a wooden desk by the window and handed it to Vince. "It was always the same number, all the years he went down there. I guess you could say Thomas was a creature of habit. If something worked for him, he never changed it."

Vince inserted the card in the back of his notebook. "I have to ask you this question, Mrs. Falcone, and I hope you won't be upset by it. Were there any problems between you and your husband before his death? Any person or persons who you feel may have come between you?'"

"You mean, other women?" She shook her head vehemently. "Absolutely not. Never, in almost twenty years of marriage, did Thomas give me the slightest reason to suspect him. You know, I had such complete faith in Thomas that it never occurred to me to call that number and find out where he was staying."

"How about his associates? Was there anyone you knew, anyone your husband might have talked about, who may have resented him, who was angry enough at him to want to hurt him?" Vince asked.

"Everyone loved Thomas," she said simply.

His gaze drifted to the framed photograph on the wall. "Is that your child I see you holding in that picture?"

"Our son, Thomas Junior. He died of meningitis when he was eighteen months old."

Vince shot a rueful glance across the room at Tommy. "I guess that'll be all, Mrs. Falcone. I hope this hasn't been too hard for you."

"Not at all, Detective Crowley. Feel free to come around anytime. There's always a pot of coffee on the stove." She accompanied them to the front door.

"One more thing . . ." Vince halted in the doorway. "Did your husband ever mention anyone named Julio?"

"Julio? I don't think so."

"Somebody he might have worked with?"

She shook her head. "There were a lot of Spanish names, I really can't recall that one in particular."

Vince and Tommy descended the front steps and climbed into the squad car. Tommy took the wheel and drove toward The Bronx. "That woman's had a lot of heartache in her life," he said. "Still, she seems pretty calm for somebody whose husband was just murdered."

"Maybe she's just a strong woman," Vince replied. "Anyway, who says Thomas Falcone was murdered? You got some information I haven't seen yet?"

"He didn't just blow himself up," Tommy protested.

"Who says he didn't? Did it ever occur to you that he might've been carrying those explosives in his car and they went off by accident?"

Tommy thought about it. "What would a guy like him be doing with dynamite in his car?"

"Beats me, but it makes about as much sense as why anybody would want to clip a middle-class family man with no enemies in the world."

Snuffy Quade passed them on the precinct steps. "You got company inside: that guy Pell from the bakery truck. He's been hanging around for a couple of hours."

Upstairs, they found Oxbridge Pell staring idly at the bulletin board in the squad room. "Can I help you, Mr. Pell?" Vince asked.

"Oh, Detective Crowley, I just thought I'd stop by and see how you were doing with your investigation." Pell followed Vince to his desk.

"Nothing new yet," Vince told him. "But it's only been a few days. Did you remember anything you forget to tell us back in the parking lot?"

Pell hesitated. "Well, I'm not sure it means any-thing, but from where I was sitting it seemed to me that the guards from that armored car had the most unobstructed view of the explosion."

"Yes sir?"

Pell reddened. "Well, just that . . . I guess you've already talked to them."

Vince looked at Tommy. "I'm sure someone got their statement. We're just in the beginning stages of this thing, you know."

"Um . . ." Pell nodded.

Street Crime deposited a computer printout on Vince's desk. "Got that information you wanted, Crowley. Seems your guy, Senji Rula, is clean as a whistle. No wants, no warrants, not even a parking ticket on his sheet."

"How about Immigration?" Vince asked.

"Man's a U.S. citizen," Street Crime said. "He was naturalized in 1987. It's all there in his records."

Vince scanned the sheet and tossed it disgustedly in the wastebasket.

"Who's that you're running down?" Tommy asked him.

"Some middle-aged scumbag my daughter's got her-self involved with—a Pakistani, for chrissake."

"Jeez . . ." Tommy shook his head gravely.

"Daughters," Steve Appelbaum groaned. "I'd raise a dozen sons before I'd raise another daughter. They give you lots of *nachus* when they're little, but then they get to be teenagers . . . *oy veh!*"

"I have a daughter," Oxbridge Pell volunteered.

The telephone rang and Street Crime answered it. "It's Hank Dornin from the bomb squad. Wanta take it, Crowley?"

Vince lifted the phone. "Whatta you got for me, Hank?"

"Your bomb was construction-grade dynamite, five sticks wrapped with duct tape and a simple electronic switch, crude but effective," Dornin said. "Somebody put the whole shmear inside a leather attaché case and just slid it under the car, then activated it by remote from somewhere in the lot."

"Any chance the dynamite was inside the car?" Vince asked.

"No way, pal. The undercarriage was blown upward through the roof of the vehicle. Like I said, somebody walked by and just slid it under."

"Gimme your best guess. What's the farthest distance they could've been from the car to set it off?" Vince asked.

A pause. "A quarter-mile, max," Dornin finally replied. "This device wasn't no work of art, Vince, just powerful as hell. My guess is whoever did this wasn't no more than a hundred yards away."

"Could they have detonated it from inside one of the buildings?"

"Maybe, but it would've been a tough chance," Dornin answered. "Like I told you, this was a pretty basic piece of work. That means the more shit your guy puts between him and the bomb, the more chance it'll be accidentally detonated by outside wiring or electrical equipment . . . or the goddam thing won't go off at all. My guess is, he was someplace near, out of sight but protected. Know what I mean?"

"Yeah, Hank. Thanks for the quick work. Do me a favor and send me a copy of your report." Vince hung up.

"What'd they come up with?" Tommy asked.

Vince eyed Oxbridge Pell. "Was there anything else you wanted to tell us, Mr. Pell?"

"Just that, about the armored car."

Vince cast a sidelong glance at Tommy. "Would you like a ride home or something?"

"Oh, no. I drove myself here."

There was a moment of awkward silence as Pell resumed reading the notices on the bulletin board.

Vince lit an unfiltered Camel and leaned back in his chair. "Would you mind my asking what you're really doing here, Mr. Pell?"

Pell shuffled his feet like an embarrassed teenager. "I don't know, Detective Crowley. Killing time, trying to find something meaningful to do. It's very hard to explain."

"Why not give it a shot?"

Pell stared at the bulletin board. "I know you're going to find this ludicrous, but ever since the explosion I've been questioning the value of my life. I don't really know why, but from the moment I found myself cringing on the floor of the truck, it was as if everything that had gone on before was meaningless. Then, when I heard that Otto Kellerman had died, it seemed like almost an obscenity to go on living. I know this sounds crazy, but I seriously thought about committing suicide."

"Maybe you're just tired and upset," Vince commented.

"No, it's more than that," Pell protested. "I know it's hard for you to understand. You've never spent half your life in a comfortable job with a comfortable family grubbing around for a comfortable life. Your jobs, your lives are vital—immediate. You can't possibly know what it's like to look forward to the same old thing day after day."

"I think maybe you got shook up worse than you thought out there," Vince suggested. "Maybe you should see your doctor, Mr. Pell."

Pell shook his head. "There's nothing wrong with me, Detective Crowley, not physically at least. As a matter of fact, I think I've been seeing things clearer since the explosion than at any other time in my life. All of a sudden it's all starting to make some sense. Everything is unfolding before me in an entirely new perspective."

"Sometimes that happens," Tommy volunteered.

"When you think you're close to death, your whole life passes right before your eyes."

Pell smiled faintly. "No, it's nothing like that. I was never really frightened—not after the initial shock, at least. I almost hate to admit this, but what I felt most of all, was thrilled . . . unbelievably excited. I don't think you can appreciate what that means to a man like me, someone who's lived his entire life in a middle-class, desensitized coma. I felt alive . . . only for a moment, but, God, what a moment! I guess I've spent the time since trying to hold on to that feeling, but the crunching boredom of my life has been chipping away at it until there's hardly anything left. It's almost back to being meaningless again . . ." His voice trailed off.

"Why not let us give you a ride home, Mr. Pell?" Vince offered.

Pell shrugged. "To what?" He sat in the chair by Vince's desk and crossed his legs resolutely. "No, Detective Crowley, if I'm ever going to get out of this rut I've made for myself, it has to be now, while I'm still thinking straight. I'm at a crossroads, can't you see that? I'm too old to be a yuppie, and I'm a failure at being a preppie. I want to start living like you do, with some excitement in my life. I want to feel something besides numbness in my soul."

Vince's telephone rang and he answered it gratefully. "Three-Seven squad. Detective Crowley."

"This's patrolman Joe Sligo, sector car forty-six. I got a mutilated female DOA out here in Secor Park. It's really fuckin' grizzly, man."

"Which end?" Vince asked.

"233rd and Baychester," Sligo answered.

"Anyone else out there yet?"

"My partner and me just found her."

"Secure everything. We're on our way."

Vince bolted from his desk. "Okay, gentlemen, we got work to do out there. Let's grab our socks and get moving!"

"Can I come along?" Pell asked.

"You stay right where you are. Got it?"

Pell nodded meekly. "It's just hard to shake this feeling. I want so much out of my life now."

Vince pointed to the empty holding pen at the rear of the squad room. "You follow us out there and you'll be spending some of it in that cage."

Pell's ringing voice trailed him down the metal stairs. "I want a *bimbo!*"

8

NYPD FORM UF 61   August 30, 1989

INITIAL REPORT OF CRIME

Det. V. Crowley   COMPLAINT # 8104

INVESTIGATION OF DOA   VISIT TO SCENE

1. At 1735 hours this date, notified by sector car #46, Ptl. Jos. Sligo and Kenneth O'Connor, of an unidentified female DOA at the eastern entrance to Secor Park, 223 St. at Baychester Avenue (Sector Dog).

2. At 1800 hours, accompanied by Dets. Ippollito, Appelbaum, and Turner of 37 PDU, I arrived at above location and accompanied Ptl. Sligo to area of occurrence, where I observed a partially naked white female DOA, approx. 25–30 yrs.

3. My preliminary observations were that the body had been severely mutilated and hidden in bushes alongside a footpath leading into the park.

4. At the scene of occurrence, the undersigned, along with Det. Ippollito, interviewed Benjamin Hooks, aka Flame, and LeRoy Hoskins, aka Badger, who reported finding the body while they were bird-watching in the park. Both were unable to account for their previous whereabouts and were subsequently arrested for possession of a controlled substance.

5. As of this report Victim has not been identified, and cause of death remains unknown.

Patrolman Joe Sligo was waiting for them at the
head of a rubble-strewn walkway that meandered downhill from busy Baychester Avenue to a sudden, unex-
pected outcrop of summer foliage. Here, the melancholy
air of disrepair and decay that infested much of The
Bronx was evident: piles of uncollected garbage and
pieces of shattered glass were dispersed like random
seedlings among the weathered cobblestones. Unidentifiable chunks of urban jetsam lined the roadway.
Pieces of broken, twisted metal that had once been
washing machines and color television sets pressed
against the cracked, graffiti-covered concrete wall of
an abandoned handball court. "KILL KIKES", the spray-
painted legend on the wall declared. "CRACK IS KING."

"This's a real bad one," Joe Sligo told them som-
berly as they headed into the park. "Whoever did this
was a fuckin' pervert." He led them past the yellow
plastic barricades to a spot not far from the park's
entrance: a leafy clump of low-lying bushes near the
walkway ringed by uniformed officers speaking in
hushed tones.

"Jesus!" Vince recoiled at his first glimpse of the
body. "What kind of animal could do something like
that?"

Tommy gagged. "I hope she was dead before he did
it."

"Close as we can tell, whoever did this took some of
her parts with him," Sligo said. "We combed the
immediate area and there's no sign of her hands and
feet. It looks like the motherfucker woulda taken her
head too, but he couldn't cut all the way through."

Vince viewed the victim's mutilated neck, a jagged
wound carved almost to the bone. What seemed to be
a pattern of ritual scarring beneath the layers of grime
and spattered blood covered her face and naked torso.
A fist-sized tuft of what looked like chicken feathers

was jammed into her open mouth. "Whatta you make of those markings on the ground, partner?" Vince asked Tommy.

"Beats me," Tommy said, observing the profusion of oddly shaped swirls scratched into the moist dirt surrounding the body. "Looks like some kind of ritualistic shit to me. Satanism maybe, something really weird like that."

"Anybody contact the D.A.'s office?" Vince asked Sligo.

"Not that I know of."

"Better give them a call. They got a cult squad now. Maybe they can make some sense out of all this."

Members of the crime scene unit began to search the surrounding underbrush, looking for footprints in the soft earth, pieces of torn material caught on broken branches, discarded clothing, shell casings or weapons—anything that could be considered relevant to the crime. Joe Sligo's partner, Kenneth O'Connor, approached with two black males in handcuffs.

"Thought you might want to talk to these scumbags," O'Connor said. "If it wasn't for the Flame and Badger here, we might not have found the body when we did."

Vince eyed the two speculatively. They were in their early twenties, gaunt and street-hard, dressed almost identically in tight leather pants, hooded sweatshirts, and black Converse high-top sneakers—the kind police called Felony Fliers. Both of them were obviously high. "They report the crime?" he asked.

O'Connor grinned. "No way. These two would swallow razor blades before they'd call the police. Joe and me were just cruising by and we saw them smoking dope with their friends. When we approached them, they tried to bolt, but we caught them. It didn't take much persuading to get them to tell us what was making them so nervous. The body was only a couple of feet from where they were hanging out."

"You're telling me they were just standing around, with that only a few feet away?" Vince asked, astonished.

"Wasn't nothing we could do about it, man," the one called Badger said in a thick, guttural voice. "She was dead anyway."

"And just what do you know about this, scumbag?" Vince stood toe-to-toe with him. "You and your partner decide to carve that woman up just for the hell of it?"

Badger glared at him with bloodshot eyes. "I don't know nothing about that, man. Me and Flame was just minding our own business when these pigs come up and start fuckin' us over. Sheeit!" He staggered, regained his balance, and spat angrily on the ground.

"What about you?" Tommy asked the one called Flame. "What the hell were you doing hanging around here in the first place?"

Flame grumbled something unintelligible.

"Elucidate, cocksucker!" Tommy grabbed him by the shoulders.

"We was watching the birds," Flame said sullenly.

"Watching the birds, huh?" Tommy said. "Yeah, you two look like real bird-watchers—don't they, Vince?"

O'Connor produced two empty crack vials. "They tried to dump these when they saw us coming."

"Yeah. Bird-watchers usually take a hit or two of rock before they watch them feathered friends," Tommy noted. "Gives them a better perspective on nature."

Vince took O'Connor aside. "Any chance these two were really involved in this?"

O'Connor shook his head. "No way. They might've whacked her over the head for her pocketbook, but they're not into that sadistic shit. Flame and Badger are just a couple of neighborhood junkies, small-time hoods. I don't think either of them's got the concentration to carve up a stiff like that."

The M.E.'s van arrived and Shem Weisen joined

them at the scene. "Whatta we got this time?" he asked wearily.

"White female DOA," Tommy volunteered. "The only sui generis aspect is that the body's mutilated."

"Sooey what?"

"Sui generis—unique," Tommy said.

"Jesus H. Christ, you never let up, do you?" Weisen shuffled off in the direction of the body.

"That guy's the most unprofessional law-enforcement official I ever saw," Tommy complained to Vince. "You'd think a guy like him would know about stuff like sui generis."

"Shem probably sees ten stiffs a day. He spends most of his time up to his elbows in blood. I think he's gotta keep things real simple so he won't end up drooling in some laughing academy," Vince said, walking back to where Weisen was kneeling, examining the body.

"How's it look?" he asked.

The coroner shrugged. "Dirty. A real nasty piece of business. They find any of these missing extremities?"

"Uh-uh, not yet at least."

"Body was butchered someplace else and dumped here afterward," Weisen said unemotionally. "There's just not enough blood for it to have happened here."

"How long ago?" Vince asked.

"Eighteen, twenty-four hours, maybe. I'll know better when I get inside and check the organs." Weisen stood and wiped his sweating forehead with his sleeve. "But the way it looks, some of them are missing too. It seems like whoever did this removed the heart and liver."

"Jeez!" Vince shook his head. "Who'd do something like that?"

"Who the hell knows?" Weisen bent over the body and removed some blood and dirt from the face. "Some kind of recent scarring here. Looks like it's concurrent with the other wounds. My guess is the markings have some kind of significance."

"You've seen markings like them before?" Vince asked.

Weisen took one of the feathers from the open mouth. "Not exact, but similar. There are all kinds of psychopaths running around who want to leave some sort of signature on their work. Sometimes it means something, sometimes not." He checked his wristwatch and entered the time in a leather-bound notebook. "We get more like this every day: voodoo, devil-worshipers, you name it. They're getting sicker all the time. I had a stiff out Prospect Park with his tongue cut out and nailed on a tree next to his body. At first it looked like Satanists or something like that, but it turned out to be Cuban drug-runners leaving a warning to the people in the neighborhood not to talk to the authorities. All this ritualistic shit means something to somebody. It's not my job to try to figure it all out."

A CSU detective returned from the wooded interior of the park carrying a plastic evidence bag. "There's some kind of ritual markings back there. Maybe you want to take a picture before we break it all down."

They corralled a videotape cameraman filming nearby and followed the detective through the tangle of shrubbery to a small clearing a few hundred feet from the body. The ground had been swept clean and a number of small stones arranged in a circle. Inside the circle, a crude drawing was scratched into the soil: a cross with what appeared to be a snake coiled around it. Beneath the drawing, seven coins were placed beside the body of a dead bird, along with a small white plate containing metal shavings.

"Whatta you make of it?" Vince asked Shem Weisen as the cameraman taped the scene.

Weisen shook his head. "I dunno. I'm getting too old for all this crap." He made his way back through the undergrowth to the road. "This job usta be easy. Stiffs got knifed or shot or hit over the head with blunt objects, and that was it. Nobody left crossword puzzles at the scene of the crime. You didn't have to be a behavioral shrink to figure it all out." He opened the door to the coroner's van. "Join me inside for a short one?"

Vince and Tommy entered the van and waited while Weisen poured three stiff bourbons into paper cups. "*Salut*," he toasted the cramped interior of the van, downed his drink, and poured another. "Seven hundred and eleven days to go."

"Till what?" Vince sipped the bourbon.

"Retirement. I'm gonna get my ass away from all of this once and for all and write a book."

"No shit?" Tommy perked up. "What kinda book?"

"Who cares?" Weisen drained his cup and tossed it into the wastebasket. "A cookbook, a comic book. Anything that'll get my mind off this garbage."

"I'm writing a book—" Tommy offered.

"I'll just bet you are," Weisen cut him off. "Try writing it in English, okay, Tommy? I think people will get turned off by all that sooey-genital shit of yours."

"Generis, asshole!" Tommy tossed down the remainder of his drink and stormed out of the van. "Maybe the city'll hire somebody with some intelligence when you're gone." His voice trailed back.

Weisen smiled. "Touchy guy, your partner."

"Tommy's okay. He just takes himself too seriously," Vince said.

"Speaking of serious, I heard you're reorganizing up there at the Thirty-seventh."

Vince shrugged. "We're getting a new C.O., but he hasn't shown yet."

"Guy named Sweeney, right?"

"Yeah, how'd you know?"

"Lieutenant Michael Sweeney, the caretaker," Weisen went on. "The guy leaves a path of destruction everywhere he goes."

"What's that supposed to mean?" Vince asked.

"Just that. He was C.O. of the old Eighty-sixth

before they shut the house down and merged it with the Eighty-ninth. Same with the old Hundred-and-fifth out in Queens."

"What're you saying, that the guy is jinxed?"

Weisen shook his head. "Not jinxed. Like I said, he's called the caretaker. They send him to wrap things up when a precinct's being eliminated."

9

TELLING A COP THAT HIS PRECINCT IS BEING ELIMI-nated is like telling a home-owner his house is being repossessed. Vince kept the information to himself until the following day, when he placed a call to Lieutenant Bill Kitzmiller at One Police Plaza.

"Crowley, I thought you were dead," Kitzmiller joked when he came on the line. "What's happening up there on those dusty Bronx streets?"

"I was hoping you could tell me," Vince replied in a low voice. "I'm getting some feedback that somebody's planning on shutting us down, maybe merging us with another precinct. You're on the fast track down there at headquarters, so I figured maybe you know something."

"Where'd you hear a thing like that?"

"Do me a favor and don't jerk me around, Bill," Vince said. "You and me went to the same interrogation lectures back at the academy, remember? I know the best way to avoid answering a question is to ask one back, and that's not what I need right now. What I'm doing is asking an old friend for some information, maybe calling in some old markers. Be straight with me, bro. You heard anything or not?"

"Nothing, Vince. I swear to God. Everybody knows there's going to be some cutbacks, but nobody knows where. Whatever happens, it won't happen until after the elections next November, you know that. No poli-

71

tician in his right mind is gonna start shutting down police precincts now."

"But the decision could've already been made, right?" Vince persisted.

"Could've. What's your point?"

"Ever hear of a lieutenant named Michael Sweeney?"

A pause. "Same Sweeney who was out at the One-oh-five in Queens?"

Vince felt the muscles of his stomach tighten. "I think you just answered my question, Bill."

"Don't go jumping to conclusions, Vince . . ." Kitzmiller was trying to sound reassuring. "Nobody really knows anything about what's going down at this point. Even if somebody's decided to merge you guys, it could all change after the elections. Those bozos are always making contingency plans based on the idea that the city's going broke tomorrow, and they always come up with the money somehow. It's all smoke and mirrors, pal, you know that."

"What I know is they closed down the One-oh-five, and the Eighty-seven before that. Sweeney came in and that was all she wrote," Vince said. "Now he's coming here. What does that tell you?"

"Lemme see what I can find out," Kitzmiller volunteered. "I'll get back to you as soon as I know anything. In the meantime, keep the faith."

"Yeah, I'll give it my best shot." Vince hung up.

Tommy approached his desk. "What's that all about?"

"Smoke and mirrors," Vince replied. "Whatta you got for me?"

"I got all that Gateway stuff you asked for, the grid and everything they picked up at the site. It's all in the interrogation room."

Vince accompanied Tommy to one of the small, windowless cubicles next to the squad room and shut the door. "You okay?" Tommy asked him when they were inside. "You look a little nervous about something."

"My stomach's been bothering me," Vince lied. "Probably some bad pepperoni, nothing to worry about." He began examining the items arrayed on the table. There was a large diagram of the Gateway lot; parked cars and adjacent storefronts outlined carefully on a blue grid background. Among the representations of buildings and vehicles, red numbers signified pieces of evidence removed from the site for further investigation. Alongside, plastic evidence bags containing those items were tagged with corresponding numbers.

Vince removed the items from the bags one at a time, examining each scrap of evidence and confirming its location on the grid. There was nothing out of the ordinary: coins, car keys, pocket combs, a crushed campaign button. "What's this?" He lifted what appeared to be a small ornament, a smooth, painted stone wrapped with wire.

Tommy shrugged. "Who knows? Some kinda good-luck charm, maybe. Why?"

Vince looked at the grid. "Just that it was found in this alleyway next to the supermarket. From what I can see, that would have been the best place for our bomber to wait out of sight, have a complete view of the lot, and be able to detonate without having outside obstructions between him and Falcone's car." He handed the stone to Tommy. "By the way, do we have statements from those armored-car guards?"

Tommy shrugged. "Somebody musta gotten them."

"Check it out for me, okay?" Vince asked. "Our friend Pell may be a fruitcake, but he's an observant fruitcake. If he says those guys had the best view, I gotta go along with him."

There was a knock. "Those guys from Contech are here," Leila Turner yelled through the closed door.

Vince replaced the items in their proper evidence bags and went back into the squad room. "I'm Detective Crowley." He introduced himself to the two middle-aged Hispanic men waiting by his desk.

"Louis Escobar." The taller of the two extended his hand. "And this is my partner, Walter Cruz. I've brought those telephone records you asked for. As far as I know, this list is complete right up to the end of last month." He handed Vince a folded computer printout.

Vince went behind his desk and offered them a seat. "Basically, what I'm interested in finding out is who Thomas Falcone did business with when he was out of your offices," he told them. "I understand he spent a lot of time lobbying for you in Washington. Can you give me the names of some people he saw when he was down there?"

"David told us you'd probably want that information." Escobar reached inside his jacket pocket, retrieved a typewritten sheet of paper, and handed it across the desk. "He saw a great many people during the time he was with us and naturally we can't know everyone, but this list should be enough to get you started. As far as we can tell, it's everyone he saw on a regular basis."

Vince scanned the sheet. There were no names immediately recognizable to him. "Can you tell me if Thomas Falcone seemed different in any way to you prior to his death? Was he unusually preoccupied or depressed? Did you have any reason to suspect that he may have been in some sort of trouble?"

They shook their heads simultaneously. "Thomas was really an upbeat sort of guy," Cruz volunteered. "He was always smiling, cracking jokes. He had a kind of infectious personality, if you know what I mean. You felt good just being around Tom."

Vince nodded. "Can you tell me when was the last time you both saw him?"

"He was in the office on Wednesday, the twenty-third," Escobar said. "We spoke briefly."

"The day before his death," Vince noted. "Can you tell me what it was you talked about?"

"Business mostly, nothing unusual," Escobar said. "He filled me in on his latest trip and we spoke briefly about his next one."

"Did he file reports? Do we have any way of tracing

his activities during the time prior to his death?" Vince asked.

Escobar smiled faintly. "Tom wasn't the kind of guy to fill out reports. He was sort of a free spirit in the manufacturing world. A seat-of-the-pants kind of salesman. To him, reports just took up a lot of valuable time he could spend working out in the field. There aren't many like him in this business anymore."

Steve Appelbaum excused himself and handed Vince a thick manila envelope. "Photographs from Secor Park yesterday," he said simply. "Pretty grim stuff."

Vince stood. "Okay, gentlemen, I appreciate you coming in like this. I'll be in touch with you if I need any more information." He walked them to the door of the squad room.

"Whatta you think?" Tommy asked when they were gone.

"Hard to tell . . ." Vince inspected the computer printout on his desk. "Falcone was a nice guy with no enemies who didn't keep any records about who he saw or what they did when he saw them. They're sure as hell not making it any easier for us. Let's run these numbers through the phone company and see where it leads." He handed the sheet to Tommy and opened the envelope Steve had given him.

"Christ!" He shuddered. "This stuff doesn't get any easier when you see it for the second time."

There was activity on the outside stairway. Several unidentified males entered the C.O.'s office, followed by Lieutenant Ed Bartow, commander of the 37th uniformed squad. Bartow stopped in the doorway and summoned Vince to follow.

"This's Detective Vince Crowley." Bartow introduced him to the same man who had been in the office a few days earlier. "Vince, meet Lieutenant Michael Sweeney, your new C.O."

Vince shook Sweeney's hand. "Welcome aboard, sir." He tried to disguise the anxiety he felt.

"Good to meet you." Sweeney returned the handshake warmly. "This's Sergeant Bob Donofrio, my assistant. He'll be helping me out during the transition." He identified the other stranger in the room, a short, unhappy-looking man in his late thirties. "I understand you've been doing a helluva job as acting C.O."

"Doing the best I can, Lieutenant. I gotta admit, it's been pretty hectic around here."

Bartow went to the door. "I'll leave you two alone to get acquainted. Let me know if you need anything." He made his way to the stairs.

"So . . ." Sweeney went behind the desk and sat. "I told Lieutenant Bartow that I wanted to meet with you before I spoke to the men, just to get a line on what's been going on during the time you've been without a commander."

"We have a couple of major cases in progress," Vince told him. "I guess you heard all about the Gateway blast, and another homicide just yesterday. An unidentified female got herself cut up out in Secor Park."

Sweeney nodded. "You've assigned men to handle them?"

"Yes sir." Vince was surprised at the naïveté of the question. "I've got a shitload of DD-5s filed away for you to look at. I'll be glad to fill you in on anything that's unclear in the reports."

"I'll take those off your hands," Donofrio broke in.

"Sergeant Donofrio will act as my liaison with the men for the time being," Sweeney explained. "Just until I've got my feet wet up here, so to speak."

"However you want it, Lieutenant." It was not a good omen.

"As far as the active cases, I don't see any reason to change the way you've been handling things so far," Sweeney went on. "Unless there are problems, let's keep the same personnel on the same cases. That okay with you?"

"I don't have any problem with it," Vince replied.

"Good. Let's just go on the way you've been going for the time being."

Vince shifted his weight uncomfortably. "Do you want me to brief you on just where things stand, sir?"

Sweeney shot an almost imperceptible glance at Donofrio.

"We'll look at those DD-5s first," Donofrio answered for him. "If we have any questions after that, we'll let you know."

An awkward silence. "Will that be all, Lieutenant?"

"I think so. How about you?" he asked Donofrio.

Donofrio shrugged noncommittally.

"Feel free to consult with me anytime," Sweeney said, accompanying Vince to the door. "I want this transition to be as easy for everybody here as possible." He dismissed him with a nod.

"What's happening?" Tommy, Steve, and Street Crime gathered around him in the squad room. "What's the new guy like?"

Vince shook his head uncertainly. "I dunno. He doesn't seem too interested in what's going on around here."

"Whatta you mean, not interested?" Tommy asked.

"Just that. He told me to keep on running things just like before he got here."

"That's great," Street Crime said.

"Yeah, maybe we finally got a C.O. who'll let us do things the way they're supposed to be done, instead of sticking his nose into everything," Steve Appelbaum agreed.

"I'm not so sure." Vince walked to his desk and shuffled through the photographs of the murdered girl. "You'd think the guy would at least want to know how things are progressing. He's got a flunkie named Donofrio in there who does most of his thinking for him."

Appelbaum shrugged. "So who says you gotta be smart to be a lieutenant?"

"Maybe not smart, but at least involved," Vince said.

"It's probably just his style," Tommy suggested. "He's probably just one of those low-key management-type guys. Maybe he feels we've all been together long enough to know what we're doing and he just doesn't want to screw up a good team."

Vince felt small animals cavorting in the pit of his stomach. "I guess that's it," he replied stiffly. "We'll all find out soon enough."

10

NYPD FORM DD-5   **September 2, 1989**
COMPLAINT FOLLOW-UP   COMPLAINT # 8104
Det. V. Crowley
SUBJECT: HOMICIDE/MUTILATION OF CHERRY DRES-
           SARD, W/F, 27. VISIT TO MORGUE.

1. At 0930 hours, above date, the undersigned
   arrived at the morgue, 520 First Avenue, N.Y.C.,
   for the purpose of viewing the body of a white
   female homicide victim (above specification).
2. I was met by Chief Medical Examiner S. Weisen
   and a black male known to me as Lionel Washington (aka Silk), a pimp, who suspected the
   victim was an acquaintance named Cherry Dressard, whom he had reported missing on 8/28/89.
3. Upon viewing the body, Washington confirmed
   that the victim was the aforementioned Cherry
   Dressard, whom he identified as a prostitute
   who had worked in his stable.

Investigation continues. Case active.

    Silk Washington felt his nose beginning to run as he
stood in the basement labyrinth of the New York City
morgue. Around him, row upon row of polished
stainless-steel vaults filled with corpses lined the corri-
dors surrounding the enormous surgical amphitheater,
a hollow echo chamber that reverberated with the
sound of his nervous sniffing.

"The inside of your nose must look like a nickel crapper with the flush stuck," Vince commented as they waited in the empty hallway for Shem Wiesen to arrive.

Silk glared at him through watery eyes. The dumb cop was probably right, he thought bitterly. The two hundred dollars' worth of high-grade cocaine he'd snorted every day for the past ten years had left the membranes like jelly. Every microbe that came to town made a beeline for the hospitable environs of his tender nostrils, settled into the warm, viscous interior, and incubated gleefully. His nose was a living halfway house for every virus known to science.

"I got allergies," he protested feebly.

"Yeah, to Colombian blow," Vince said. "Wipe your nose, for chrissake. There's snot dribbling down your chin."

Silk wiped his nose resentfully on the sleeve of his embroidered shirt. "This place gives me the heebie-jeebies, man. How much longer we gotta stand around here waiting? I got a business to run."

Vince checked his watch. "Not even ten A.M. yet. Your girls are probably still tucked away in bed, getting their beauty sleep. There isn't any business out there this time of morning."

"You don't know nothing about my business, cop."

Vince shrugged. "What's to know? You push table-grade poon on the East Side. I don't have to be no Einstein to figure out how that works."

"I'm a promoter, man," Silk said.

"Yeah, a pussy promoter," Vince shot back.

The elevator door opened and Shem Weisen stepped out into the hallway. "Crowley . . ." He nodded curtly and handed Vince a plastic envelope. "These are the personal effects we took off that guy Falcone's body before we autopsied him. I figured you might as well take them with you as long as you're down here."

Vince placed the envelope in his jacket pocket. "This here's Silk Washington, Shem. Silk runs whores uptown in The Bronx."

"I hope you got a strong stomach, Mr. Washington," Weisen said, leading them down the hallway to one of the closed vaults. "This is not a pretty sight." He opened the vault and slid the drawer toward them.

"Sheeit!" Silk covered his mouth with his hands as Weisen removed the sheet that covered the body. "Oh, God! Who'd do something like that?"

"Can you I.D. her?" Vince prodded.

He nodded. "Yeah, that's Cherry. Used to be her, at least. That's the worst fuckin' thing I ever saw, man."

"Are you a relative of the deceased?" Weisen asked.

"No." Silk turned away. "I just knew her, man. She was like a sister to me, like a wife. I dunno what I'm gonna do without her. This is the worst thing that ever happened to me."

"Do you know if she has any living relatives?"

"I dunno. I don't think so. I was all she had in the world, man. I took care of her, if you know what I mean."

Weisen slid the door shut. "Okay, there are some forms upstairs you'll have to fill out before I can release the body."

"And you'll have to come uptown with me and give me a statement," Vince added.

"Statement? What kinda statement?" Silk demanded.

"You've gotta tell me all about Cherry there, then you're gonna tell me what you were doing at the time she was being butchered."

"What *I* was doing? What the fuck you mean, what I was doing? I was looking for her, man," Silk protested as they took the elevator to Weisen's office. "That girl there was one of my principal assets. You think I'd be dumb enough to blow away one of my best girls, then report her missing? What kinda asshole you take me for?"

"Ask Shem. He's the doctor."

"I'm a pathologist, not a proctologist," Weisen said, handing Silk a sheaf of release forms. "Fill in whatever you know about the deceased and specify where you want the body to be sent. We'll have it there sometime tomorrow."

"Huh?" Silk eyed him dumbly.

"The mortuary. You are going to have her buried, aren't you?"

Silk paled. "Buried?"

"Yeah, you know. They put her in the ground and shovel dirt on top. You heard about that."

"Hey, wait a minute . . ." Silk backed off. "That's her family's job, not mine."

"She was like a sister to you," Vince reminded him.

"Your principal asset," Weisen added.

Silk groaned. "I ain't got that kinda money, man. It costs a fuckin' fortune to plant a stiff these days."

"What'd she make for you in a night, Silk—six, seven hundred?" Vince asked.

"What of it? She's dead, man. I don't got no money to go throwin' around on no dead lady."

Vince eyed his eight-hundred-dollar lavender silk suit, embroidered shirt, and flowered tie. "You know, that kind of loyalty gets me right here." He pressed his chest.

"Sign here." Weisen shoved the form in front of Silk. "We'll use what we can and bury the rest in potter's field."

Silk scrawled his signature at the bottom of the page. "Yeah, maybe somebody can use her parts. We gotta help out those less fortunate. It's the least I can do."

"The man's all heart," Vince noted.

"A regular humanitarian," Weisen concurred.

Back at the precinct, Vince emptied Thomas Falcone's personal effects on his desktop. "Look at this, Falcone wore a wedding ring," he commented to Tommy, who was sprawled at his desk fanning himself with a blank DD-5.

"What's so strange about that?" Tommy asked. "He was married, wasn't he?"

"I dunno. For some reason I got the idea he didn't wear a ring."

"Can we get on with this?" Silk moaned. "I got

more important things to do with my time than sitting around this shithole."

"Oh, yeah, I forgot you were such an important person. What you need is an office." Vince walked to the rear of the squad room and unlocked the empty holding pen. "Detective Ippollito, would you mind escorting this captain of industry to his new office?"

"What the fuck do you think you're doing?" Silk howled as Tommy muscled him to the pen and shoved him inside. "I know my rights. You gotta charge me with something before you can lock me up!"

"Whatta you want to charge this douche bag with?" Vince asked Tommy. "Pandering? Dressing in bad taste?"

"How about dribbling snot all over the squad room? Tommy suggested.

"You motherfuckers! I wanna see my lawyer," Silk wailed.

Vince walked back to his desk, extracted the envelope containing Thomas Falcone's morgue pictures from the drawer, and leafed through them. "Take a look at this, partner." He handed Tommy a Polaroid close-up of Falcone's left arm and hand.

Tommy checked the photograph carefully. "What about it?"

"Look at the ring finger. It's completely tanned. No white spot where his wedding ring used to be."

Tommy handed back the Polaroid. "So?"

"So, that ring was on him when he got blown up. They removed it when he was autopsied. That means he had it off sometime prior to that—off long enough to get that finger tanned all over."

Tommy thought about it. "Whatta you think?" he asked hesitantly.

"I'm not sure. Would you take your wedding ring off if you were going someplace to get a tan?" Vince asked.

"Doesn't make a whole lotta sense," Tommy admitted.

"Unless you wanted to hide the fact that you were married."

"You get me a lawyer or I'll have your goddamn badges," Silk screamed from the holding pen. "You'll be counting Cadillacs on the fuckin' Triborough Bridge when I get through with you cocksuckers!"

Across town, at Pratt Institute in Brooklyn, Katie Crowley sat on a wooden stool behind a large easel and eyed her charcoal drawing nervously. It was all wrong, she decided, observing the sketches of her classmates out of the corner of her eye. The hips were too large, the legs grotesque and out of proportion. She looked again at the nude female model who was posed in the center of the room and shuddered inwardly. Her first class in anatomical drawing was turning out disastrously. She clenched her teeth and prayed for the closing bell.

"Would you mind waiting a minute?" Senji Rula asked her as the bell rang. "I'd like to discuss your drawing with you when the others have left."

Panic gripped her. Here it was, she thought. Not even her friend and mentor could tolerate her crude, incompetent scrawls. He would look at her pitiful drawing and shake his head hopelessly, she decided.

"It's not very good," she admitted to him when everyone had gone. "I just don't know what I'm doing wrong."

Senji Rula stood behind her, looking at the drawing. "I wouldn't be so hard on myself if I were you," he said in a softly accented voice. I see a lot of promise here."

"I think you're just being kind to me." She could smell his after-shave or cologne as he bent near her; a spice smell, something exotic and Eastern.

"Your basic anatomy is a little off, but I sense a kind of strength in your drawing, a passion I don't often see in the beginners I teach."

Katie could feel herself starting to blush. "Maybe I could fix it with a little work."

He reached forward, over her shoulder, and took

the charcoal from her hand. "The sweep of line here
. . ." He accentuated the curve of the model's back.
"Remember, tone, shadow, and balance; those are the
keys to drawing the human body. The body must
always be fluid, sensuous. To draw the naked form is
to have something like an erotic experience." She
could feel his hips tightening against the arch of her
back—an almost imperceptible movement, a hardening.

"Think of your own body," he went on, subtly
shading the drawing with a few deft strokes of his
forefinger. "Your body isn't a wooden representation
of a woman. It's alive, undulating, full of vibrancy
. . ." He ran his fingers across the drawing, defining
the soft shadow of the breasts. "When you draw, think
of how you feel when you touch your own body. Do
you feel warmth? Passion? That must be reflected in
your art. You must always draw as if you are touching
yourself in the most intimate places . . ." He let his
hand drift sinuously downward, across the line of buttocks on the drawing. His gracefulful, seductive fingers
caressed the voluptuous thighs, the shadowed recesses
hidden in between, kneading, tantalizing, like an ar-
dent lover seeking to arouse. Katie could hear only his
soft, captivating voice and the newly aroused rhythms
of her own heavy breathing.

Senji Rula was pressing against her now. The penetrating aroma of his scented skin captivated her, envel-
oped her. His soft, cooing words melted her anxiety,
her resolve. Before her, the textured sheet of charcoal
paper seemed to come alive as the naked drawing
trembled underneath his touch. She saw it writhe,
inhaled its musky smells of sweat and desire, and felt
herself slipping, plummeting, unable to halt her dizzy-
ing descent.

11

STANDING AMID A GAUDY ARRAY OF PAINTED PLASTER statues, crucifixes, candles and fetishes, Beata Ruiz watched with apprehension as the two detectives approached the front door of her Fordham Road *botánica*. "*Buenas tardes.*" She nodded curtly as they entered the store.

"Excuse me, ma'am. Is there anyone here who speaks English?" Vince asked, looking around at the cluttered store at the display of religious articles. "*Perdón, ¿habla usted inglés?*"

She shrugged. "*Un poquito . . .* a little bit, not much." In fact, Beata Ruiz spoke fluent English, but there was no reason for the police to know that. Whatever they were after, it would be far easier for her to get rid of them if they believed she was simply another dumb spick, she reasoned. Beata distrusted the police, as did almost everyone else she knew in the Hispanic community. It was not that they acted cruelly, or even with insensitivity—only that they were different, outsiders. The *policía* did not understand her people's beliefs and traditions. The sooner she could satisfy them and get them out of the *botánica*, the better it would be for everybody.

"I'm looking for some help," Vince said hesitantly. "*¿Puede usted ayudarme, por favor?*" His Spanish was poor, a few rudimentary phrases he had picked up in the streets and alleyways of The Bronx barrios. He handed Beata several Polaroid photographs that had been taken at the Secor Park murder scene. "Can you tell me if you've ever seen markings like these?"

"Santa María!" She gasped instinctively at the color shots of Cherry Dressard's mutilated body. "*¿Qué significa esto?* Why are you showing this to me?" She shoved the photographs back into his hand.

"*Excúseme, señora*," Vince apologized. "I'm sorry if I've upset you. Can you tell me if you've ever seen any symbols like the ones scratched into the ground in those photographs?"

Beata reluctantly took the pictures back from him and inspected them. "Who would do something like this?" she asked.

"That's what we're trying to figure out." Vince found himself speaking slowly and distinctly. "We think those markings on the ground next to the body might be important, so we're trying to find out what they mean. Have you ever seen symbols like them before?"

She studied the photographs. "They are not santero, if that is what you think."

"Ma'am?" Vince shot a sidelong glance at Tommy, who was studying the array of religious talismans and relics in the display case. "I'm not sure I understand."

She caught herself. "What makes you think I would know anything about strange markings on the ground?"

Vince noticed that her English was becoming remarkably clearer the more agitated she became. "We're into something we don't really understand here, ma'am. Maybe some kind of religious ritual—some sort of human sacrifice maybe."

"Sacrifice? We sell religious articles here. What do you think we are, savages?"

"*Perdón*, I'm very sorry if I've given you that impression." Vince glanced at Tommy and grimaced. "We've been told that the markings may have some religious meaning, and I was hoping you could give us a hand interpreting them. I never meant to suggest that you were responsible in any way."

She seemed satisfied. "They are unfamiliar to me, but perhaps they have some symbolic meaning." She looked again at the pictures. "I have heard of things such as this, but they have nothing to do with us—"

"The *santeros?*" Vince interrupted her.

"There are devil-worshipers," she went on, ignoring his question. "Satanists, who are known to perform rituals with symbols, but I have no personal knowledge of them."

"And there's nothing about those shots that would have any meaning to you?" Vince asked again, taking the photographs back from her and replacing them in his jacket pocket.

"I would say it is the work of Satanists," she said resolutely.

Vince turned to Tommy. "Okay, partner, I guess we've learned about as much as we're gonna find out. Can you think of anything else we should cover before we leave?"

"What're these things?" Tommy asked, pointing to a shelf filled with pungent dried leaves, flowers, and herbs.

"*Plantas,*" she told him. "*Flores* that are used in healing." She scooped up a handful of fragrant, dried flowers and held them in front of Tommy's nose. "Here is *verbena* for the care of the hair . . ." She replaced the flowers and ran her fingers through a display of seeds. "And *anís* for hysteria or indigestion. Almost all of them are also used to ward off evil spirits, sometimes with charms or talismans." She indicated an adjoining tray filled with small wooden and metal carvings. "The magic is strongest when both are used."

Vince scanned the display case indifferently. "Well, let's get our show on the road, partner."

"Hold it!" Tommy grabbed him by the elbow. "Do you see what I see?" He pointed to a small charm nestled among the others in the tray.

Vince spotted it immediately: a smooth, painted stone wrapped in wire. "Can I see that, please?" he asked Beata.

"It is nothing but a good-luck token," she told him, handing the stone across the counter.

Vince took it in his hands. "Damn near identical to the one CSU picked up in the Gateway lot. Do you sell many of these?" he asked Beata.

She shrugged. "Like I said, it's a good-luck charm. Many people carry charms just like it."

"Do you by any chance keep records of your customers?" Vince asked hopefully.

"What do you think this is, Montgomery and Ward?"

He grinned. "Okay. How much for this one?"

She stared at him dumbly.

"I want to buy this. *¿Cuánto cuesta esto?*"

"For you, free." She was happy to be rid of them. "Maybe it will help you get lucky in your investigation."

"I think it already has." Vince deposited the talisman in his pocket and followed Tommy outside to the car.

Steve Appelbaum was alone in the squad room when they returned. "Silk Washington's shyster lawyer sprung him while you were out," he reported laconically. "He says he's slapping you both with unlawful-imprisonment suits, and that you'll both be working in the pits at Jiffy Lube by the time he's finished with your asses."

"Anything else?" Vince checked his phone messages.

"Yeah, that Brink's guard you wanted to interview is waiting for you in room sixteen."

Vince took Thomas Falcone's file from his desk and led Tommy down the hall to the interview room. "I'm Detective Crowley," he introduced himself to the uniformed Brink's guard inside. "This's Detective Ippol-lito."

"Bernie Coppolla." The guard extended his hand. "I understand you wanted to talk to me about that car explosion in the Gateway parking lot."

"Thanks for coming in, Mr. Coppolla." Vince leafed through the sheets of testimony in the file. "It's about the deposition you gave to Detective Vargas on the day of the explosion. You saw a suspicious black male in the area prior to the occurrence."

"Well, that's not exactly what I told him," Coppolla hedged. "I don't remember saying he was suspicious, just that he was hanging around near the supermarket."

"Yes sir. That's what it says here, but it also says that you saw this black male 'lurking' in the alleyway between the bank and the supermarket. Is that correct?"

Coppolla paused. "Near as I can remember, that's about it. He didn't seem to be doing anything suspicious, though. I can't say for sure that he was lurking. Maybe just standing would be a better way of putting it, you know what I mean? He just kinda walked into the mouth of the alley and was standing there, like he was waiting for someone."

"Standing, not lurking?"

There was confusion in Coppolla's eyes. "Yeah . . . He didn't lurk—at least not while I was watching him."

Vince nodded. "And this description you gave Detective Vargas . . . Do you have anything further to add to it now that you've had a couple of days to think about it?" Vince handed him the typewritten deposition.

"Nope, that's it. About six feet, two hundred pounds, no apparent scars or contusions, close-cropped hair, with a full beard and mustache."

"That's a pretty thorough description," Vince observed. "You must've gotten a good look at him to be that definite."

"I'm trained to identify suspects. It's my job," Coppolla responded haughtily.

"Then you considered this man suspect in some way?"

Coppolla handed the sheet back. "I didn't say that. What I said was I observed the man, and I saw what I saw, and that's not gonna get any clearer as times goes by. You and me are both in law enforcement, and we know that first impressions are always the best."

Vince smiled at him. "I appreciate that, Mr. Coppolla, and thanks again for coming in. I'll call you if we need any further clarification on this." He closed the folder.

"Like I told Detective Vargas, I eyeballed this guy all the way, had him in my sights from the time he left the cash machine to when he went into the alley."

"Hold everything!" Vince hurriedly checked Coppolla's deposition. "It doesn't say anything here about any cash machine. Are you telling me that this guy used the outdoor cash machine at the bank?"

Coppolla frowned. "It don't say nothing about that? That's fuckin' weird, man. I coulda swore I told him I saw the guy make a withdrawal from the Twenty-four Hour Banker. It ain't like me to leave out an important piece of evidence like that."

"So he did use that machine, Mr. Coppolla?" Vince persisted.

"Sure, he walked up to the bank, made a withdrawal from the machine, and went to the alley. I can't hardly believe I left that out."

Vince saw Tommy's eyes widening. "Could you tell me roughly what time it was he made that withdrawal, sir?" he asked, calmly.

"Sure, he was standing there when we pulled up to the bank." Coppolla retrieved a copy of his trip manifest from the inside breast pocket of his jacket and checked the time. "That woulda made it seven-fifty-two A.M."

Vince could feel his chest tightening, an unmistakable quickening of his heartbeat. "It's okay, sir. Some things just slip our minds in the confusion of the moment." He tried to disguise the excitement he felt. "Is there anything else you remember now about that morning that you'd like to add to your previous recollections?"

Coppolla shook his head. "Nope, that's about it."

Vince escorted him to the door of the homicide room. "Thank you for coming in, Mr. Coppolla. I'm glad we had a chance to clear this all up."

Coppolla eyed Vince conspiratorially. "You're not gonna tell my boss about this little slipup, are you?" he whispered.

"Don't worry, Mr. Coppolla." Vince patted him reassuringly on the back. "I just wish all our eyewitnesses were as sharp-eyed as you are."

"It's my training." Coppolla grinned and headed down the stairs.

Tommy was already on the telephone when Vince returned to his desk. "I got the bank running down that deposit now. Can you imagine that asshole forgetting to tell Street Crime something as important as that?"

Vince shrugged. "What the hell can I tell you, partner? I guess Brink's isn't recruiting their security guards from Scotland Yard these days."

Tommy raised a hand, balanced the telephone receiver between his cheek and shoulder, and began writing. "Thanks a lot for the information. We'll send somebody right down there to get a hard copy of this from you." He hung up the phone.

"Well?" Vince asked impatiently.

"A withdrawal was made on eight, twenty-four, at seven-fifty-five A.M. in the amount of sixty dollars, and debited to account number 017-63642. Name on the account is Rafael Rosa, 365 East 209th Street, The Bronx, New York *fucking* City!" He punched the air triumphantly.

"They don't come much prettier than this, partner." Vince thumbed through the telephone book and verified the name and address. "Let's run our friend Rafael Rosa through BCI and see if he's dirty. Then let's get our asses out there and find out just what he was doing in the Gateway lot that morning. If we're lucky, he may just be the key that'll bust this thing wide open for us."

"Are we moving in for the kill?" a disembodied voice echoed through the squad room.

Vince looked up to see Oxbridge Pell standing in the doorway, a hopeful grin creasing his face.

12

CITY OF NEW YORK
BUREAU OF CRIMINAL IDENTIFICATION
Date: 09-06-89   Time: 2323 Fax #: M020756
Confidential to: NYCPDU 37. Det. V.Crowley.
WANTED SYSTEM SEARCH RESULTS
Based on the inquiry of 9/5/89 for Rosa, Rafael, a
wanted search has produced the following arrest
and disposition information:
11/22/84. Criminal Trespass 2nd. Dismissed, Crim.
           Ct. Bx.
04/03/85. Poss. Burglar tools. Dismissed, Crim.
           Ct. Bx.
09/13/85 Assault Brd. a misd. Dismissed, Crim.
           Ct. Bx.
04/28/87 Poss. ctrld. sub., fel. No disposition
           reported.
10/03/87 Poss. marijuana, C fel. Convicted,
           Queens Cr. Ct. Sentenced to 90 days,
           Men's House of Detention.
05/16/89 Violent felony: NYPD Pct. 46. Suspect
           released on bail, failed to report Bx. Crim
           Ct. 7/02/89. Docket # N053309. Bench
           warrant issued.
Alias(es): Robert Townes, Pedro Martínez.

   The apartment was in a middle-class neighborhood
of ethnic whites, blacks, and Hispanics who were
struggling to withstand the steady advance of hookers,

junkies, and vagrants encroaching from the south. Vince and Tommy parked at the foot of a sloping street and waited until their backup units had arrived before climbing the hill to the ornate brown-brick-and-sculpted-concrete entrance. They were armed with a bench warrant for the fugitive suspect, Rafael Rosa, a small-time career criminal who had jumped bail on a charge of armed robbery several months earlier. Street Crime, Leila Turner, and two uniformed patrolmen accompanied them up the worn marble staircase to the third-floor landing and took up positions along the hallway as Vince rang the doorbell at apartment 3D.

"¿*Quién*?" a tentative female voice responded.

"Police, open the door," Vince shouted.

There was a flurry of activity inside; urgent, scrambling footsteps and muffled shouting.

"Open up now or we'll break it down," Vince repeated.

There was a fumbling of locks before the door opened slowly inward. "*Sí*?" A scrawny, unkempt girl of about seven stood in the entrance. Her face, hair, and clothing were spattered with dirt and grease.

Tommy stepped carefully past her into the hallway and accustomed his eyes to the darkness. "Anybody else in here?" he yelled.

There was no response. Vince and the others followed Tommy into the apartment and began searching the darkened corridor.

"This place fuckin' stinks," Tommy whispered hoarsely to Vince as they made their way from empty room to room. "What the hell are they doing in this place, anyway, raising goats?"

The smell of livestock mixed with the permeating aromas of dirt and decay hung in the suffocating heat of the apartment. They saw the unmistakable residue of animals as they edged from room to room: sheets of newspaper soaked with urine, random heaps of fly-infested excrement spread across the bare wooden floor, dog and cat hair everywhere, mounds of down and chicken feathers swept into the corners, billowing in imperceptible wind currents.

"Out! Everybody out, before I blow your goddamn heads off," Street Crime shouted from the rear of the apartment.

A disorganized stream of small children began to exit one of the bedrooms, each seemingly as grimy and neglected as the little girl who had met them at the door.

Vince entered the bedroom behind them and flicked the light switch, but the room remained dark. He walked to the window and drew the closed draperies. "Jesus Christ, look at that, will ya?"

"Omigod!" Leila Turner paled at the sight of the rotting, decapitated sheep's carcass on the bedroom floor.

Vince could feel his stomach turning as the sour-sweet smell of decaying flesh penetrated his nostrils. He threw open the window and inhaled greedily. "Anyone find an adult around here?" he asked, covering his mouth and nose with a handkerchief.

"Just the kids," Street Crime said. "It looks like they've been alone in this place for days with nothing to eat or drink. The water and electricity are both shut off."

"What's your name?" Vince knelt next to one of the frightened girls. "¿Cómo se llama usted?"

She stared at him through terrified eyes, but remained silent.

"Can any of you tell me what happened in here?" Vince asked the others.

"They're not going to say anything," Street Crime volunteered. "They're scared out of their wits."

"I don't want to imagine what they've seen in here." Leila Turner shuddered.

"Go get me the super," Vince instructed the uniformed patrolmen. "I wanta find out what kind of bastard would leave these kids up here in this hellhole without water or electricity." He stepped out of the bedroom into the relatively fresher air of the hallway.

"Get a load of this," Tommy shouted from another bedroom. "Looks like we got ourselves some real weirdos, partner." He pointed to an array of articles spread on the bare floor of the bedroom as Vince entered. Candles burned almost to the bottom were set in shallow glass cruets. Several bowls were filled with dead flowers, insect-covered candies and chocolates were arranged in a terra-cotta dish surrounded by a dried rind of coconut, some coins, several unlit cigars and the headless remains of a gutted chicken.

Vince shook his head, bewildered. "What in hell do you make of all this?"

"*Santería*," Street Crime said simply. "Latin-American black magic. My mother told me stories about it when I was growing up."

"You know about this shit?" Vince asked him.

"Not very much," Street Crime admitted. "Where I grew up, people were too afraid to talk about it a lot."

"What we do with the kids?" Turner broke in.

"Notify the Bureau of Child Welfare. Have them send a bus out here to take them to the New York Foundling Hospital," Vince instructed her. "They'll know what to do with them out there."

The uniformed patrolmen arrived with the superintendent of the building; a sweating, unshaven Hispanic in his mid-fifties. "This here's Enrique Arroyo," Patrolman Tim Sheer said, pushing the man ahead of him into the room. "Enrique runs this cesspool."

"You the janitor here?" Vince demanded.

"*No hablo inglés*," he muttered.

"You don't speak American, huh?" Vince backed him against the wall and gripped his grimy undershirt with a clenched fist. "Well, let me tell you something, scumbag, you just better learn to speak it quick or you're gonna end up like that chicken on the floor there."

Arroyo eyed the gutted bird nervously. "I don't know nothing about that." His breath came at Vince like a punch to the jaw: a combination of unwashed teeth, decaying gums, rum, and garlic. "These people are *loco,* crazy people. I try to have them thrown out, but they tell me I gotta get a court order. Where am I gonna get a fucking court order, you tell me that?"

"Slow down." Vince backed away from the offending breath. "Are you telling me you knew they were slaughtering animals up here?"

"Everybody knows it. I call the cops and they come three, four times maybe. They tell me they can't do nothing because these people are religious.'"

Vince shot a quizzical look at Tommy. "You mean the police came here, saw what these creeps were doing, and never arrested them?"

Arroyo shrugged. "Arrested them? Sure, they arrested them, but the *oficiales* let them loose. I call them time after time and they tell me these people are a religion, that they're protected under the Constitution."

"The Constitution lets them get away with that?" Tommy looked at the grisly scene on the floor.

Arroyo shrugged. "It's your Constitution, not mine."

"What about the children?" Vince asked. "You left seven unprotected minors up here without food, water, or electricity. They could've starved to death up here, thanks to you. You know what we can do to you for that?"

"I didn't know nothing about no kids," Arroyo wailed. "I ain't been near this place in weeks, because these people scare the shit outa me, man. I figured they were gonna carve me up like one of them animals." He wiped his sweating face with a pudgy, grease-stained hand. "I didn't shut off no water or electricity either. Those *loco* bastards ripped out all the wiring and plumbing and sold it to buy dope."

Vince removed Rafael Rosa's mug shot from his pocket and gave it to Arroyo. "Is that the man who lives here?"

"He's one of them," Arroyo said. "There's maybe a dozen or more who use this place. They come, they go, they do that shit—" He looked at the display on the floor and spat. "I don't even know who holds the lease on this apartment. All I know for sure is they ain't paid no rent in the last six months."

"When was the last time you saw the man in that photo?" Vince prodded him.

"Who knows? A couple of weeks, a month maybe."

Several Child Welfare officers arrived at the apartment and began examining the children in the hall.

"How's it look?" Vince asked a stout, heavy-breathing black woman who was administering to one of the crying boys.

"This is one of the worst cases of child neglect I've seen in twenty years on this job," she said, shaking her head sadly. "Some of these children are so seriously malnourished I'm afraid they might have suffered permanent brain damage."

"How long would you say it's been since they were taken care of?" Vince asked.

"Properly taken care of?" She looked up at him with tired eyes. "Who knows? Years probably, for most of them. I wouldn't be surprised if some of them have never had a decent meal or worn clean underwear or slept in a clean bed in their entire lives. Just look into their eyes. Whatever they've seen, or lived through, has turned them into caged animals."

Vince and Tommy watched as the pitiful procession of children and caseworkers made its way out of the apartment and down the stairs to a waiting van.

"They don't get much rougher than this, partner," Vince muttered. "I don't give a shit what those bastards do to one another; I could even live with the animal crap if I had to. But kids, jeez! If that's religion, I don't want any part of it."

"Detective Crowley?" A short, distracted-looking man in a rumpled polyester suit entered the apartment. "I'm James Kroll from the district attorney's occult-crime unit. BCW phoned us about all this and we came right out."

"Cult cop, huh?"

Kroll smiled. "Yeah, sometimes they even call us Ghost Busters. What's going on here?"

Vince shrugged his shoulders. "I dunno. This is all new territory for me. You're the expert. Maybe you can tell me what this is all about."

Kroll looked at the ceremonial display on the floor. "It looks like *santería*, or some variant of it. How much do you know about them?"

"Whatever you tell me will be it."

Kroll examined the ritualistic items carefully, took one of the cigars from the floor, and lit it. "Pretty good smoke," he said, exhaling a lazy column of blue smoke toward the ceiling. "Cuban, maybe."

"Hey, that's evidence, man," Tommy protested.

"Smells a lot better'n that shit on the floor, though, doesn't it?" Kroll walked to the other bedroom, where the rotting sheep's carcasss lay in a corner. "This sort of thing is pretty common—the animal sacrifices, I mean," he explained. "They're meant to appease a bunch of gods and spirits in their hierarchy: Elegguá Olokun, Ochosi . . . They've got a god for just about every aspect of their lives and a complete set of rituals set out to make sure they're getting the right kind of magic."

"Sounds like a lot of mumbo jumbo to me," Tommy commented sourly.

"Maybe it is to you, but there are hundreds of thousands of *santeros* who swear by it," Kroll said. "And they're not all a bunch of uneducated savages either. They've got all kinds of followers: doctors, lawyers, college professors—people who believe they can get absolute control over their lives, attain any goal they want, as long as they have the right magic and the gods are on their side."

"Doctors and lawyers didn't do this," Vince said.

"Probably not, but whoever did it is no less devout

in their beliefs than you may be in yours. Some of them even call themselves Christians, after a fashion."

"How can that be?" Tommy asked.

"*Santería* is a synthesis," Kroll told him. "Sort of a combination of African voodoo brought over by slaves and the Christianity they were told they had to practice by the slaveholders. Being innovative people, they just mixed it all together in a cooking pot and out came *santería*."

"No Christian ever told them it was okay to rip the guts out of a helpless animal, let alone chop up some poor hooker and do magic over her dead body." Tommy argued.

"You have a human victim?" Kroll asked.

"A prostitute was carved up out in Secor Park," Vince told him. "There were a lot of these same symbols and markings at the crime scene."

Kroll nodded thoughtfully. "The animal sacrifices are one thing; they're practiced by all *santería* as part of their general rituals. As far as the other, it happens, but not very often, and you're almost always dealing with some offbeat, quasi-religious sect that utilizes bits and pieces of a lot of occult practices—voodoo, Satanism, even *santería*. If this is all the work of the same group, my guess would be that you're looking at a bunch of out-of-control renegades here, and if that doesn't scare you, I gotta tell you, it scares me."

The sight of Cherry Dressard's severed, mutilated body flashed before Vince's eyes. "It scares me, pal. It scares the shit out of me."

13

POLICE DEPARTMENT
CITY OF NEW YORK

09-12-89
From: Commanding Officer 37th Pct. Detective Unit

To: Police Jurisdiction Concerned

Subj: Request for Field Information

1. Attached is a surveillance photograph of a suspect in a homicide being investigated by this command.
2. It is requested that any field information possessed by you re: the possible location of this individual be forwarded to this command.
3. Description: male, black, Hispanic descent. 5 ft. 11 in. 27 yrs. Good build. Black hair, close-cropped. Black beard (goatee type), close-cropped. Brown eyes. Subject may be dressed in a short leather jacket (black or brown) and may be wearing several gold or silver chains around his neck.
4. Subject may be driving a late-model Cadillac or Chrysler sedan bearing personalized license plates CHANGO.
5. Subject is to be considered armed and dangerous. Do not approach or attempt to apprehend this individual!

6. Subject is sought for a homicide/bombing carried under 61# 8081, case # 1717. Dets. V. Crowley and T. Ippollito assigned. Kindly telephone any pertinent information to 37 PDU at (212) 920-6712, 13 or 19.

Luck was with them. The bank's surveillance cameras were running at the time of Rafael Rosa's withdrawal from the cash machine, giving them an updated photograph to go with his past mug shots and placing him irrefutably at the scene of the Gateway explosion. Further investigation uncovered the information that Rosa was a member of the Engineering Corps of the United States Marines from March of 1980 to April of the following year, had received a summary court-martial and dishonorable discharge, and spent eighteen months in federal prison resulting from a charge of theft of government property—six dynamite caps—a fact inexplicably missing from his New York City arrest records. The flyers and photographs were in the mail, the computers were humming, and sooner or later the network of law-enforcement agencies seeking him would close in and he would be captured or killed. It was that simple. Nobody remained a fugitive forever.

For Vince it was a day off, and he had spent most of it lounging in front of the bedroom TV watching the Mets lose to the Pirates in twelve innings, and consuming the better part of the Genoa salami and a six-pack of Schlitz. It was one of those days when doing nothing seemed like a pretty good idea; when he'd reached the limits of time and patience and endurance, and it was time to uncoil, time to mellow out for a few hours and think of nothing more challenging and disturbing than extra innings and extra calories. He surveyed his stomach, bulging beneath the maroon Detective's Endowment Association sweatshirt he wore, and sucked it in reflexively. Connie would spot the cans and wrappings when she came home from work and remind him that he was killing himself with inac-

tivity and cholesterol. And he would solemnly promise
to stop eating garbage and get to the gym the following day—swim fifty laps in the pool or play racquetball
with Walt Cuzak. It was all bullshit, they both knew, a
fiction they needed to maintain if they were to appear
responsible to themselves and to each other. Vince
belched contentedly and switched channels with the
remote control. He could live with it if Connie could.

The telephone by the bed rang and he answered it:
a call for Connie from a frosty-voiced female.

"Can you ask her to call District Attorney Quinlan's
office?" she asked when Vince told her Connie was
out.

"Can I take a message?"

"Just ask her to return the call, please."

Vince hung up the telephone. What the hell was
Tom Quinlan calling Connie at home for? The D.A.
had been getting entirely too chummy with her lately,
he thought, flicking through the TV channels morosely. Quinlan was current news and Connie was in
the business of gathering news, he knew, but the city
was full of reporters just as competent and just as
eager for a story. So why the calls at home, the hur-
ried conversations?

Politicians and newspeople made strange bedfellows
. . . He was angry at himself for the suspicion. Vince
had made it a point never to pry into Connie's work,
and she had done the same for him. Part of what they
felt for each other had to do with professional respect.
All it took was maturity and resolve. He decided to
shelve his misgivings and be adult about it.

Connie arrived an hour later and collapsed on the
bed next to him. "God, it's been a day. What's happening here?"

"You had a call from Tom Quinlan. You and him
are getting kinda chummy, aren't you?" So much for
maturity and resolve.

She frowned. "What's that supposed to mean?"

"I dunno. It's just like all of a sudden you're his

favorite reporter in New York. What'd you do to get such special treatment?" He immediately hated himself for asking.

Connie kicked off her shoes and stretched her toes. "You know what us women do. Who needs brains and spunk when you've got a body, right?"

"That was dumb, I'm sorry," he groaned.

"If you want to know the truth of it, I think D.A. Tom Quinlan is an egomaniacal asshole," she said. "I find him shallow and devious and manipulative, and I'd be thrilled if he just crawled back into whatever hole he slithered out of and left me alone."

"Hey, you're talking about a friend of mine."

She retrieved her address book from her purse and thumbed through it. "I don't expect you'd feel the same way about him as I do. After all, you have to wade through all that male bonding before you start looking for substance in a person." She found Quinlan's telephone number and dialed. "Rest your fears, Crowley. Unshaven and sloppy and smelling like Oktoberfest at the New York Deli, you're still better than Tom Quinlan on his best day, hands down."

Connie's conversation with the D.A. was cryptic and unemotional. "Want to know what it was about?" she asked when she hung up.

He shrugged. "Hey, it's none of my business."

"It just might be, if what he's been telling me over the past few weeks is true."

"What's that?" Vince asked.

"Basically, that his opponent in the upcoming election is a crook."

"So? All politicians say that about their opponents in one way or another."

"True, but Quinlan's starting to get specific," Connie said. "Like telling me that Julian Santiago inherited a network of bribery and theft, extortion and securities fraud from his mentor, the late congressman, Guido Derosa, and that he's kept it going at full tilt."

"He got any proof of this?"

"Nothing he's giving me," Connie replied. "So far just a lot of unsubstantiated charges that I haven't been able to verify."

"Sounds like my buddy is taking the low road," Vince observed. "He ought to know better than to think any responsible newsperson would report stuff like that."

"I don't think he expects me to report it at all," Connie said. "I think he's looking for me to investigate it, maybe make his case for him."

"What's wrong with the D.A.'s department? If they think the guy's dirty, they should investigate him themselves."

Connie shrugged. "I gave up trying to figure out politicians a long time ago." She took the remote channel changer from Vince and turned off the set. "This much I have been able to verify, though: whether this is true or just another campaign smear, yours truly seems to be the only member of the fourth estate it's trickling down to."

"Why you?" Vince asked.

"That, I have not yet figured out." She stood and began undressing. "On to more prosaic matters, Crowley. I'm about to take a shower, and you and only you are being invited to participate. Care to respond?"

"Um, this preparatory to anything else?" he asked casually.

"You're the investigator, investigate!" She disappeared into the bathroom.

Vince left his clothes in a heap on the bedroom floor, checked his naked profile in the bureau mirror, satisfying himself that he was still reasonably trim, salami and beer notwithstanding, before joining Connie in the shower.

"You smell nice." He nuzzled her steamy neck and shoulders, closing his eyes instinctively against the stream of warm water. "We oughta do this more often." He pressed his chest and hips against her naked back, reached around her gently, took the bar of scented soap from her hand, and began to rub it on her body, forming frothy circles on the tender skin of her abdomen, lathering her aroused breasts.

Connie stiffened, then relaxed, submerged in his heady, lubricating touch, his urgent, throbbing hips poised and pumping against her yielding buttocks. She felt safe in his grasp, reassured by the knotted sinews of his encircling arms and his heavy breathing blending with the resonance of water droplets cascading off the tiles around her.

"I'll be waiting." Connie parted the plastic curtain and stepped outside.

Vince soaped his body hurriedly and allowed the soothing flow of hot water to wash over him, easing his tightened muscles but not his desire. He envisioned Connie waiting for him in the bedroom, her still-steaming body naked beneath the sheets. She would pretend to be sleeping when he came to her. Her closed eyelids would flutter imperceptibly, then open slowly and register mock surprise as he stood above her, toweling off. He would be a stranger, intruding on her, forcing his attentions on her as she lay helplessly in her bed, ravaging her, compelling her to submit. It was a fantasy that had probably endured as long as there had been lovers and lovemaking, they knew, but it worked, and neither of them was embarrassed by their lack of originality. Good sex was good sex. There was no point in analyzing it.

What was harder for him to understand was why Connie wanted to be with him in the first place. That was a mystery that merited analysis, but he was no closer to understanding it now than he had been when they first got together. He was a decent-enough-looking man, he realized, eyeing the indistinct outlines of his naked form in the steamy full-length mirror on the bathroom door. He was also reasonably bright, sometimes witty and amusing, but he was a New York City cop, and getting involved with a New York City cop was bad business. Connie knew that, just as Jessy came to know it before her, and still she wanted him. Strange. Somehow Connie saw something in him that he was unable to see in himself. For now he could only hope it stuck, whatever it was—at least for the next couple of minutes.

Connie's eyelids fluttered and she opened them in mock surprise. "Sir, do I know you?"

Vince smiled. "I'm gonna unhook the telephone so we don't get any in-flight calls from anybody."

Connie rolled and stretched. "God, yes," she agreed. "The last thing I need now is another surprise call from your buddy the district attorney."

"Tom's got more sensitivity than that," Vince commented, climbing into the bed next to her.

"Not when it comes to Julian Santiago and the Contech Corporation."

"The what?" Vince sat bolt upright.

"The Contech Corporation. That's the outfit that's supposed to have him on the payroll."

Thoughts of sex evaporated with the bathroom steam.

14

ON FRIDAY THE THIRTEENTH, THE HEAT WAVE FINALLY lifted after more than a month. Vince found several messages on his desk when he arrived at the Three-Seven for the four-to-twelve shift: a call from Jessy wanting to know what he had learned about Katie, a return call from James Kroll at the occult-crimes unit, another from Lieutenant Bill Kitzmiller at headquarters. He lifted the receiver and dialed Brooklyn.

"We're not here right now, but we want desperately to talk to you," the recorded message droned. "Please leave your name, number, and a brief message at the tone, and we'll get right back to you."

"Katie, it's Daddy," Vince said at the beep. "Call me back when you have a chance. Your mom's worried about you." He thought a minute. "And what's this *we* stuff? I thought *we* were living alone." Vince hung up.

He was immediately sorry he'd said it. It would put Katie back on the defensive, and that would widen the gap between them even more. He wished there was a way to erase the message, but it was like an ill-conceived letter already in the mailbox. There was nothing he could do about it now. He phoned James Kroll.

"Thanks for calling me back," he said when Kroll came on the line. "Any chance we could get together soon and compare notes on this santería stuff? I gotta tell you, this is pretty much brand-new territory for me and I can use all the help I can get."

"I'd be glad to help any way I can," Kroll replied. "It's nice to be taken seriously by somebody from NYPD for a change."

"They been giving you a tough time?"

Kroll laughed. "Well, I can't say that I blame them. We are a little way out, and sometimes what we have to tell them makes their jobs harder. No offense, Detective, but let's face it, cops don't like working in areas they don't understand."

"Does anybody?"

"You called me, didn't you?"

"I guess so, but I didn't know I was letting myself in for more problems than I already got," Vince admitted. "Let's just say I want to know more about these guys. What do I have to do for starters? Is there any way I can get inside and talk to them, ask them some questions, maybe get to go to one of their ceremonies?"

"As far as questioning them, forget it," Kroll said. "They don't want anything to do with the police. By them, the police are there to harass them, put them out of business. And if you want to attend one of their ceremonies, you'll have to become a member, a *santero*. That means you go through an elaborate ceremony called the *asiento* and become a saint."

"Hold it. I'm not interested in sainthood. All I want to know is what kind of people will carve up a woman and starve a bunch of kids. I don't want to be converted or anything."

"What you want is some answers," Kroll corrected him. "And they're not easy to come by when you're dealing with *santería*. What kind of people are they? Most of all they're people who hold an absolute belief that they can control their own destinies on this earth if they practice the right magic. Their gods are not like what we think of God. Their gods can be manipulated, even tricked, if you know the right formula. They use their gods to get what they want in their lives, or to get back at their enemies. The mutilations are just part of the magic, something to appease whatever god they're looking to exploit."

Vince thought about it. "To tell you the truth, it doesn't sound like something I want to spend my life studying. Just suppose I want to find out who's practicing it around this neck of the woods. Who would you suggest I see to get that information?"

"I can't give you anyone specifically. We're pretty new at all this ourselves, and our intelligence isn't that good yet. If I were you, I'd talk to anybody up there who's involved in the occult: fortune-tellers, palm readers, numerologists. They're not *santería*, but they're closer to the pipeline than we are."

Vince spotted Steve Appelbaum coming in the door. "Okay, thanks for your help. I'll get back to you if I have any more questions."

"Or if you come up with any answers," Kroll added. "Like I said, we're pretty new at this ourselves, we can use all the help we can get."

"What'd you find out about Santiago?" Vince asked Appelbaum when he hung up the telephone.

Steve sat by Vince's desk and checked his notebook. "Well, for starters, nobody down at the D.A.'s office will even admit there's an investigation going on. My gut feeling is that they don't want to stir up any shit before November. You know New Yorkers: they'd consider it dirty pool for Quinlan to indict his opposition just before the election. They'd probably elect Santiago out of sympathy, crook or no crook."

Appelbaum turned the page of the notebook. "I had better luck down at the U.S. attorney's office, though. I pulled in a couple of markers and found out that they've been investigating Guido Derosa for about a year now."

"How about Santiago?" Vince asked.

"Nothing that I could find out, but that business about the Contech Corporation seems to check out. Apparently it has to do with the Small Business Administration channeling federal contracts to the company without competitive bidding. It looks like ex-Congressman Derosa was influence-peddling and Contech was buying."

Vince shrugged. "Derosa's dead. Santiago's the guy I'm interested in now." He sifted through the papers on his desk and found the list of Thomas Falcone's Washington contacts that the Contech executives, Escobar and Cruz, had given him. "Do me a favor and check these names out for me Steve, okay? It might be interesting if one of them turned up on the congressman's payroll." He handed the sheet to Appelbaum and dialed Bill Kitzmiller at Headquarters.

"What's the word, my man?" he asked.

"I wish I had better news for you, Vince, but you told me to give it to you straight," Kitzmiller answered. "It looks like there's a contingency plan in front of the board of estimate that'll merge twelve precincts, and the Three-Seven is one of them."

"That's definite?" Vince asked weakly.

"You know nothing's definite in this city, pal. Right now there's a budget crunch and an election all at the same time. Every half-assed politician in New York is running around with his head up his keister looking for answers, and this just happens to be one of them. You know how it works, Vince. Every time they look to save money they cut the cops; then they scream their fuckin' heads off when crime goes up. What can I tell you?"

"Not much, Bill. Thanks for getting back to me." Vince hung up the phone.

"Trouble?" Tommy asked from his desk.

Vince hesitated. "I dunno, maybe . . . I'll let you know after I've checked it out more." He grabbed his jacket. "Let's get the hell outa here."

"Where to?" Tommy asked, following him down the stairs.

"Anywhere, just away from here." Vince climbed into the front seat of the unmarked squad car as Tommy started the ignition. "Let's go uptown and have a talk with our friend Silk Washington. Maybe he knows something about those voodoo markings out in Secor Park where Cherry Dressard was killed."

They drove silently, Vince engrossed in thoughts and projections. He would retire if the Three-Seven closed up, he decided, even though he knew that was what the city wanted in the first place. Veteran cops would take their pensions rather than go through the hassle of working in another command, and they would not be replaced. The pols saved money on real estate and attrition and nobody was the worse for it, except for maybe a few beat-up old cops who'd worn themselves out in the service of their city anyway. It was no big deal.

Vince knew it wasn't that he would miss the precinct so much. Most of the old guys were gone anyway, and the new breed of cops coming in would be the same no matter where he was: scraggly, arrogant, and unprofessional, caring nothing for the bond of brotherhood cops before them had forged with their sweat and blood. The rookies thought of old-timers like Vince and Walt and Steve as throwbacks to a time when being a cop was a bigger deal than just a paycheck and a dental plan. Being an anachronism in the Three-Seven was bad enough. Vince knew he could never hack being one anywhere else, where he would have to start winning the new guys' respect all over again. No way! He was getting too old for that crap.

"Three-eleven West 103rd, partner." Tommy's voice shook Vince out of his reverie. "And if I'm not mistaken, that's Washington's pimpmobile parked in front of the apartment." He pointed to a silver Mercedes sedan standing in a no-parking zone, unticketed.

"Looks like Silk's got some friends down at the parking violations bureau," Vince noted as Tommy pulled to the curb. "Let's try not to make a big splash on the way in. Maybe we can catch the slimebucket with his pants down."

No such luck.

"You musta just missed him," the voluptuous young black woman who answered the door said coyly, fluttering her long black eyelashes at them as they stood in the doorway, seemingly undaunted by their gold shields and credentials. "Try calling next time. Silk's a busy man, you know."

Vince rolled his eyes at Tommy. They both should have known that the jungle drums would give them away before they got to the front door. "Okay if we come in and have a look around, Miss—?"

"Violet." She shrugged and stood aside.

"We're investigating the murder of Cherry Dressard, Violet," he told her as Tommy walked from room and room. "I don't suppose you knew her."

Violet paled. "She was a friend of mine. I hope you catch the bastard that did her."

Vince removed his notebook. "Would you mind answering a few questions as long as we're here?"

"Sure, if it'll help catch that motherfucker."

He poised his pencil. "Were you aware of anyone who had reason to kill her? Was she receiving any threats that you knew of?"

Violet laughed bitterly. "She was in the life, man. Girl meet all kinds of weirdos when she's in the life. Some of them are violent, some get it off just acting like they are. I dunno, man . . ." Her voice trailed off.

"Did she ever tell you she was afraid of anybody in particular, maybe someone with a background in *santería*?" Vince asked.

Her eyes went wide. "That black-magic stuff? No way Cherry was going to get herself involved with some lowlife voodoo turkey. Cherry wasn't no street hooker, you know. She had a pretty sophisticated clientele."

"I'm sure." Vince stifled a smile as Tommy returned from one of the bedrooms, signaling that his search for the elusive Silk had been unsuccessful. "I don't suppose you could provide us with a list of her customers—a little black book maybe?"

"You must be outa your cotton-picking mind!" Violet grinned broadly. "I will tell you this, though: Cherry wasn't taking no regular tricks lately. She did a vacation gig, a couple of rich old men out on a yacht in the Caribbean. She made enough money in one week on that gig to take some time off and just relax."

"And just when would that trip have been?" Vince asked.

Violet paused. "Oh, I'd say along about the end of July, beginning of August."

"Can you be more specific?"

She shrugged. "First week in August, thereabouts."

"And she was gone how long?"

"A week, maybe. Trixie Lee could tell you better than I could."

"Trixie Lee?"

"She was the other girl hired to go on the trip," Violet said. "But don't ask me where she is. I ain't seen her white ass since they came back. Probably took the money and stuck it up her nose."

Vince wrote down the information. "Can you tell me if this Trixie Lee was working for Silk?"

She shook her head resolutely. "No way. Neither was Cherry at that point. Silk's okay at handling the small-time stuff, but he ain't got the brains to set up no Caribbean cruises, no sir. Whoever handled that piece of business was probably connected with somebody important downtown, somebody who knows what rich white folks want and how to get it. That's way out of Silk Washington's league."

"Got a name for me?"

"You just gotta be kidding me, man," Violet howled. "If Id'a knowed that, I woulda been on that trip myself."

Vince closed his notebook and headed for the door. "Maybe it's a lucky thing for you that you didn't. Look where Cherry Dressard ended up."

15

SERGEANT BOB DONOFRIO STOOD IN THE DOORWAY of the C.O.'s office and signaled to Vince that Lieutenant Sweeney was ready to see him. Vince cleared his desk, swallowed hard, and went in.

"You wanted to see me about something?" Sweeney asked from behind his desk.

"Yes sir . . ." Vince tried to keep from fidgeting. "It's about the reports that they're planning to shut down the house, sir."

"Reports? What reports?"

"Well, sir, it's just that the word is going around that we're gonna be merged with another precinct after the election. I just thought I'd verify it with you before I let the men know."

Sweeney leaned forward on his elbows and rested his chin on his folded hands. "Where'd you hear a thing like that, Crowley?"

"You know the grapevine, Lieutenant. These things have a way of getting out."

"The grapevine, huh?" Sweeney stood and walked around his desk. "Nothing substantial? No corroborating evidence? We're just going on hearsay here, right?"

Vince shuffled his feet uneasily. "I guess you could say that, Lieutenant, but it's pretty good hearsay."

"Good hearsay . . ." Sweeney thought about it. "What would you say if I told you that this precinct was about to be renovated and enlarged, that our complement of officers was to be increased twenty-five

116

percent, that all the plumbing and electricity was going to be fixed, that our toilets and air conditioners were finally going to work the way they're supposed to work?"

"I'd say that's pretty good, Lieutenant. Is that gonna happen?"

"No, but you might just as well start spreading it around on that grapevine of yours," Sweeney said. "There's just about as much validity to it as there is to that other cockamamy story you're ready to tell them."

Vince could see Donofrio out of the corner of his eye, grinning broadly. "Begging the lieutenant's pardon, but it's hard for me to find a lot to laugh about here. I'm not saying that the information is absolute, but the word that's going around is that you're just here to mop up before they shut us down."

"And you believe that?" Sweeney asked.

"If I can be frank, sir, you haven't exactly plunged into the precinct caseload."

"Um . . ." Sweeney nodded. "Well, maybe I'd better change that. Why don't you have a report on my desk by tomorrow morning outlining everything in the house, who's assigned to what and current disposition. I'll read it as soon as I can and get back to you on it, how's that?"

Vince felt like a panzer division had just driven up his asshole. "If that's what you want, sir."

"That's what I want. Anything else?"

"No sir, Lieutenant." He exited the office.

"What was that all about?" Street Crime asked him when he got back to his desk.

"Do me a favor, willya? Next time I ask to go in there and see that guy about anything, cuff me and send me off to the flight deck at Bellevue." Vince placed a blank UF-49 form in his typewriter and stared at it morosely. "I oughta know better than to try to get a straight answer out of a politician by now."

"Steve left this for you while you were out." Street Crime handed him the computer list of Thomas

Falcone's Washington contacts. One of the names and telephone numbers had been circled in red grease crayon with an arrow leading to a note in the margin, written in Appelbaum's unmistakable scrawl: "This guy used to work for Guido Derosa. Now he's a member of Santiago's staff." The name circled was Daniel Keliher.

"Very interesting . . ." Vince walked to the robbery room, where Steve was eating his lunch. "You do any follow-up on this?" he asked, brandishing the list.

"I called," Steve mumbled through a mouthful of his cheeseburger. "Somebody down there told me he'd get right back, but I'm not counting on it. Snuffy and me are going over to Santiago's Bronx office after lunch and shake the trees a little bit to see if anything dirty falls out."

"Sounds good." Vince turned to leave. "Oh, by the way, Sweeney asked me for a list of current cases and everyone assigned. I'm not saying he'll do it, but don't be surprised if he pulls you off this one. I get the feeling he's gonna stir things up just so he can start looking like a commander."

His telephone was ringing when he got back to his desk. "Crowley here, Three-Seven precinct," he barked.

"Daddy, it's Katie." She sounded far away.

The call surprised him. "Katie . . . How's everything at school?"

"Okay. You called me, left a message on my machine."

"Oh, yeah. I just wanted to know how you were making out. Your mom called and wanted to know what was going on with you."

"You said she was worried about me," Katie corrected him. "What does she think I'm doing anyway, turning tricks on street corners?"

He winced. "She's just being a mother, you know that."

"And you're just being a father when you start growling about my use of the word 'we,' right?"

"Hey, let's not start a fight here, honey. Unless I'm mistaken, you did say you were living alone," Vince pointed out.

"I have a roommate," she said coolly. "Her name is Karen."

Vince rolled his eyeballs. "Look, honey, I'm glad everything's good with you. I'll pass that message along to your mother."

"I'm sorry. It's just that I need you both to trust me right now," Katie moaned.

"I know, honey," Vince reassured her. "When am I going to get to see that place of yours anyway?"

"Soon, Daddy, as soon as we have it straightened out. I'll call you in a week or so, okay?"

"You got it, 'Bye, baby." He hung up.

Tommy entered the squad room and handed Vince a folded computer printout. "The rap sheet for Trixie Lee," he explained. "Nothing really spectacular."

"What the hell happened to you?" Vince eyed Tommy's hair, uncharacteristically close-cropped.

"Don't ask," Tommy scowled. "I made the mistake of going to that old guinea down by the diner, the one who cuts your hair, right? I tell him, 'Just a trim, motherfucker, none of that white-sidewall shit you usually give the cops who come in here. I'm watching you,' I tell him. 'So don't try to pull a fast one.'

"So I sit down in the chair and this mook starts snipping, real easy like, you know? Pretty soon I'm all settled in. The old man is lulling me to sleep with talcum and witch hazel and Brylcreem. He's cutting my nose hair like this is the Waldorf or something and I'm relaxed as hell. All of a sudden the son of a bitch comes at me with the electric clipper like a chain-saw murderer. Before I can stop him, he's halfway up the right side of my head like he's mowing a goddamn lawn or something." Tommy sat down hard at his desk. "I shoulda arrested the motherfucker for something. I swear to God, Vince, those old dago barbers aren't happy unless everybody looks like 1945."

Vince scanned Trixie Lee's rap sheet: several dozen arrests for soliciting, prostitution, and possession of drugs and drug paraphernalia, dating back to the late seventies. "Looks like your basic whore here. Were you able to find out if she's got a pimp?"

"I'm checking it out now, trying to find out who posted bail for her the last time she got busted."

"Good. Let's get as much of this shit done now as we can," Vince told him. "Sweeney's liable to start rattling our cages in a couple of days."

"What for?" Tommy asked.

"Call it a hunch." He leafed through his book, found Andrea Falcone's telephone number, and dialed.

"I'm sorry to bother you, Mrs. Falcone," he apologized. "I was hoping you wouldn't mind answering a few more questions."

"Not at all, if you think it will help," she replied.

"Okay if my partner and I drive out there now?"

"I'll put a pot of coffee on the burner."

Downstairs, Tommy backed the patrol car out of its parking space, made an illegal U-turn, and headed for the Boston Post Road and Yonkers. "Why didn't you just ask her whatever you wanted to ask her over the phone?" he asked Vince.

"Mostly, because we'll be asking a bereaved widow if she knew her husband might've been cheating on her," Vince replied. "The least we can do is look her in the eye when we do it."

"You know something I don't?" Tommy asked him.

"Only that Thomas Falcone was somewhere warm and sunny the last week of his life. Steve and Snuffy tried to find out where from his bosses out at Contech, but they're stonewalling. They say he was in Washington the whole week, as far as they know."

"So? Washington's warm and sunny in August," Tommy reminded him.

"But Falcone removed his wedding ring and left it off long enough to get his whole finger good and tanned, and that smells fishy to me."

"A tanned ring finger's pretty shaky evidence," Tommy pointed out.

"It's not as shaky as it seems. I called that hotel number in Washington that Andrea Falcone gave us, and they hadn't seen him in more than a month. His telephone credit card is blank from August fourteenth to the twenty-first—no calls to his office, none to his home. None of his other credit cards was used during that period either. As far as I can tell, he didn't do any business, nobody saw him, and nobody talked to him for an entire week. It's like he fell off the face of the earth."

"Except he showed up in time to get himself blown away by a petty hood named Rafael Rosa," Tommy added.

"Allegedly blown away by Rosa," Vince corrected him. "Who, by the way, just happens to be carrying a voodoo charm that is practically identical to one we find on a dead, mutilated hooker in Secor Park, and turns out to be a practitioner of *santería*, which may or may not having something to do with this whole thing."

"You saying Falcone was into that shit?" Tommy asked.

"Just thinking aloud," Vince replied. "But it wouldn't surprise me. Nothing would at this point."

Tommy turned onto MacLean Avenue in Yonkers. "You gonna tell his wife about the wedding-ring thing?"

Vince shrugged. "What choice do I have?"

"You're gonna break her heart," Tommy moaned as he parked the car in front of the Falcone house. "This really stinks, man. It really fucking stinks."

Less than ten miles away in Brooklyn, Katie Crowley joined the group sitting cross-legged on her apartment floor and watched nervously as the others passed a glass pipe in a circle. They inhaled the curling white smoke captured inside the transparent bowl through a slender glass tube with short, sucking gasps, drew it deep into their lungs and held it there.

The room was semidark, suspended in hushed whispers and the unsteady flutter of candles, the penetrating aromas of spice and incense. At the center of the circle, Senji Rula handed the pipe among the participants, cradling the glass bowl in his slender hands reverently, like a necromancer divining the unknowable with a crystal ball. He softly chanted as he removed the pipe from one trembling hand and handed it to the next in line, sometimes reheating the admixture in the bowl with a lighter.

Across the circle, silhouetted in the flickering halflight, Katie saw her roommate, Karen, rocking back and forth on the floor, moaning softly in response to Senji Rula's chanted cadence. His sensitive artist's fingers unbuttoned her blouse, unhooked her bra, and slid it down into her lap. Katie felt a thrill as Senji cupped the small, firm breasts in his hands and kissed Karen's aroused nipples tenderly. She found herself touching her own breasts in a way she had never allowed herself outside of the privacy of her bedroom. Others in the room began to sway and to touch one another, mildly at first, almost ritualistically, then with greater and greater fervor as Senji Rula's chant grew in cadence and intensity: *"Chango mani cote, Chango mani cote olle masa, Chango arabari cote ode mata icote. . . "*

"Come, my child." Rula knelt before Katie and pressed the pipe gently in her hands. "Partake of this sacrament if you are to be whole again."

Katie looked into his sensitive eyes, set deeply beneath a ridge of paint-daubed brow, glistening with sweat in the reflected light of the candles that burned in the center of the circle. She took the glass mouthpiece between her lips and drew some smoke into her lungs, holding it there as she had seen the others do until she felt a heat wave rising out of her stomach and spreading throughout her body like a flight of frolicsome birds beating their wingtips against the tender membranes of her nervous system. She felt them coursing through her bloodstream, lighting up millions of incandescent bulbs she had never known were there, sockets she had never known were there to plug them into . . . glowing hot and red all over like the sun had suddenly been plucked from the sky and planted in her head.

16

"DANIEL KELIHER, THAT NAME MEAN ANYTHING to you?" Vince sat in The Bronx D.A.'s office and put the question to him bluntly.

Tom Quinlan's eyes flickered, but he remained impassive. "You talking about the Dan Keliher who happens to be the chief aide to my worthy opponent?"

"Yep. I'm getting information that could tie him in with a current homicide investigation, and I thought you might have something I can use," Vince said.

"Homicide? Jeez, that's serious stuff."

"That's what I do for a living, in case you forgot," Vince reminded him.

"Dan Keliher, huh? I knew he was a crooked son of a bitch, but I wouldn't have pegged him as a murderer."

"I didn't say he was a murderer. I said I was getting information tying him in with a case I'm on."

"Murder case, huh?"

Vince expelled a long, low breath of air. "When you're finished jerking me off, Tom, would you mind telling me what it is I'm supposed to know about this guy?"

"Supposed to know about him? Whatta you mean by that?" Quinlan asked.

"Come on, Tom, don't play dumb with me," Vince said. "You've been feeding crumbs about Santiago to Connie for the past month, and it doesn't take a genius to figure that you knew some of them would get back to me. Now we can play Bust Vince's Balls

124

here and put me through the hassle of digging up what I need all by myself, or we can get serious. Somehow this guy Keliher is tied in with Thomas Falcone, and that could mean he's tied in with a lot of other stuff I'm trying to sort out. Want to help me out here?"

Quinlan leaned back in his office chair and surveyed the view from his window. "You gotta understand, Vince. Anything I tell you has to be just between the two of us, at least until after the election. You can use it any way you want, but don't involve me. You do and I'll deny I ever talked to you about it, okay?"

"Fair enough."

Quinlan reached into his top desk drawer, removed a thin manila folder, and placed it on the desk in front of him. "In a nutshell, Keliher was a bagman for Guido Derosa when he was alive, and he's got the same job with Santiago. If you want to know the truth of it, I guess you could say that Keliher's the guy who makes the whole operation work. That strunz Santiago wouldn't have the brains to lift an apple from a fruit stand."

"And how does Contech figure into all of this?" Vince asked.

Quinlan allowed himself a slight smile. "Basically, the whole operation isn't much more than a high-class pongee scam. Contech would bid low to obtain government contracts, fake their books to show a paper profit even when they were losing money, then use those phony figures to borrow more money and compete for new contracts. Ex-congressman Derosa was the guy who siphoned new business off to them, and they returned the favor with illegal campaign contributions and gifts of stock to members of his family. Now Derosa's heir apparent, the distinguished Julian Santiago, has retrieved his fallen banner and keeps the scam alive."

Vince shook his head. "Look, Tom, this is pretty much all Greek to me. All I want to know is whether you've established some kind of link between Thomas

Falcone and this bird Keliher. If so, what was the connection and could it have had anything to do with Falcone's murder?"

"Keliher is Santiago's man. Contech needed Santiago's blessing if they stood any chance of getting those juicy government contracts, and your guy Falcone spread the grease for Contech," Quinlan said. "I don't think I can make it any plainer than that."

"I can see that." Vince nodded. "What I can't see is why you don't just move in on these guys and bury them? If what you say is true, you can wipe Santiago out in the press long before election day."

"If it was strictly up to me, Santiago and the whole Contech bunch would be in jail right now," Quinlan said. "Unfortunately, this is a lot bigger than just a local Bronx issue, and a lot of other agencies are breaking their asses for a piece of the action: the FBI, the attorney general's office, the Treasury department, you name it. It's a goddamn legal and procedural nightmare. Right now, the way things are going, Santiago'll be retired back in San Juan before anybody gets around to indicting him."

"So goes the bureaucracy—"

"And I'm sitting on enough shit to blow these bastards right out of the water and I'm bound by professional ethics not to release it. It really pisses me off." Quinlan shook his head sadly and pushed his chair away from the desk. "Hang on a minute, okay, Vince? I gotta take a wicked leak." He nudged the manila folder forward on the desk with his forefinger.

Vince waited until Quinlan had closed the door to the lavatory adjoining his office before he lifted the folder and looked inside. It contained a single eight-by-ten photograph in black-and-white, grainy and slightly out of focus but unmistakably a picture of Thomas Falcone and a male companion relaxing on the rear deck of a luxurious yacht, tanned and grinning in swim shorts and gaily colored Hawaiian shirts, hoisting icy drinks in a mock toast to the unseen cameraman.

Vince removed it from the folder and slipped it under his jacket just before the bathroom door opened and Quinlan returned to his desk.

"Are we okay here?" Quinlan asked him, slipping the empty folder back into his desk drawer. "Can I get on with my campaign now, or do you want to waste any more of my valuable time here?"

"I'm okay, unless you have something else you want to let me in on," Vince answered.

"I'm afraid I can't help you there, pal." Quinlan stood and extended his hand across the desk. "I think our business here is over."

Vince smiled. "You're some piece of work, you know that?"

"Hey, just another civil servant like yourself, trying to make the world a better place to live in."

Downstairs, Vince climbed into the passenger seat of the squad car and directed Tommy to drive across town to Madame Sabatini's Gypsy fortune-telling parlor, a ramshackle storefront in the barrio section of The Bronx, where Madame Sabatini, aka Myrna Grosfinger, a twice-convicted grifter, read palms for five dollars a hand, assayed astrological charts, interpreted tea leaves, and acted as a collection depot for Nick the Spic's numbers runners. She was less than overjoyed to see Vince and Tommy entering her establishment.

"What's the beef this time?" she asked wearily.

"Hey, what kind of greeting is that for an old friend?" Vince protested unconvincingly. "Can't I just stop in and see how you're doing?"

"Stop busting my chops," Madame Sabatini grunted from the small, bare card table where she was seated. "I got a business to run here, so say your piece and scram, okay? Cops are bad for business."

"Never one to chitchat, were you, Myrna?" Vince observed. "Okay, let me lay it out for you." He handed her several photographs of Cherry Dressard's mutilated body, the surrounding area of Secor Park, and the grisly display found in Rafael Rosa's apartment. "I'm looking to make some sense out of those markings on the body and that ritualistic stuff on the ground there. You ever seen markings like those?"

She shuddered involuntarily. "What makes you think I'd know anything about that?" She pushed the photographs away.

"Look again, Myrna," Vince urged her. "And this time remember how close Tommy and me are to your parole officer. I'm sure he'd love to get in on a little of Nick the Spic's action, if you catch my drift."

Myrna eyed the photographs reluctantly. "Look, I got me a nice little operation here," she moaned. "I don't cause no trouble for anybody, and nobody gives me any trouble. I don't want to get involved with people like this. It gets around that I'm talking to the cops about them and I could be in real big trouble."

"We talking about *santerías*?" Vince asked.

"First of all, let me tell you that I've never been involved in this crap—at least not until I started doing business with these greasers. Believe me, half of them are really into it and the other half are too scared to talk about it."

"We're talking about *santería*, right?" he asked again.

"Honestly, it scares the shit out of me, too," she went on, ignoring his question. "But some of my best customers swear by it, so I gotta go with the flow here."

"Santería," Vince repeated. "What can you tell me about the markings in those photographs?"

Madame Sabatini went to the back of the store, sifted through a pile of dusty books and magazines and returned carrying a small paperback. Opened it on the card table, and began thumbing through the pages, comparing the illustrations and plates in the book with the scenes in the photographs. "Near as I can make out, these look like offerings to the god Chango," she told them, settling on an illustrated portion of the book. "Chango is a very powerful god to the *santería*: the god of fire, thunder, and lightning. Chango is the god they usually summon when they want to conjure an evil spirit on an enemy, or cause havoc and unhappiness in somebody's life. He's a dangerous and fickle god, and you don't screw with him unless you know what you're doing."

"Well, whoever filleted that lady there sure knew what they were doing," Tommy suggested.

"Weird, though, there are plenty of animal sacrifices, but I haven't heard of a human sacrifice in years," she noted.

"Well, you heard of one now." Vince scooped up the photographs and returned them to his jacket pocket. "You got any idea what they hope to accomplish with all this?"

She shrugged. "It's hard to say. They could be looking to gain strength by eating parts of the victim's body, maybe take on some aspect of her life for themselves—"

"Jeez, that's disgusting," Tommy broke in.

"Or they could just be out for revenge. They got a god for everything, and every god's got about a hundred uses. They can conjure up spells for just about anything they want, and if you ask them, they'll tell you that the magic never fails if it's done properly. They're a superstitious buncha bastards, but I swear, Crowley, I've seen things that'd turn your hair gray. Whatever magic it is they're using, I don't want them using it against me."

"So you think it really works?" Tommy asked her.

"I don't even want to think about it . . ." She threw her hands in the air. "And if you're smart, you shouldn't either. Just do me a favor, okay? Whatever you're planning, just leave me out of it. I got trouble enough in my life as it is."

"So where's that leave us?" Tommy asked when they were back in the car. "Right back where we started, right?"

"Not by a long shot." Vince leafed through his notebook until he found what he was looking for. "Well, whatta you know? I think we might just have hit paydirt here, partner. It says here that our friend Rafael Rosa was known to drive a vehicle with the license plate CHANGO. How's that grab you for an interesting coincidence?"

The squawk of the short-wave radio prevented Tommy from answering: "All available units to 814 East 233rd Street. See the man about an unidentified male DOA . . ."

"That's us, partner." Tommy shoved the car into gear and squealed from the curb. "Just what we need, another stiff in the Three-Seven."

17

NYPD FORM UF61   Sept. 16. 1989

INITIAL REPORT OF CRIME

Det. V. Crowley

HOMICIDE/MUTILATION,
UNIDENTIFIED B/M   COMPLAINT #8246
                    VISIT TO SCENE

1. At 1036 hours, this date notified by 911 Central of a DOA in the Eastchester section of The Bronx at 233rd St. (Sector Charlie).

2. At 1107 hours, accompanied by Det. Ippollito of 37 PDU, arrived at above location, an automobile graveyard near Eastchester Creek, and observed a human body inside an oil drum on the property of Anchor Springs & Welding Company.

3. First officers on the scene, Ptl. Garrity and Leach, 37 PDU, stated to the undersigned that they were directed place of occurrence by Dominick Testa, owner of the property who reported that he had noticed a strong odor coming from the oil drum and a number of stray dogs prowling about the site.

The area had been abandoned to the slow deterioration of waste metal, mostly derelict automobiles and parts of automobiles stacked on top of one another and forged into mountains of jagged metal by giant bulldozers, then strewn randomly across the yellow earth like the lifeless aftermath of a World War Two tank battle. Twisted, peeling skeletons of once-proud Buicks and BMWs had been picked clean by scavengers who simply appeared at any hour of the day or night to remove anything worth selling. It is said here that an unattended vehicle can be stripped to its chassis in a matter of minutes, chopped and carted off for parts in less than a half-hour.

Vince and Tommy parked in an elevated area of 233rd Street overlooking the sprawling auto graveyard. Winding downward behind a surrounding chain-link fence festooned with hubcaps and horns, they could see farther down the hill police and medical personnel gathering next to Eastchester Creek, a reeking slash of stagnant mud and effluent that wound sluggishly through the wreckage, and the beginnings of a crowd of curious onlookers being restrained behind draped lines of yellow plastic tape. They clipped their shields and credentials to their lapels and made their way carefully down the rubble-strewn embankment until they reached the creek.

"Is that the water or the stiff I smell?" Tommy asked, covering his nose with a handkerchief.

"Probably a little of both." Vince wedged through the cordon of uniformed policemen gathered around the crime scene and led Tommy to a spot by the water's edge, where Walt Cuzak and a team of ESU personnel were examining an overturned oil drum.

"Body's in there," Walt told him indistinctly through the handkerchief he held cupped over his nose and mouth. He jerked his head and indicated the oil drum on the ground, partially submerged in the brackish water, and pointed to a circling pack of dogs on the outskirts of the area. "Those mutts out there were tearing at it when we got here."

They watched as several muscular ESU volunteers waded into the water and began rolling the drum onto the dry embankment with considerable effort, unleashing new, more pungent waves of miasma from inside. Once on shore, CSU detectives gingerly began to remove the body, coughing and gagging at the penetrating aroma of putrefication that hung in the sultry air.

"Jeez, that's fuckin' awful!" Tommy recoiled as the bloated corpse of a black man was dragged from the confines of the oil drum, rump and legs first, unfolding like a jackknife to reveal what was left of his head. "You think those dogs did that?"

"Not likely," Walt Cuzak commented. "He was shoved in the drum headfirst. "From here it looks like somebody blew his face away with a shotgun."

Members of the D.A.'s video unit arrived at 1152 hours and recorded the scene from various angles while CSU detectives went about the grisly business of removing bits of hair, fingernails, torn remnants of clothing, and other unidentifiable pieces of debris from the body and sealing them in clear plastic evidence bags. The M.E.'s van arrived at 1219 hours, and Shem Weisen made his way cautiously down the slope toward them. "Whatta we got here?" he asked Vince as he approached, winded from his descent.

"Black male, stuffed in an oil drum," Vince replied. "Looks like he might've been here for a while from the smell of him."

Weisen sniffed the air. "Maybe not as long as you think. Putrefication sets in pretty fast in the kind of weather we've been getting." He knelt over the body, brushed aside the detectives who were gathering and cataloging evidence, and began probing the head and upper body with his fingers. He worked his way carefully downward toward the abdomen and lower pelvis, and finally the legs and feet. "Too early to say for sure, but right now my guess would be death by gunshot, probably no more than four days ago."

"Blew his head off with a shotgun, huh?" Tommy said.

Weisen stood, steadied himself against the rusted side of the oil drum, and wiped his hands with a paper towel. "I don't think so. He's been shot a couple of times in the ribs. Probably took at least one slug directly in the heart, judging from the amount of blood that's pooled up in his chest cavity."

"What about his head?" Vince asked. "From here it looks like somebody blasted him between the eyes with a load of buckshot."

Weisen tossed the towel on the ground and got another. "No sign of gunshot to the head. Unless a full examination proves different, I gotta think someone took a blowtorch to his face after he was dead. Same with the fingertips of both hands." He crouched next to the corpse and lifted one of his limp hands, revealing the charred flesh burned almost through to the bone. "Someone went to a lot of trouble to see that this guy won't get I.D.'d."

"Whatta you think?" Tommy asked Vince as they headed back up the hill toward Anchor Springs & Welding. "Gang hit?"

"Looks like it," Vince concurred. "It just wouldn't be a summer without at least one dumper out here in this cesspool."

It was hardly an exaggeration. Vince had recovered murder victims there before, killed by goons from one of the local crime families and dumped in the remote environs of the auto graveyard, sometimes disfigured like this one to prevent identification. It was almost as routine to the police as it was to the surrounding population of poor tenement dwellers and struggling businessmen. Children scouring the area, searching for metal scrap to sell, found bodies regularly and stripped them of any valuables they could find. Merchants like Dominick Testa, the proprietor of Anchor Springs & Welding, reported them only when they made life uncomfortable, as this one had.

"Whatta you want from me?" Testa howled as Vince and Tommy confronted him in the bay doorway of his

233rd Street garage. "I done what I was supposed to do, right? I called you guys as soon as I saw the stiff. Well, I didn't really see him. More I got a whiff, if you catch my drift."

"This place always stinks," Tommy reminded him.

"Yeah, but not like that. Also I saw those mutts trying to get inside the drum. I guess you can't hardly blame them. Meat is meat. They like it gamey."

Vince ran the toe of his shoe across the multilayered grease stains on the cement floor of the bay. "You did a real public-spirited thing, reporting the crime like that, Dominick. Now how about telling us how the body got inside that drum in the first place?"

"Maron!" Testa threw his hands in the air. "How dumb do you think I am anyway? I'm gonna waste some *mulinion*, stuff him inside an oil drum on my own property, and then call you up and tell you about it, right?"

"I didn't say you wasted him personally. I just figured you probably saw something suspicious going on when whoever did him was dumping his body," Vince explained. "I know you got a pretty good view of everything around here from that upstairs bedroom window of yours. Nothing much happens of a suspicious nature around here without you knowing about it."

"Suspicious?" Testa rolled his eyes. "You gotta be fuckin' kidding me, Crowley. Everything that goes on around here is suspicious, for chrissake. Whatta you think we got in this neighborhood, Olympic hopefuls?" He walked to the door and pointed to the denuded carcass of an automobile across the street. "You see that? That was an intact Mercedes two days ago." He peered out across the auto graveyard toward Eastchester Creek, past the idle, graffiti-covered stacks that had once belched smoke from vigorous cinderblock foundries, past the rusting skeleton of Eastchester Bridge silhouetted against the early-afternoon sky. "Do I know what happened to it? No. Do I give a shit? No again. Nobody gives a shit what happens in this neighborhood, you guys know that—"

"You're breaking my heart here," Vince moaned. "Now how about telling me what you know about that body on your property."

"I don't know nothing. You want a cuppa coffee, maybe a little *grappa*?"

"You didn't see anybody park right in front of your garage, lug a body all the way down the hill, and jam it into an oil drum?" Tommy asked disbelievingly.

"I got some Genoa and cheese, a little homemade guinea red," Testa offered.

"Thanks, Dominick, but I'm trying to drop a couple of pounds," Vince said. "Give it to the guys on the beat."

"That's another thing, Crowley." Testa grabbed Vince's elbow as he turned to leave. "What kinda *gibrones* you got working out of the Three-Seven these days? This guy pulls up in front of my place last week in a new Cadillac and walks in here smelling like cop all over. 'I wanta get rid of that car out there,' he tells me. 'You chop 'em up, right?' I say, 'No way, man. That's fuckin' illegal.' 'No shit?,' he says to me, 'you know somebody who does that kinda work?' " Dominick Testa was shaking his head in disbelief. "I'm not kidding you, Vince, I can practically see the wire coming outa this dumb shit's collar. What ever happened to smart cops anyway?"

Vince shook his head sadly. "I dunno, Dominick. The department isn't what it used to be."

"Assholes," Testa exclaimed. "It usta be fun being a criminal in this neighborhood. At least the bulls made it challenging."

Vince grinned. "I'm gonna pretend I didn't hear that, Dominick. Don't forget to call if you remember anything more."

"Sure, or if I see anything suspicious." Testa guffawed.

Shem Weisen met them outside on the sidewalk, where ESU policemen were depositing the plastic body bag in the coroner's van. "Join me inside for a pop?" he asked.

Tommy made a face. "Not unless you're supplying nose plugs in there. No body bag is heavy enough to block that smell, man."

"I guess you're right. I must be getting desensitized to it after all this time." Weisen shrugged and stepped resignedly into the van.

"You'll send me your report, right?" Vince reminded him.

There was a slight smile at the corners of Weisen's mouth. "Maybe you want to come downtown for the autopsy on this one, Vince. That way you can get a head start on solving this crime and relieving the public clamor for an arrest." He closed the van door behind him.

"Smart-ass," Tommy said as they walked to their car. He knew, as Vince did, that they would probably never find the killer of the man in the drum. He was nameless and he was black, and the likelihood of discovering any clues to his killer among the evidence was next to negligible. Mob hits were hardly ever solved for just that reason, and for the simple fact that there was no public clamor to arrest their killers. It was routine and it was irritating paperwork that would end up gathering dust in some file drawer until the mandatory annual review of unsolved homicides, when it would be carelessly updated and forgotten for another year. It was just the way it worked in the City of New York, and none of them could afford to spend too much time worrying about it.

Besides, there was a more immediate problem to worry about: both rear tires were missing from their vehicle.

18

OXBRIDGE PELL STARED AT THE TELETYPE MACHINE
in the squad room of the Thirty-seventh Precinct and
examined the incoming communication. It was nothing
extraordinary: a domestic dispute in the South Bronx
and the arrest of one black male for breach of peace
and possession of illegal firearms. "Slow day," he
commented to Vince, who was seated at his desk.

"Yeah," Vince responded, "you get them like that
sometimes." He returned to the travel brochure on
the desk: a slick, full-color promotional folder herald-
ing the good life to be had at Buccaneer's Key: "A
Retirement Community for the Young at Heart." The
brochure was filled with photographs of happy retirees
golfing, playing tennis, fishing, enjoying the nightlife
in one of three recreational centers. Next to the brochure, Pete Yorio's letter lay open on the desk:

Hey, old buddy,
How much longer are you going to bust your
ass up there in the Führer Bunker? Take your
pension and start enjoying a piece of the good life
for a change. I shit you not, Vince, I really never
knew what living was all about until Marge and I
retired down here last year. This place is a para-
dise! I fish off my front dock every day, and head
out to deeper waters about once a month—tarpon,
marlin and bonefish practically jumping into the
boat! I've lost ten pounds since I stopped eating

that shit from Finger's Diner and started eating
normal meals and playing racquetball every day.
Don't die fat and unhappy, you old fart. Come on
down!

Tarpon, marlin, bonefish . . . Vince put the letter
and brochure in his drawer. Retirement was beginning
to look better and better to him as the months rolled
by, especially now that it seemed the precinct was
about to close. He glanced around at the familiar
chipped metal desks with drawers that wouldn't open,
patched vinyl chairs with squeaky, unsymmetrical wheels
that charted their own course along the worn linoleum
floor, the bare concrete block walls painted sickening
green, bulletin boards layered with out-of-date notices, postings, yellowing photographs . . . the empty
holding pen, the lazy, unspectacular smells of dust and
grease and fingerprint ink. This was what was holding
him here, he thought. This, and the sordid, uncompromising streets and alleyways of The Bronx, filling him
with terror and elation, killing him slowly with tension
and fast food.

Vince shifted his glance to the paperback book he
had purchased that afternoon, *Myths, Legends, and
Rituals of Santería*, and thumbed through the pages
until he reached an illustrated section titled Signs and
Symbols. There were a half-dozen pages of drawings
of stars and serpents and designs of indeterminable
origin. Each was representative of a particular god or
spell, each with a power of its own, a special magic
designed to produce a desired effect or enhance a
special rite. He compared the designs with the Polaroid
photographs taken at Secor Park. There were similari-
ties, but there were also significant differences: nothing he could establish as an absolute link between her
violent death and the cult of *santería*.

Balmy weather and fishing all day: Connie would
never go for it. As much as she complained about Cherry
Dessard's job, Vince knew she could never be happy

away from it. She'd never be able to adjust to the ease and languor of a life in retirement—same as him. They both needed the energizing tempo of the streets to keep them going, he knew. They needed to feel that what they were doing was somehow useful, if only to themselves. It was what made them tick, gave them a sense of who they were. Both of them would grow to hate each other and themselves on the white sand beaches of Florida. They would simply forget what made them happy in the first place.

Vince leafed through the chapters of the book, searching for some previously unseen clue to pop out of the pages at him: The Legend of Santería . . . Magical Rites . . . The Black Arts . . . Gods and Spirits . . . It all seemed like mumbo jumbo, based in superstition and fear, but he knew enough about it now to take it seriously. People murdered other people in all sorts of weird and illogical ways for all sorts of weird and incomprehensible reasons, and it wasn't the homicide detective's job to try to make sense of it all. All he needed to do was to find a disconnected piece of the puzzle that corresponded to a face, an address, a social-security number, an arrest record, or a set of finger-prints that established an identity.

"You think you're onto something here?" Oxbridge Pell asked over Vince's shoulder.

Vince closed the book. "Nah, just something Tommy picked up in one of his night-school courses." He was wary of telling Pell too much, even though he knew, along with everyone else at the Three-Seven, that he was certainly no threat. As a matter of fact, most of them had come to genuinely like the diminutive, bespeckled auditor who now spent a good part of almost every day hanging around the precinct. He was harmless and seemingly lost in a world that he felt had let him down. Something had snapped inside his brain on the morning of the Gateway explosion that had brought him face-to-face with the reality of his life, and that reality had been too much for him to handle.

Tommy had diagnosed Pell right away, his textbook memory recalling some obscure night-school lecture in human behavior. Pell was a classic anal-regressive personality, playing out his childhood cops-and-robbers fantasies, Tommy had told them, and nobody had argued, but then nobody took Tommy any more seriously than they did Oxbridge Pell. Whatever reasons the auditor had for shitcanning his life's career and immersing himself in the day-to-day routine of policework were his business, they reasoned. Better he be allowed to hang around the precinct playing cops-and-robbers than wandering the streets all day like a lost soul. They had come to care for him too much to let that happen.

Steve and Snuffy entered the squad room, saw Pell, and signaled for Vince to join them in the robbery room. "What's up?" Vince asked when they closed the adjoining door.

"Just got back from Santiago's headquarters," Steve said. "Just how much do you know about this guy?"

Vince shrugged. "Just what I read in the papers, why?"

"I dunno, there's something weird going on out there. Nobody wants to talk to us about anything."

"You get to see that Keliher guy?" Vince asked.

"There's a real cutie," Steve said. "Everybody on Santiago's staff but him is Spanish, look like they just climbed off the banana boat. But this guy Keliher is slick as goat snot, like he belongs on the quad at Harvard instead of grubbing around The Bronx. The whole time we were talking to him he had his nose in the air like he was sniffing shit or something."

"He'd have to be able to move in pretty highfalutin circles if he was collecting for Santiago. Did he tell you anything about his Contech connections?"

"You gotta be kidding." Steve grinned at Snuffy. "The man is serious, partner. I think he really expected Santiago's bagman to just break down and spill his guts to us when we confronted him."

"I'll take what you got when you're finished jerking me off," Vince said.

"Keliher's a real scumbag," Snuffy volunteered. "By that I mean your basic politician. The only thing he was willing to admit was that he knew Thomas Falcone, that they saw each other occasionally when Falcone was in Washington, and that he was shocked and saddened at Falcone's death."

"We ran a background check on Santiago and came up with some interesting stuff," Snuffy said. "Like the fact that this bird was teaching junior high school less than six years ago and he's a U.S. congressman today. I'd call that a pretty fast rise up the ladder of success, if you know what I mean."

"Maybe he's just smart, or lucky," Vince suggested.

"Take a look at this." Snuffy spread a handwritten sheet on his desk for Vince to read. "November 1983, three members of Bronx School Board 82 are killed in a car crash on the Saw Mill River Parkway; Santiago is appointed to fill out one of the unexpired terms. April 1984, the wife of State Assemblyman Warren Hines is blinded in an acid attack by an unknown assailant. Hines flips out, ends up drooling in a mental institution, and Santiago fills out his term in Albany. January 1986, Julian Santiago steps in to take the seat of City Councilman Al Gottlieb, who sticks a butcher knife in between his ribs after he's indicted for bribery and racketeering. And finally, our eight-term congressman, the beloved Guido Derosa, has a heart attack on the golf course and guess who gets his job?" Snuffy looked up at Vince. "You starting to detect a pattern here?"

Vince played a hunch. "Either of these guys look familiar to you?" He handed Snuffy the photograph he had taken from Tom Quinlan's office.

Snuffy examined the picture. "The guy on the left looks like Thomas Falcone, and if the other guy isn't Daniel Keliher, I'll eat my badge. What's that all about?"

"I'm not sure." Vince took the photograph from Snuffy. "If I had to guess, I'd say that our friend Falcone was sucking up to Keliher to get at the congressman, but that's strictly guesswork at this point."

"Knowing what I know about Santiago, I can't imagine anybody wanting to get close to him. People who get in his way seem to end up dead."

Tommy opened the door of the robbery room. "Sweeney's in and wants to talk to you, partner," he told Vince.

Vince walked the length of the squad room and entered the C.O.'s office. "You wanted to see me, Lieutenant?"

Sweeney sat behind his desk. "It's about this caseload report you gave me. I'd like to review it with you, if you have a minute."

"Yes sir, is anything wrong with it?"

"No, no." Sweeney shook his head. "I just want to make sure we're both operating on the same wavelength here, so to speak." He lifted the report and examined it. "The way I see it, we have three active homicides that we're working on right now; Thomas Falcone, Cherry Dressard, and the unidentified DOA we found out by the Eastchester Bridge. Am I correct there?"

"Yes sir."

"And the assignments are as follows," Sweeney went on. "Appelbaum and Quade assigned to the Falcone homicide; Cuzak and Ippollito to the Dressard murder, and Turner and Vargas to the unidentified DOA, is that right?"

"Pretty much, Lieutenant," Vince replied.

"And you?"

"I'm sort of overseeing the whole shooting match, sir."

"Um." Sweeney stared at the sheet. "That corpse out by the bridge was a black male, wasn't it?"

"Yes sir, I believe it was."

"Turner and Vargas, they're both black, right?"

Vince nodded uncertainly. "Yes?"

"Don't you feel that might be seen as condescending —putting black detectives in charge of the only black homicide in the house?" Sweeney inquired.

"Condescending, Lieutenant?"

Sweeney raised a reassuring hand. "Don't get me wrong, Detective Crowley. I'm not saying that you personally have any racist motives in assigning the case that way. It's that it could be misinterpreted. Do you agree?"

"I'm not sure I understand what you're saying," Vince answered weakly.

"Let's reassign that case, Detective," Sweeney went on, ignoring Vince's discomfort. "Put Cuzak and Ippollito on that one. A Polack and a dago—nobody can accuse us of any bias on that one, eh?"

Vince felt the muscles in his stomach beginning to tremble.

"And the Dressard case, give that one to Turner and Vargas . . . No, wait a minute, Cherry Dressard was a woman. I don't want the goddamn feminists breathing down our necks. Better give that one to Appelbaum and Quade," Sweeney corrected himself.

"Maybe I should get a pencil and paper and write this all down, Lieutenant," Vince suggested.

"Put Turner and Vargas on the Falcone thing," Sweeney went on, "but keep an eye on them. Falcone is an important homicide, so I want you to maintain overall supervision." He surveyed the report. "Let's see, have I covered everything?"

"Pell, sir?" Vince said evenly.

"Who?"

"Pell. You forgot to assign Pell, Lieutenant."

"Oh yeah." Sweeney's brow creased. "Put Pell on the phones. He's good on the phones, right?"

"The best, sir."

Sweeney shook his head satisfactorily. "Then that will be all, Detective. Carry on."

Back in the squad room, Tommy approached him cautiously. "How'd it go in there?" he asked.

"About the way I figured it'd go," Vince replied. He turned to Oxbridge Pell. "You're out new phone guy."

"I'm what?" Pell looked like he was about to swoon.

Vince grinned. "You're our new communications expert, pal. Welcome to the Three-Seven."

19

CITY OF NEW YORK

Office of the Medical Examiner

AUTOPSY REPORT

S. Weisen, M.D., D.F.M., pres. Sept. 19, 1989

The victim is a black male, approx 25–28 yrs., of possible Hispanic origin. Height: 5′11″, weight 167 lbs., with multiple gunshot wounds to the chest and incendiary injuries and mutilation of the face and manual extremities. Other (nontraumatic) scars and lesions on the body include one keloid-type scar of indeterminate origin on the upper right shoulder blade (approx. 9 cm.), one area of apigmentation (approx 3 × 3 cm.) on lower front neck area, one visible tattoo (purple color) on upper right biceps, resembling a double-edged ax . . .

Vince reread the opening paragraph of Shem Weisen's autopsy report on the unidentified DOA and hurriedly thumbed through his book on *santería* until he found what he wanted. There, in the chapter titled Signs and Symbols, he saw the unmistakable drawing of a double-bladed ax, the symbol of the god Chango. He compared the drawing with the attached Polaroid photographs, clearly showing the same symbol tattooed on the victim's arm. "You got the file on Rafael Rosa?" he asked Tommy.

Tommy sifted through the piles of unattended paperwork on his desk, found the manila case record, and handed it across the desk to Vince.

"Remember Chango?" Vince asked Tommy as he sorted through the arrest records and the request for field information that had gone out earlier, verifying that Rosa's vital statistics were roughly the same as those of the unidentified body.

"Chango, wasn't he that voodoo god Madame Sabatini told us about?" Tommy recalled.

"The same, and now it looks like that stiff out by the creek had a tattoo of Chango's symbol on his right arm."

"Chango, huh? Wasn't he supposed to be a real bad-ass?" Tommy asked.

Vince scanned the book. "Says here that he's the god of fire, thunder, and lightning . . . a real mean mother-fucker if you happen to be on his shit list, but powerful as all hell if you use the right magic on him."

"Jeez." Tommy shook his head. "You believe that crap?"

"I don't, but it seems Rosa and our DOA both did."

Vince dialed the medical examiner's office.

"You run a dental on that guy we dragged out of the oil drum?" he asked Shem Weisen when he came on the line.

"Dental, what the hell for?" Weisen asked.

"Is it too late to get a chart on him?"

"No, but what's the big deal? This guy is a dumper, right?"

"Maybe nothing, but I'd appreciate it if you could draw one up for me," Vince told him. "There's a chance this guy could be a murder suspect we've been looking for."

"Terrific," Weisen grunted. "I was just wondering

what I could find to keep me busy for the next couple of hours."

"You're a buddy." Vince hung up.

"Whatta we got?" Tommy asked.

Vince leaved through the paperwork. "We got Rafael Rosa at the scene of the Gateway blast, where he drops a *santería* talisman in the alleyway. We got an apartment that was the listed address for the same Rafael Rosa, filled with half-starved kids, animal sacrifices, and all kinds of ritual *santería* garbage on the floor. We got a murdered prostitute with some of those same markings and symbols carved into her body and on the ground where she was dumped. We got a stiff crammed in an oil drum that matches the physical description of said Rafael Rosa, right down to his tattoo and the name on his license plate. I don't know what it all means yet, but it's starting to add up to something."

"You want me to run a check on local dentists to see if we can come up with some X rays of Rosa's mouth?" Tommy asked.

"Yeah, get some help and make it citywide," Vince told him. "And check under his other aliases: Pedro Martínez and Robert Townes . . ." He shuffled through the paperwork on his desk. "Anybody seen the file on that Eastchester dumper? I gotta file this stuff."

Walk Cuzak handed him the file, marked JANITOR IN A DRUM across the front in glaring red grease pencil. "Very funny. What makes you think he was a janitor?" Vince asked.

"I told you we shoulda wrote Jigaboo in a Jug," Walt told Tommy. "That other's just sloppy policework."

"I heard that!" Leila Turner screamed from the other end of the squad room. "You guys are just determined to remain a bunch of ignorant peckerwood assholes, aren't you?"

"No fair," Cuzak protested. "We didn't call you no nasty names."

"What do you call Jigaboo in a Jug?" Leila howled. "That's an insult to every black person alive!"

"That's why we wrote Janitor in a Drum," Cuzak said. "We're sensitive to ethnic feelings here—"

Vince's phone rang and he answered it gratefully. "Crowley here."

"Vince, it's Jessy." His ex-wife's voice was tight, controlled.

"Hi, Jess, what's up?"

"Vince, I'm really worried about Katie. I've called her place a dozen times and all I ever get is that recording of hers. I've left messages and she's never answered them."

"She's in school, probably real busy." Vince tried to sound convincing.

"She's busy all right, busy getting stoned," Jessy said. "She answered when I called today and I swear she was high as a kite."

"Come on, Jess," Vince groaned. "Aren't you just being a mother here? Maybe the kid had a cold. Maybe it was just a bad connection—"

"You're talking to a former alcoholic here," Jessy reminded him. "I know when somebody's stoned and when they've got a cold. I've been there, remember?"

"Look, if it'll make you feel any better, I'll check it all out, okay?" he offered. "We were going to have dinner anyway, as soon as she got her place squared away."

"Would you do that, please?" Jessy sounded desperate. "I just have this sinking feeling that something is terribly wrong."

"Stop worrying," Vince said. "I'll go out there if I have to, but I can practically guarantee you that everything's just fine. Katie's a good kid, she's got good instincts. We brought her up to know better than to get involved with drugs. You know that."

"I only know what I feel," Jessy said. "And it scares me to death."

"It's gonna be fine, trust me." Vince hung up.

His next call was to Brooklyn: "We're not here right now, but we want desperately to talk to you . . ." He slammed down the receiver and headed for the door of the squad room. "I'll be out in Brooklyn if anybody wants me," he shouted back over his shoulder.

Jessy was probably overreacting, he thought as he pulled the unmarked patrol car from its parking slot and headed for the southbound Major Deegan Expressway and the Triborough Bridge. Jessy was a mother and she would be a mother long after her daughters had children of their own. It was a mother's job to worry . . .

Spring Valley, New York, had been their first home, a brand-new, split ranch he'd purchased with a small down payment he managed to borrow from Jessy's father. They were home-owners, he'd realized, masters of their quarter-acre plot in the middle of what had once been an apple orchard and now lay bare in heaps of unlandscaped rubble and stone. Thirty-two houses in what had been the orchard, all alike in every detail except for the texture and quality of the lives inside . . . families, beginnings . . .

Kelly was three or four, Katie just an infant learning to pull herself up in her crib: earnest, resolute, directed by whatever biological force tells babies that it's time to start being people. Jessy had noticed the spots on Kelly first, then on little Katie; red pinpoints on their skin that grew into angry, itching pustules, confirming their worst fears. Both children had chicken pox. The girls suffered for what seemed like most of that first summer, especially Katie, who was too young to tell them where it hurt or how much.

Katie with hair like corn silk . . . Daddy's little girl sobbing in her crib, her tiny hands swathed in cotton cloths to keep her from scratching herself. Vince remembered standing there, feeling completely helpless, wanting to cry along with her, but knowing he had to be brave for Jessy's sake. Jessy was beside herself with worry that the girls would end up disfigured, or that the pustules would become infected and pump poison into their little bloodstreams, or that she wouldn't be there when they cried at night, or that there might be something to ease their pain that she had left undone. Mothers always worried . . .

He located a parking spot not far from Katie's apartment. Brooklyn had changed since his days as a foot patrolman in the old Seventy-third Precinct in Brownsville, he thought as he walked along the littered sidewalks. People seemed angrier, more suspicious of one another. There was less banter, less buoyancy, less of the swagger and boisterousness Vince remembered from his days as a rookie.

"Daddy?" Katie answered his knock, shocked to see him standing in the hallway outside her apartment. "What are you doing here?"

"Okay if I come in?" Vince asked, averting his eyes from an expanse of milky cleavage exposed by her carelessly wrapped bathrobe.

"Why didn't you call?" Katie sputtered, reluctantly allowing him to enter. "I would've straightened up the place."

Vince looked around the tiny apartment: a jumble of heaped clothing, partially filled wineglasses and stained coffeecups, ashtrays overflowing with cigarette butts. "It looks like you had a party," he commented dryly.

"You should have called, Daddy." Katie began to retrieve cups and glassware from the tables and carry them into a small kitchenette off the living room. "I wanted to have this place all cleaned up when you came."

"I was in the neighborhood," he lied.

"Can I get you something—coffee, maybe?" Katie asked nervously.

Vince looked at his watch. "It's almost four in the afternoon, baby. I'm all coffeed out by now."

Katie wrapped the bathrobe around her self-consciously. "Some wine?"

"Uh-uh." Vince eyed the almost-empty half-gallon of burgundy on the kitchen counter. "Must've been some party."

"Just some friends." Katie was reddening. "Look, I'm running real late, Daddy. I have to get dressed and be at school in less than an hour."

Vince could sense the panic in her voice, the tone and tremor he had heard a thousand times from people who had something to hide. He could see Katie edging backward toward the bedroom, her eyes darting reflexively to the closed door. "You okay, baby?"

"Sure. Why shouldn't I be okay?"

It didn't take Charlie Chan to figure out that there was somebody in the bedroom. His mind raced through the possibility of bursting through the door and confronting whoever was in there, but he dismissed the thought. Katie was a woman now. He had no power over her anymore. "Your roommate, Karen, still asleep in there?" He hated himself for asking.

Katie stood across the room from him, anxious and afraid behind a growing mask of defiance. "I'd love to talk, Daddy, but this is just a really bad time for me. Call next time, please?"

Vince went to her and put his arms around her, felt her muscles stiffen beneath his touch. "Call me if you need me, okay, honey?"

"Okay, Daddy." She stood numbly until he released her.

Downstairs, Vince returned to his car and headed for The Bronx. What would he tell Jessy? he wondered as he drove through the spiritless streets of Brooklyn. Would he tell her not to worry, that her daughter was growing up and searching for a life of her own, or would he convey the churning in his gut? He would be reassuring, he decided, because that was what Jessy wanted him to be, even after all these years. She wanted him to tell her everything was fine, even when it wasn't. And it wasn't, and they both knew it.

He crossed the Triborough Bridge, through the intricate webwork of steel cables and beams, knotted together like a child's toy suspended above the vastness of the city . . . like the metal swing set he had laboriously assembled in the backyard of their Spring Valley home. Nothing had worked the way it was supposed to, he remembered. Nuts and bolts and miscellaneous pieces of steel tubing that mocked him, defied the incomprehensible set of directions the company had provided. He had sweat and he had cursed and he had sworn he would never again buy anything that had to be put together, but somehow, by sheer will, he had managed to complete the job.

Katie had been tentative at first when he strapped her into the wooden child's seat, then grew in confidence as he gently rocked her higher and higher, her silken hair pressed against her face in the cradling wind—higher, farther out into the air until she squealed with innocent delight.

20

VINCE EXITED THE ELEVATOR AT THE THIRD SUBBASE-
ment of One Police Plaza and negotiated the maze of
hallways to the police photo unit, a forgotten place
where forgotten police personnel labored night and
day in darkrooms, developing raw negatives of everything from crime scenes to pictures of the commissioner's nephew celebrating his bar mitzvah.

"Hey, Crowley, what brings you down here to the
bowels of the earth?" Sergeant Ray Butz asked him
when he entered.

"Dickey's got something for me inside," Vince said.
"Okay if I go on in?"

Butz checked the electronic panel on his desk, where
even rows of flashing red lights signified which darkrooms were in use. "He's in twelve. Just knock before
you go in, in case he's got a chippie in there with
him."

Vince walked to the rear of the floor and knocked
on darkroom twelve. "Who's out there?" Dick Gutbaum's
disembodied voice demanded from inside.

"It's Vince, Dickie. Zip up and let me in."

Gutbaum appeared at the door pale and red-eyed,
looking like a mutant from some sci-fi thriller about
underground civilizations. "Jesus Christ, Dickie, don't
you ever get out into the sunlight?" Vince asked,
stepping inside the blackness of the darkroom.

Gutbaum switched on a light above the developing
tanks. "Lucky for you I don't, buddy," he replied

154

wearily. "Otherwise shit like yours would never get done, what with all the demands on my time from the guys upstairs."

Vince grinned. "Got you hustling, huh?"

"You kidding? Two inspectors had daughters get married this month, and guess who got to take all the pictures?"

"Most be tough being an artist," Vince observed.

"Artist, shit!" Gutbaum scowled. "Those gonifs would let you take the pictures if they could get them on the arm. I'm telling you, Vince, graft ain't what it used to be when you and me came in. Nobody's got no subtlety anymore."

"You called. You got something for me?" Vince asked.

"Yeah, hold on." He began rummaging through the stacks of enlarged photographs stored on shelves beneath the tanks. "Crowley . . . Crowley . . . here it is." He slid a flat brown envelope from the shelf and placed it on a nearby table. "I remember it real good 'cause it's part of a legitimate criminal investigation." Gutbaum smiled at the irony. "I don't hardly ever get to work on those anymore."

He removed an eight-by-ten glossy photograph from the envelope; the scene of Thomas Falcone and Daniel Keliher Vince had taken from Tom Quinlan's office. "Whoever took this shot was a real bad photographer," he said, removing a number of subsequently larger prints of the same scene, blown up to show detail that was too minute or indistinct to see on the original. "The quality's real bad to begin with, and it doesn't get any better when you blow it up." He handed the final print to Vince.

Vince squinted at the shot in the half-darkness, an enlargement of a section of the boat eight to ten feet behind Santiago and Keliher, where the bottom portion of a life preserver hung next to the stern hatch leading belowdecks. "Looks pretty good to me," he said, reading the fuzzy but discernible legend written on the life preserver: HANKY-PANKY, CAPTIVA, FLA.

"Took some work," Gutbaum said. "What you're seeing there is really a computer enhancement. The original enlargement would've been worthless."

"But it's the real thing, right?" Vince pressed him.

"You could take it to court." Gutbaum shrugged.

"That's great, Dickie." Vince pressed his hand. "I can take this, right?"

"Take it for chrissake." Gutbaum winced. "They'd hang me by the balls if they thought I was doing real police business down here."

There was someone waiting by his desk when he returned to the precinct: The tall, slenderly built young white male sported eight or nine hundred bucks' worth of double-breasted blue gabardine suit, enough gold jewelry to finance a third-world revolution, and a thatch of well-oiled black tresses that cascaded down his back like a lava flow.

"This is Mr. Guy Giuliani," Tommy introduced him. "Mr. Guiliani is the gentleman who posted bail for Trixie Lee the last time she was a guest of the city." He handed Vince the arrest record.

"Trixie's pimp, huh?" Vince eyed him speculatively.

"Miss Lee's business manager," Guiliani said haughtily.

Vince sat at his desk. "Oh, yeah, business manager. Well, you know we're looking for your client, Mr. Giuliani. Got any idea where we can find her?"

"I haven't seen her in over a month," Giuliani said. "She's probably booked some out-of-town engagements."

"You're her manager. You'd know about anything like that, wouldn't you?" Vince suggested.

Giuliani shrugged. "Not necessarily. She's free to pursue lucrative business opportunities on her own if they present themselves."

Vince nodded. "I see . . ." He scanned Trixie Lee's arrest record. "These out-of-town engagements, would you say they might be in any way similar to her past business opportunities?"

"I'm not sure I follow," Guiliani said warily.

"Well, let's just take this last one, for example. It says here that Miss Lee was engaged in performing an exotic dance at the Black Pussy nightclub in Lodi, New Jersey, during which time she apparently was given the opportunity of performing fellatio on a number of male customers in her audience—"

"If you're talking about that debacle out at Le Chat Noir, that was a bum rap," Guiliani broke in. "I'm sure your record there shows that the case against her was thrown out of court."

"I can see that," Vince allowed. "Entrapment, it says here."

"You bet your ass," Guiliani said. "Those vice goons were sitting there through her whole performance with wires and hidden cameras."

"I'm sure they were just doing their jobs," Vince pointed out.

"Sure, like the four of them had to sit there and wait until she'd finished them all off before they busted her, right?" Guiliani scowled.

"Maybe they were amassing evidence, strengthening the case against her," Tommy suggested, stifling a grin.

Vince raised a conciliatory hand. "Hey, what's past is past, right? What we're interested in now is finding your client so we can ask her some questions about a homicide we're investigating."

"Homicide?" Guiliani paled. "What would Trixie know about any homicide?"

"That's just what we want to find out," Vince replied. "Now, you don't seriously expect us to believe that you haven't had any contact with her in over a month, do you?"

Guiliani shrugged. "Believe what you want. The last time I saw Trixie she told me she had agreed to do a special gig down in Atlantic City. A couple of rich old farts wanted tour guides for a couple of days."

"Tour guides?" Vince almost choked.

"Whatta you want from me?" Giuliani groaned.

"Guides, that's plural," Vince pointed out. "Was somebody else involved in this business venture with her?"

"She had another girl, I never met her."

"Got a name for me?" Vince asked.

"Sherry, Cherry . . . something like that."

"It wouldn't be Cherry Dressard, by any chance?"

"Maybe . . . That sounds about right."

Vince shot a sidelong glance at Tommy. "Were you aware that Cherry Dressard was found murdered a couple of weeks ago?"

Giuliani stiffened. "How would I know about a thing like that?"

"Do you have any reason to suspect that Trixie Lee may have experienced the same fate?" Vince asked.

"Jesus, no!"

Vince paused. "Atlantic City . . . You didn't book any business engagements for her after that?"

"I swear to God . . ." Sweat broke out on Giuliani's brow. "She just kinda disappeared. If I knew where she was, I'd tell you."

"Okay, Guy. I don't think we'll be needing you anymore today." Vince stood and accompanied Giuliani to the door. "You will stay available to us if we need to talk to you, though, right?"

"Hey, anything I can do to help—"

"I got a question," Tommy broke in as Giuliani turned toward the stairs. "How'd a young guy like you get into a business like this anyhow?"

Giuliani shrugged. "I dunno, I guess I just kinda fell into it after I was cashiered out of divinity school." He bounded down the steps.

"You see the gold on that son of a bitch?" Tommy groaned when Giuliani was gone. "He couldn't have been as old as I am, and he was wearing more on his chest than I got in the bank. Kinda makes you wonder what we're doing busting our humps out here for nickels and dimes, don't it?"

"You think you'd be happy running whores?" Vince asked.

"Shit, yeah, if I had that guy's bankroll I would," Tommy replied. "I'd call myself a business manager like Guy there, or an agent . . . something with a little class. Get fat and rich sitting around all day while the bimbos did all the work . . ."

"I had an uncle who was a business manager," Snuffy broke in. "He represented some big names in show business; Sophie Smucker, Fred Adaire—"

"You don't mean Fred Astaire, do you?" Tommy asked.

"Fred Adaire, the Chicken Man. He had a beak instead of a nose. My uncle got him on the *Ted Mack Amateur Hour* one time. He pecked out 'Embraceable You' on cow bells."

"And we're not talking Sophie Tucker here, right?" Vince hated himself for asking.

"Sophie Smucker, the Alligator Girl, had skin like tree bark."

"There ain't no call for shit like that anymore," Tommy remarked. "Whores are where it's at now."

"Mind if I break in here with some precinct business?" Vince handed Tommy the blow-up photograph he had brought from downtown. "Let's check this out, okay? Get on the horn to the Florida coast guard or whoever's in charge of boat registration down there and see if we can come up with an owner for this tub."

Tommy looked at the enlargement. "Where's Captiva?"

"South Florida," Oxbridge Pell volunteered. "It's an island off the coast of Fort Myers. My wife and I vacation there almost every winter."

"Man, that's class," Snuffy said. "South Florida— the keys, rum swizzles, limbo . . . Whatta you want to hang around a stinking sewer like this for when you can be in a place like that?"

Pell shrugged. "It's not all that wonderful. The same old people saying the same old things. Everybody down there is so white, if you know what I'm saying."

"Hey, we're white," Tommy protested. "At least most of us." He shot an apologetic glance at Street Crime.

"No, no. You've all got texture, coloration to your lives. There's some inner vitality to you all," Pell explained.

"Kishkes," Steve Appelbaum said.

"If that means what I think it means, you're right," Pell went on. "People like me are tissue-paper-thin. Just scratch the surface and you break right through. You guys all have something underneath, and that's what I want for myself. I know you all must think I'm crazy hanging out here like this, but it's the only way I know of to break away from what I am."

"I never heard nobody describe 'white' quite like that," Street Crime observed.

The telephone rang and Pell answered it. "For you, Detective Crowley. The district attorney's office."

"What's up, Tom?" Vince asked when the D.A. came on the line.

"Just a word to the wise." Quinlan's voice was clipped, urgent. "Things are starting to move on the Contech thing faster than I thought they would. It looks like the feds might move anytime now to start making their case."

"So, isn't that what you want?" Vince asked.

"Not if all they're going to do is move in there and seize the company's records. By the time their auditors have gone through all the figures and they're ready to seek an indictment, we could be drinking up our pensions."

Vince hesitated. "I'm not sure what you're trying to tell me here, Tom. What exactly is it you want me to do?"

"What you do is your business," Quinlan answered. "All I'm telling you is that those records are probably critical to your Falcone homicide, and if the feds get their hands on them first, you can kiss your investigation good-bye."

"So you give me a warrant to go in there and we'll get them out before the feds get there."

"Can't do that. No probable cause."

"So what the hell are you yanking my chain for?" Vince exploded. "First, you tell me I need this stuff and then you tie my hands so I can't get it. What am I supposed to do, break in there and steal it?"

"Come on, Vince. You're talking to an officer of the court here."

"What you're saying is you just don't want to know about it, *correcto*?"

"I have faith in your resourcefulness." Quinlan hung up.

21

UNDER THE CIRCUMSTANCES, A CALL FROM HIS EX-wife, Jessy was not a ray of sunshine breaking through Vince's already overcast day. There was only one reason she would be calling, to find out what he'd learned about Katie and what he was doing about it. It would do no good for him to try to reassure her, Vince knew. Jessy was convinced that something was very wrong out in Brooklyn, and to make matters worse, she was probably right. Vince knew his daughter well enough to be able to tell when she was holding something back from him. Katie had no talent for dishonesty, and that made her vulnerable in a dishonest world.

Like Katie's inability to lie, Jessy had no talent for dealing with discomfort, especially when it came to her daughters. Almost twenty years of being married to a New York City cop had done virtually nothing to diminish the impact of her pampered Connecticut upbringing.

"Hi, Jess. How's it going?" He faked a hollow bouyancy.

"Vince, did you see Katie?" she asked.

"Uh-huh, I was out there day before yesterday."

"And?" He could hear the impatience in her voice.

"And there's nothing bad going on that I could see," he replied.

"That you could see," she repeated. "What about what you felt?"

"What I felt was that our daughter is a college girl

now. She's out on her own, doing what college girls do," he lied. "We've gotta give her some room here, Jess."

"What kind of room are you talking about?" Jessy demanded. "Room to take drugs and kill herself?"

"Come on now. There's no evidence that she's taking drugs. That's all in your mind, Jess."

"You're sounding like a detective again, Vince." Jessy moaned. "This is our daughter, not some suspect in a homicide you're investigating. Stop talking about evidence and start acting like a father."

"What do you want me to do, Jess?" he asked weakly.

"I want you to start acting like a father," she repeated.

"You got it. Anything else?"

"There you go, shutting down again," Jessy said acidly.

"Gotta go, Jess. There's a call on my other line." He hung up.

"Trouble with your ex?" Walt Cuzak asked.

"Trouble, period," Vince said. "Jessy's worried about our daughter, Katie. Thinks she's taking drugs and hanging around with some Pakistani twice her age."

"Pakistani, huh? That's bad news," Cuzak said. "Those sons of bitches are always setting their women on fire."

"On fire?"

"Women got no status in those countries," Cuzak explained. "They're like chattel, if you know what I mean. A guy gets tired of his wife, flicks his Bic underneath her sari, and its Barbecue City. Happens all the time."

"Oh, shit," Vince moaned.

"Why not just pull the greasy bastard in and we'll put him in the chair for a couple of hours?" Cuzak suggested. "Nothing like a common-sense talk to get scumbags like that to be reasonable."

"He's out in Brooklyn," Vince said.

"So you know guys out in the Seven-Three. They'll pull him in for you."

"For what? He's a professor out at Pratt. I checked him out; no wants, no warrants, no record of any kind. The son of a bitch is squeaky clean."

Walt Cuzak scowled. "Nobody's squeaky clean, you know that, Vince."

"Knowing it and proving it are two different things," Vince pointed out.

Cuzak rolled his eyes. "Jeez, you're starting to sound like one of those ACLU pussys. You wanta nail this creep or what?"

"If I can."

"So call Pratt security. I can practically guarantee they'll have something on him out there."

Vince leafed through the Brooklyn telephone book, found the number for the Pratt Institute security division, and called. "This is Detective Crowley from the Thirty-seventh Precinct in The Bronx," he told the sleepy male voice that answered. "Can I talk to whoever's in charge?"

A pause. "We don't talk to pissy-assed rookies out here," the voice snarled.

Vince stiffened. "Who the hell is this?"

"Who the hell do you think?" the voice shot back.

He shot a glance at Walt Cuzak. "This isn't no crank call, mister. I *am* the New York Police Department, and I will have your nuts if you fuck with me."

"The whole goddamn department, is that what you are, Vinny?"

There was a faint Irish lilt to the voice that jarred Vince's memory. "Kayo?" he asked.

"Sure, it's Kayo, you little turd."

"I'll be dipped in shit . . ." Kevin O'Grady had been his rabbi, Ben Volpe's partner back during the days when Vince was a rookie in Brownsville. He'd retired years ago, after Ben had been killed on duty, and Vince had simply lost touch. "What the hell are you doing at Pratt?" he asked.

"I'm running security out here," O'Grady answered. "I have been for the last nine years."

"If that don't beat all. Ever hear from any of the old guys?"

"Not many anymore. Most of them are dead or living in Florida," O'Grady said. "It's good to hear your voice after all these years, though. What can I do for you?"

"I'm running down information on one of your employees out there, guy named Senji Rula," Vince told him. "He's some kind of instructor in the art department."

"I know the guy," O'Grady said.

"Anything you can tell me about him?" Vince asked.

"Nothing you can take to the bank. Whatta you want him for?"

"I'm not sure yet. I'm just kinda fishing around here," Vince admitted. "I got a suspicion about him, but I can't nail it down."

"Well, if you're looking for hard evidence, forget it," O'Grady said. "Rula's sharp as ratshit, and there ain't no way anybody could pin anything on him."

"But you think he's dirty," Vince finished the thought for him

"I think he's a sleaze, but there's no crime in that," O'Grady went on. "He's got himself a kind of harem out here, a bunch of young girls who follow him around, lapping at his lapels like he's the Second Coming or something. They treat him like some kind of prophet, like he's got some mystical power over them. I got no hard evidence, but if I had to make a guess, it'd be that he keeps them in line by giving them drugs."

Vince felt his heart sink into the pit of his stomach. "Christ, Kayo, why haven't you done anything about the son of a bitch?"

"What's to do? He hasn't committed no crime. Walking around the campus with a bevy of gorgeous young chicks hanging all over you wasn't a punishable offense the last time I checked. I don't know too many guys who wouldn't want a piece of that action if they could figure out how to get it."

"How about the drugs?" Vince persisted.

"Like I said, it's just a guess."

"I know your guesses. You and Ben taught me just about everything I know about playing hunches," Vince reminded him.

"Yeah, but it's a little different out here," O'Grady said. "Out here I can't just pull somebody in every time I get a gut feeling. This ain't the police department, Vince. This is campus security. It's a nice safe, secure job, but I got no real power to arrest people. I'm just here to keep things quiet."

"But you could call the cops if you had probable cause to suspect him, right?"

"You said the magic words, Vinnie—'probable cause.' If I'd gone around calling the cops every time I suspected some staff member of taking drugs or porking some juicy young coed, I would've been history around this place a long time ago. By me, most of the staff out here are scumbuckets, and most of the students are spoiled little brats with nothing better to do than play with their crayons and sniff glue. They deserve one another, and good riddance to them."

"Yeah, well, one of those spoiled little brats is my daughter Katie, and I think she's also one of the groupies hanging around this Rula character," Vince said.

"Oh, shit, I'm sorry," O'Grady moaned. "What can I do, Vince?"

"Sounds to me like you can't do much, Kayo."

"I can keep my eyes open, maybe have a talk with her, or him," O'Grady suggested.

"I'd appreciate anything you can do," Vince told him.

"I'll do what I can, pal, you know that."

"Thanks, bro. I'll be here at the Three-Seven if you have any word for me." Vince hung up.

Oxbridge Pell was signaling him from the other end

of the room. "Detective Ippollito calling from Florida on eight-two."

Vince lifted the receiver. "Hey, partner, how's everything down there in the Sunshine State?"

"Sunny," Tommy replied. "I wish to hell I had more time to enjoy it."

"Well, you're down there on business," Vince reminded him. "What'd you come up with?"

"Plenty," Tommy said. "I interviewed the owner of the *Hanky-Panky*, a guy named Roger Butler. He runs party excursions all along the East Coast, and he positively identified Daniel Keliher and Thomas Falcone as the ones he took out on a magical cruise to nowhere the week of August fourteenth."

"The two of them went on a magical trip to nowhere?" Vince asked. "What does that make these guys?"

"There were two bimbos with them. Butler picked them all up at Ocean City, New Jersey, on the fourteenth and they just cruised off the coastline for a week, as far south as Norfolk and back again," Tommy said.

"Just the four of them?" Vince asked.

"Two in a stateroom, but from what Butler says, they switched around a lot," Tommy replied. "They did a lot of drugs and alcohol too. The bill for the booze alone came to over six hundred bucks."

"Who paid for everything?"

"Falcone paid in U.S. greenbacks, according to Butler. I guess so the payments couldn't be traced."

"Any names for the bimbos?"

"Yeah, Butler said they called themselves Sandra and Louise, but he also told me Keliher and Falcone were named Tucker and Vásquez, so you can figure it out for yourself."

"Everyone used an alias," Vince acknowledged.

"One other thing. Butler said that the girls looked like pros, not some high-school chippies these guys picked up at some bar and talked into taking a trip with them. If I had to guess, I'd guess there's a pimp someplace down in Jersey who made a bundle up front on this deal."

"Okay, we're gonna need a sketch on both of them. See if you can get the Fort Myers cops to let you use their artist, if they have one. Better still, a photomontage if they have the equipment.

"How about my idea on the pimp?" Tommy asked. "Want me to spend a couple of days nosing around the fleshpots down in Jersey to see what I can stir up?"

Vince laughed. "You can nose around the fleshpots of The Bronx, how's that?"

"Seriously, wire me a C-note and I'll split my winnings at the crap table with you," Tommy said.

"Crap tables? They got gambling in Ocean City?"

"No, but they got it in Atlantic City, and that's about a half hour away." Tommy said.

Vince felt his muscles tense. "You get the sketch of those two hookers to me pronto," he told Tommy. "Atlantic City was the last place Cherry Dressard went to before somebody carved her up."

22

NYPD FORM DD-5   September 26, 1989

COMPLAINT FOLLOW-UP   COMPLAINT # 8081

Det. V. Crowley

SUBJECT: BOMBING/HOMICIDE, THOMAS FALCONE. RE-INTERVIEW OF LUIS ESCOBAR AND WALTER CRUZ

1. At 1023 hours, this date, along with Det. Ippollito, 37 PDU, I visited the Contech Corporation for the purpose of re-interviewing the subjects re. new evidence in the above-mentioned homicide.
2. Questioned about the victim's apparent connection with Con. Julian Santiago, and the matter of a boat excursion made by the aforementioned victim, during the week of 8/14–8/21, this year, accompanied by Daniel Keliher and two female companions, both subjects refused to answer and recommended to Det. Ippollito and myself that all further questions re. the above matter be directed to company attorney, J. Sánchez.
3. When asked if we might be given access to the company's records in order to verify certain facts pursuant to our continued investiga-

tion, we were told by the subjects we could
not access company ledgers without power of
subpoena.
4. In the opinion of the undersigned, both above-
mentioned subjects were uncooperative and of
a suspicious nature.

Investigation continues. Case active.

Tommy hit the jackpot without ever going to Atlantic City. One of the artist's sketches he brought back
from Florida, drawn from the description provided by
Roger Butler, was almost a dead-ringer for Trixie
Lee's mug shot. The second was close enough to the
morgue photograph of the battered Cherry Dressard
to leave no room for doubt that they were the hookers
who had accompanied Thomas Falcone and Daniel
Keliher aboard the *Hanky-Panky*.

"This Roger Butler's keeping himself available in
case we need him to identify Trixie Lee in a lineup,
right?" Vince asked Tommy.

"He's not going anyplace but out on the boat, and
the coast guard can get him anytime on ship-to-shore,"
Tommy said. "How about Keliher while we're at it?
Why don't we bring him in and ask him some questions. Maybe have Butler pull him out of a lineup just
for the hell of it."

"We got nothing on Keliher," Vince said. "Whatta
you want to do, have half the chiefs in New York
breathing down our necks?"

"He was one of the last people to see Falcone
alive," Tommy protested. "That makes him a witness,
no matter how big a shot he happens to be."

"Let's not outrun our interference here," Vince cautioned him. "It looks like we're finally starting to get
somewhere on this case and I don't want to blow it all
by being overanxious."

"Cases, plural," Tommy reminded him. "If what we
got here holds water, the Falcone homicide and the

Cherry Dressard homicide are probably linked some-how. Two people who just spent a week together don't all of a sudden get murdered right after that by accident."

"Not to mention Rafael Rosa," Vince pointed out. "He was heavy into *santería*, and Cherry Dressard's murder looks like one of their ritualistic sacrifices."

"Maybe they're all tied into *Santería* somehow," Tommy agreed. "You gotta figure Rosa set the charge under Falcone's car and he was sure into that shit. Aren't you starting to get the feeling that this is all part of the same case, that somehow all this *santería* gobbledygook is responsible for all three homicides?"

"Nothing would surprise me at this point, but I gotta ask myself why. What's the motive here? *Santería* is a religion, and religions don't commit murders. People commit murders, and they usually have reasons for doing them."

"Yeah, but these loonies are doing human sacri-fices," Tommy noted. "Maybe that's motive enough for them. Whatta we know? You and me never got ourselves involved in none of this occult crap before."

"Four people go for a joyride on the love boat. About a month later two of them are flatout murdered and another one is missing," Vince said patiently. "To me there's nothing mystical or occult about that. To me, that's reason to suspect that something about that romantic cruise to nowhere was hazardous to these people's health. Somebody, somewhere, had a real stake in seeing these people dead—a real person with a real motive, not some thunder god with an ax to grind."

"Double-edged ax," Tommy reminded him. "So what do you think the motive was?"

"One thing at a time." Vince grabbed his jacket. "I think it's time for you and me to pay another visit to those guys out at Contech." He chalked them both out.

They drove to the Contech plant and were ushered into Luis Escobar's office after a few minutes' wait.

"Sorry to keep you waiting, but it's a madhouse around this place." Escobar shook their hands and offered them a seat. "You should have called first."

"Well, we were just driving around reviewing what we know about Thomas Falcone's death, and a couple of questions came to mind," Vince told him. "I don't suppose we could get your partner, Mr. Cruz, in here, could we? It'd save us all a lot of time."

Escobar pressed a button on his telephone console. "Walt, would you mind coming in here for a few minutes? Those detectives we talked to a while back have some more questions." He replaced the receiver. "Are you any farther along on this thing than you were the last time we spoke?"

"We're starting to put together a few bits and pieces," Vince said. "Mostly what we've found out has given us more questions than answers."

Escobar smiled thinly. "That's usually the case in our business too. The minute we think we're on the verge of a breakthrough, something happens to set us right back where we started."

Walter Cruz entered the office and shook hands all around. "How's the investigation going?" he asked, sitting in the only remaining chair.

"Like I was telling your partner here, we keep running up against a lot of questions that we're going to need answers for," Vince said.

"Well, if there's anything we can do to help you out, just ask," Cruz offered. "I don't think I've had a good night's sleep since Tom was killed. I'm sure I speak for Luis as well when I tell you gentlemen that things just haven't gotten back to normal here since Tom's death. It's cast a terrible pall over everybody."

"I'm sorry to hear that," Vince said, removing his notebook from his jacket pocket and thumbing through the pages. "I'll try not to take up too much of your time: I just have a few questions . . ." He poised his pencil above the notebook. "Can either of you tell me what you know about the *Hanky-Panky?*"

Cruz went white and Escobar's left eye twitched involuntarily. "I'm not sure I get your meaning," Escobar said finally, clearing his throat.

"*Hanky-Panky,* sir," Vince repeated.

The partners studiously avoided looking at each other. "You're going to have to be clearer than that, Detective Crowley," Cruz said.

"The *Hanky-Panky* is an excursion boat," Vince told him. "Thomas Falcone hired it out for the entire week of August fourteenth, the week before he was killed, to take a romantic cruise to nowhere with Congressman Julian Santiago's aide, Daniel Keliher, and a couple of hired chippies. Would either of you mind telling me what you know about that?"

"Do you have proof of this allegation?" Cruz asked.

"You don't think we'd just walk in here and make up a story like that, do you?" Tommy asked them.

"There's plenty of proof: eyewitness testimony, credit card and telephone receipts," Vince exaggerated. "Even photographs of Thomas Falcone and Keliher on the boat together."

Escobar drew himself up behind his desk. "If what you're telling us is true, the person you should be talking to is Daniel Keliher not us. Tom Falcone knew a lot of people, and if he chose to take a trip with Keliher or anybody else that was his business. Nobody here ever asked him to file a flight plan with us before he took off."

"You're saying that neither of you had any knowledge of this trip, before or after it was taken?" Vince asked.

"That's precisely what we're saying, Detective." Cruz looked to his partner for reinforcement.

"Just what is it you're trying to infer here?" Escobar demanded.

Vince rested the notebook on his lap and removed a

pack of unfiltered Camels from his shirt pocket. "Okay if I smoke?"

Icy silence. "Are you saying you think this company had something to do with that?" Cruz asked finally.

Vince lit the cigarette and blew a lazy column of smoke across the desk. "Why don't you tell me?"

"This is preposterous!" Escobar stood and glared at Vince and Tommy. "Are we being accused of something, Detective . . . ?"

Vince raised his hand. "Hey, let's not lose it here . . . any of us. Nobody's accusing anybody of anything. My partner and I have learned about certain things and it's our job to check them out. If you don't know anything, then you've got nothing to worry about, right? I mean, if you both tell us you know absolutely nothing about the *Hanky-Panky* and that trip, we got no alternative but to believe you. We're not out to railroad anybody here."

Escobar returned to his seat slowly.

"Actually, what we were hoping was that you gentlemen could fill us in on Thomas Falcone's relationship with the congressman: how long they'd known each other, what kind of business dealings they had, that sort of thing."

The partners looked at each other. "I wasn't aware of any relationship," Cruz said. "If Tom had any dealings with Congressman Santiago, I can assure you they had nothing to do with Contech."

"I find that hard to believe, sir," Vince said, checking the earlier entries in his notebook. "The fact is that Thomas Falcone's last correspondence from your offices was to someone he called Julio, recalling what appears to be that very boat ride and mentioning the fact that they had a great time with some unnamed companions."

"Julio is a common Spanish name," Cruz responded icily. "I don't know whether the Julio in that correspondence was the congressman or not, but if it was, it was not related in any way to his employment here."

Vince shot a sidelong glance at Tommy. "You're asking us to believe that Thomas Falcone, who acted openly as a lobbyist for the Contech Corporation in Washington, never did any company business with a man who could practically guarantee you guys a big hunk of government business?"

"I'm not asking you to believe anything," Cruz told him matter-of-factly. "The areas we're getting into now are areas we're not permitted to discuss with anyone but our own counsel. I wish we could be of greater help to you, but our hands are tied." He stood and motioned toward the door. "Now, if you don't mind, we have business to attend to."

"Wait a minute," Vince protested. "I just told you nobody's suspected of anything here. What's this counsel stuff? Innocent people don't need lawyers when they're not being charged with anything."

"By you," Escobar said. "I'm sure you're not unaware that there are several other agencies investigating our company. I'm afraid we're just not at liberty to discuss our business dealings with you or anyone else until this whole matter is cleared up."

"And we have been vindicated," Cruz added.

"Your business is your own affair," Vince said. "I'm not interested in proving anything against your company or against either of you. I have a homicide to solve here, the murder of a man you say you both loved. I'm gonna need your cooperation in order to get anywhere on this thing."

"I wish it was that simple." Cruz opened the office door. "Unfortunately for all of us, certain politically motivated government officials have decided to make Contech a cause célèbre in order to advance their own narrow self-interest. We are an easy target, Detective, a couple of spicks who just happened to have the ambition and the balls to make it in the *yanqui* marketplace. That pisses off a lot of people who want to see us stay where we belong, back in the barrios drinking homemade *ron* and munching on bananas.

People like that are willing to believe anything about us, Detective Crowley. The politics of race still pays off in this country."

Vince stood and nodded to Tommy. "I don't suppose you'd be willing to let us take a quick look at Thomas Falcone's credit-card receipts, just so we can verify dates and locations?"

"That information would be in the hands of our accountants, and they've been instructed not to talk to anyone until our legal entanglements are cleared up." Cruz ushered them out into the hallway. "Please understand, detectives, we'd like to be more cooperative if we could, but we're dead in the water here if we tell you anything we're not supposed to. You have to understand that we're fighting for our corporate lives here. There are millions of dollars at stake."

Vince nodded. "I guess the murder of a man you loved doesn't mean much when it's stacked up against those kind of bucks."

Cruz eyed him coldly. "Your people made the rules, Detective. Don't blame my partner and me if we play by them."

23

"THIS IS A DIFFICULT STORY TO COVER, A STORY that should never have been allowed to happen in a civilized society, but one that happens all too often in this city . . ."

Vince settled back in a wooden chair and watched a videotape of Connie's televised report from the day before.

"We are standing just outside the pediatric critical care unit of Misericordia Hospital, where one of the children taken from a Bronx apartment on September sixth has already died and two others are still in serious condition from malnutrition, dehydration, and a number of other problems stemming from their forced incarceration in a 'house of hell' at 209th Street. The images you are about to see are stark and unpleasant, not for the squeamish or faint-hearted, so we suggest you change the channel if scenes of violence and child-neglect and abuse upset you . . ."

The picture on the screen dissolved into a series of shaky images of the interior of the apartment, taken by the district attorney's video unit on the day officers of the Thirty-seventh precinct had first discovered the horror: close-ups of the mutilated animals on the floor, the mounds of dirt and feces, the emaciated children staring hollow-eyed into the camera's lens.

"All of the children found in the apartment bear the scars of beatings and neglect," Connie's voice continued shakily over the footage. "As well as the unmistakable evidence of sexual abuse by adults. Tests taken at this hospital indicate that many of the children are suffering from vaginal and anal gonorrhea and herpes. Two of the children have tested positive for AIDS . . ."

Vince cast a sidelong glance at Leila Turner, who was fidgeting uncomfortably in the only other chair in the precinct viewing room. He could see her lips and jaw tighten as the graphic scenes of wanton violence prodded her memory of that day. Her eyes moistened as the grim procession of children passed before her on the screen, zombielike.

"I've seen enough!" She stood and faced Vince. "What're we watching this all over for, anyway?"

Vince turned off the VCR. "It's an active case, Leila. I'm just trying to refresh our memories here. Maybe we'll see something we missed the first time around."

"I didn't miss anything," Turner volleyed. "I'll never forget the look on those kids' faces as long as I live."

"Yeah, but we're looking at a homicide now," Vince reminded her. "One of those kids died, and we may be looking at more before this thing is over. You heard the report."

She shook her head. "I don't understand what you're getting at here, Crowley. Don't you think I know how bad this thing is? I don't need a videotape of yesterday's news to get me moving on this case. I hate the bastards who did that to those kids."

"I never said you didn't," Vince replied evenly. "I just want to make sure we're exploring every possible lead here, that's all."

"We already have names and descriptions for five of the people who lived in that apartment, and we're working on the others," Turner said. "Wherever they are, they can't stay holed up forever. Sooner or later they've got to surface, and when they do, we'll nail them."

Vince turned on the lights and opened the case

folder he was carrying. "That's pretty much what this is all about: nailing these bastards when they come out in the open." He handed Leila mug shots of the suspects, obtained from the BCI after they had been identified by the landlord and neighbors in the building. "These five and the others are heavy into this *santería* stuff—"

"They're heavy into starving and abusing children," she interrupted him.

"Whatever. Maybe that's all a part of their weird rituals," Vince suggested. "The point is, we gotta start anticipating where they're going to surface, and be there, ready to bust them when they do."

Turner eyed him suspiciously. "Just what's that supposed to mean, Crowley? You got something up your sleeve that you're not telling me about?"

"Maybe . . ." Vince retrieved the photos and placed them back in the folder. "I got a feeling that these slimeballs can stay underground for a real long time unless we start going out there after them."

"Why is it I get the impression that when you say *we* should go out there after them, what you're really saying is *I* should go out there after them?" she challenged him.

Vince smiled. "We're all in this, Leila. You know that."

Her eyes narrowed. "I know you too well, Crowley. You're setting me up for something, right?"

He sat, facing her. "How'd you like to become a member of the cult of *santería* for one night?"

Silence. "Oh, my," Leila groaned finally. "What've you got cooking up in that sick brain of yours, Crowley?"

"Remember that cult cop, James Kroll?"

She nodded uncertainly.

"Well, he phoned me about an hour ago and told me his intelligence sources had learned there was going to be an important ceremony out in Flushing Meadows Friday night. He said they were expecting maybe a thousand people from all over the country, so it wouldn't be a big deal to slip somebody in there undercover."

"Oh, Jesus." Turner shook her head. "Let me see if I can figure this one out, okay? *Santerías* are mostly black people, so you'd want to send in someone who was black. And a woman would attract less attention than a man, so you'd probably want to send in a black woman. Now, how many black women do we have in the Three-Seven detective squad?"

He grinned. "I always said you were a quick study."

"Oh, man, those people are crazy," Leila moaned.

"You said you hated the bastards who did that to those kids."

"So that was what that TV show you just put on was all about. You weren't looking for anything new, you just wanted to make me good and mad all over again before you sprang this on me, right?" Turner demanded.

"You don't have to do this, Leila. You know that."

"Sure, like I'm gonna refuse after all that."

"It'll be a piece of cake, I promise." Vince waded in while she was still vulnerable. "You're just there to observe, nothing more. You won't have to wear a wire, no walkie-talkie, nothing that could give you away if you were challenged, which you're not going to be. You just keep your eyes open and report what you saw after you get out."

"And what if I happen to spot any of those creeps from the apartment? Do I get any backup when I go to bust them?" Turner asked.

"You're not going to bust anybody. We'll be nearby, outside someplace where we can't be spotted. You just try to keep them in sight and point them out to us when you're outa there."

She eyed him cynically. "You know, you didn't need to go through the whole TV bit. I would've done this without all that."

Back in the squad room, there was a message that Ramón Rosado, an old snitch from Vince's days at the Seventy-third Precinct in Brooklyn, had returned his call. Vince dialed the number on Oxbridge Pell's hand-written note.

"Ramón, how goes the old pill mill?" Vince asked when the drug merchant came on the line.

"Hey, man, I ain't into that shit no more," Rosado protested. "That what you called me for, just to bust my chops, Crowley?"

"Hey, calm down, my man," Vince said. "I know you're a righteous dude. Why do you think I'm calling you in the first place? When I need a pipeline out there in Brooklyn, who's the first name I think of? Ramón, I say to myself. I could always count on good old Ramón when the chips were down."

"Oh, man, the shit is piling up so deep I can hardly breathe here," Rosado groaned. "Why don't you just tell me what's on your mind and forget the hand job, okay, Crowley? I'm a busy man."

"Okay, I want you to take a hypothetical situation," Vince went on. "Just suppose you were still in the pill business. I know you're not, but for the sake of this argument let's just suppose you were—"

"What's this all about, man?"

"Hear me out, Ramón. Believe me, I got your best interests at heart here. Like I told the guys at the Seven-Three, I said, 'Ramón, he's a stand-up guy, and if you got any idea about squeezing the poor dude's stones, forget it. Ramón and me do square business.' Word of God, Ramón, that's just what I told them."

A low moan. "Whatta you want, Crowley?"

"We're back to that hypothetical situation," Vince continued. "Now, suppose you were still pushing illegal pharmaceuticals, which we both know you are not, and suppose you were dealing with the same sophisticated clientele you once dealt with, but which we know you now have nothing to do with. My question is this. Given that unlikely set of circumstances, would you be doing business with an instructor out at Pratt named Senji Rula?"

There was a pause. "Strictly between me and you, I

have no personal knowledge of anyone like that," Rosado said gravely. "But a savvy guy like me hears things every now and then, if you know what I'm talking."

"And you've heard about this Senji Rula?"

"I hear stuff, you know. Rula, shmoola, who the hell knows from names? Some guys are saying there might be a teacher from that place that's into high-grade psychedelics—morning glory, peyote, psilocybin— strictly mind-fuck stuff. You know these intellectual types."

"A name. I need a name," Vince pressed him.

"I told you, I don't know from names. He's some kinda Indian, that's the best I can do for you?"

"Pakistani maybe?"

"What's the difference, they're all scumbags."

"That's good enough. Thanks, Ramón." Vince hung up, took a deep breath, and dialed Katie. Eight rings, . . . nine, ten. Katie wasn't answering, not even the stupid machine telling him how desperately she wanted to hear from him . . .

What Katie desperately wanted was for Senji Rula to emerge from the faculty lounge and walk her back to the apartment. She stood forlornly in the hallway of the Pratt administration building and tried to appear nonchalant to the passing students and instructors, desperately needing a cigarette to calm her jittery nerves, but afraid that if she stepped outside she would miss him.

"Miss Crowley?" The voice startled her. "Migod, you look just like you're old man."

Katie turned to see a chubby man with white hair and an elfin grin standing behind her. "Were you talking to me?" she asked tentatively.

"I'm sorry if I frightened you," he apologized. "My name is Kevin O'Grady, an old friend of your father's. He asked me to stop by and say hello to you."

"Daddy asked you to say hello to me?"

"In a manner of speaking. Your dad and I are old friends from the days when I was on the force. He knew I was working here at Pratt and he asked me to see how you were doing."

"Are you an instructor here?" Katie asked.

"No, more of a caretaker, I guess you'd say. I'm in charge of campus security."

Katie found herself fidgeting uncomfortably. "Well, it's nice of you to look me up. I'll tell Daddy I spoke with you." She turned to leave.

O'Grady caught up with her and walked alongside. "To tell you the truth, your dad's a bit concerned about you. He asked me to have a talk with you about some of your friends."

Katie stopped, clenched her fists and teeth. "I don't believe this is happening? I knew he didn't trust me, but I didn't think he'd sent his police buddies to check up on me."

"Be fair to your father," O'Grady warned her. "He loves you very much, and from what I can see, he has good reason to be worried about you. We both think that maybe you've gotten yourself in over your head here . . ."

Katie resumed walking at a fast pace, staring straight ahead, pretending not to hear him.

"It's not for myself I'm talking to you, Katie . . . or for your dad either . . ." O'Grady was panting, trying to keep up with her. "It's for your own good, young lady."

"Why is it every time someone is trying to horn into somebody else's life, it's always for their own good?" she challenged him as they descended the front steps of the administration building. "You can report back to my father that I'm doing just fine, and the next time I need his help I'll call. In the meantime I'd appreciate it if you'd both butt out!"

"You're not giving your dad a chance . . ." O'Grady puffed.

"I'm trying to give myself a chance!" Katie began

running, slowly at first, then faster and faster, widening the distance between them as it became apparent that O'Grady was no match for her. His shouted entreaties were lost beneath the exaggerated sounds of her own labored breathing, her quickening heartbeat surging in her ears like the sound of a runaway locomotive. She felt the damp kiss of tears washing her cheeks, deep, reflexive spasms of twisting pain, and waves of nausea that refused to go away even after she stopped running, rising in her chest to overwhelm even the fear and guilt.

Senji would have something for that, she knew. All she had to do was make it through the next few minutes until he came home.

24

From: Commanding Officer 37th Precinct
Detective Unit
To: Police Jurisdiction Concerned
Subj: Request for Field Information

1. Attached is a photograph of a fugitive witness being sought by this command.
2. It is requested that any field information possessed by you re: the possible whereabouts of this individual be forwarded to this command.
3. Name: Trixie Lee, aka Thelma Gruenwald.
4. Description: female, white, 5 ft, 4½ in., 24–27 yrs., Light blond hair (platinum), may also be dyed darker. Identifying marks: heart-shaped tattoo (blue) on upper left front shoulder. 3″ scar (knife type) on left buttock. May possibly be suntanned.
5. Subject is sought for information in connection with three homicides being investigated by this command. She was last seen on 8/12 this year.
6. Subject is not considered to be dangerous and should be apprehended if possible.
7. Matter is carried under 61 #8081, case #1717. Dets. V. Crowley and T. Ippollito assigned. Kindly telephone any pertinent information to 37 PDU, (212) 920-6712, 13 or 19.

"Am I disturbing something important here, or can we get on with a little precinct business?"

C.O. Michael Sweeney stood in the squad-room doorway. "I'd appreciate your attention for a minute," he announced to those seated outside. "I have an announcement to make that affects everyone in this squad as well as everyone in this precinct."

Vince could see the C.O.'s flunkie, Bob Donofrio, leaning smugly against Sweeney's closed office door, a half-grin on his face. It was the kind of grin that greedy, incompetent little men got when they caught someone classier than them in a run of bad luck. "Bad shit's coming at you," it said, "and it's gonna hurt like hell."

"I know there's been speculation among you that this precinct is on the list of those to be phased out." Vince noticed the startled reaction to Sweeney's disclosure out of the corner of his eye. Everybody began looking at everybody else, uncertain whether they were really hearing what they were hearing.

"I've always tried to discourage this type of hearsay information," Sweeney went on, oblivious to the shocked reactions around him. "But in this case the speculation has some merit. The way it now looks, there will be a major realignment of existing precinct structure in The Bronx. As part of that realignment, this precinct, the Thirty-fifth, and Thirty-eighth are to be gradually phased out over a period of months and replaced by a single unit that will encompass all three jurisdictions."

He looked out over the strained sea of faces. Donofrio could barely suppress a giggle.

"Nothing has been resolved as of this moment." Sweeney stared hard at them. "Let me repeat that. Nothing is happening right now. Nobody is out of a job, nobody is going to be working anywhere but right here for the foreseeable future. What we're talking about here is a plan that may not be fully implemented for several years. It won't even begin before the first of next year.

"I've chosen to tell you all about this now rather than waiting until the last possible minute in order to forestall any charges that may arise over the unfair treatment of individual officers during this period of readjustment. As someone who has been involved in operations like this in the past, I am fully aware that officers are resistant to being reassigned, whether or not their reassignment is beneficial to the department they are sworn to serve. I fully expect that there will be grumblings, that people will be put-out and angry, and that they will make their dissatisfaction known to me and my superiors. That's okay, as long as the grumbling and dissension remain here inside the department where they belong. The police department has a big-enough image problem among the press and public at large without anybody here adding to it."

Sweeney looked around the room. "Any questions?"

Stunned silence.

"All right, then. In closing, I can tell you that any requests for transfer by members of this squad will be inspected and processed. I can't promise that you'll all end up where you want to go, but I am sensitive to your needs and will do everything I can to see to it that this transition is as painless for everybody concerned as possible. That will be all. Carry on." Sweeney went back into his office, followed by a sneering Donofrio.

"What now?" Tommy asked weakly after a while.

"I dunno . . ." Vince looked at Steve and the others and shrugged. "I don't see that there's much any of us can do."

"Anybody filing a fifty-seven?" Walt Cuzak asked, referring to the standard departmental UF-57 form requesting transfer of duty.

"That'll get you shit," Steve remarked. "Ask for a transfer in this department and they automatically put you down as a troublemaker. The chiefs'll have you counting dead trees on Staten Island if you're lucky."

"You know it, bro," Walt concurred. "My bother-in-law Louie was out in the old Eight-Three when they merged it and he asked to be sent over here to The Bronx. Next thing he knows, he's out at Kennedy Airport with a pot-sniffing dog, rummaging through people's luggage."

"You're fucked no matter what you do," Snuffy Quade muttered

"I don't know about you bozos, but I'll be glad to get out of the Führer Bunker," Leila said halfheartedly. "Maybe I'll end up in a place where there's a little chance for advancement instead of watching my career go down the tubes in this outhouse."

"Oh, yeah, they'll probably end up making you chief of the department, when they hear you're available," Tommy sneered. "The only reason they probably ain't offered you the job up to this point is they figured it'd be a letdown from what you got here."

"A dangerous career move," Snuffy concurred.

"Laugh all you want." Leila pouted. "You all know this joint is a one-way ticket to oblivion."

"*If* you plan on remaining a cop," Tommy reminded her. "Me? I'm outa here, man. No way these chicken-shits are shuffling my ass all over this city. It's law school for me, and a little respectability for a change. I was just looking for an excuse to bag this cops-and-robbers shit anyway."

"Retirement for me," Vince said. "I owe it to myself to get in a little recreation before I die. Twenty-four years cooped up in pigpens like this place, eating stale food and listening to assholes like you guys. What I need to do is expand my horizons. I got a few good years left in me."

"I'm with you," Walt agreed. "I'm getting my ass down to Florida, and spend the rest of my days sucking on piña coladas and basking in the sun. A guy's really gotta be half-nuts to spend his old age in this place when he can have it all down in the tropics."

"Hey, there's not one of us that won't end up better-off once we're out of this shithole," Tommy cried.

"Fuck the Führer Bunker!" Snuffy raised an imaginary glass and toasted them all.

"To a little fun in our lives for a change." Vince toasted him back, his eyes sweeping the familiar room with its antique furniture and peeling paint. Tommy was right, he knew. They would all end up better-off somehow.

So how come it hurt so much?

25

Flynn's Shanty was what saloons were all about: standing sentinel among the proliferation of Irish saloons that abounded in the Castle Hill section of The Bronx. What Flynn's brought to the business of being a legitimate Irish watering hole in a legitimate Irish neighborhood was an unapologetic sense of self, an understanding that it could never be more than what it was, and that was fine with the homely band of working-class regulars that gathered there each day, secure in the knowledge that they would be accepted there, wanted there. They knew that in an age of glitz and insincerity, they were in a place where people called a spade a spade, and if they called it something else, it was an acceptable lie and not a deception. Irishmen are, after all, nothing if they cannot lie sincerely, and the rowdies that ringed the age-worn oak bar at Flynn's each night were nothing if they weren't Irishmen.

What the regulars brought to the saloon night after night was a part of themselves they had kept buried inside until they got there: an outpouring of jokes and anecdotes and vague reminiscences, arm wrestling, liar's poker, coarse shouted insults and raucus laughter, stentorious belching and hard-boiled-egg farts that hung in the air with the timeless smells of beer and whiskey; the trailing, melancholy strains of blended tenor voices rising above the hubbub, commanding everyone there to stand and share a memory, to shed a tear. They brought with them the certain knowledge that they were where they belonged, in the company of friends they wished to be with. If everything they saw outside was distant and uncertain, here in Flynn's they were safe, and nothing would ever change.

The drinks were shots and beers, dispensed by Eamon Flynn to the genial crowd of regulars who passed them in precarious waves of overflowing froth over, under, and around the three-deep gathering at the bar. Spilled beer and whiskey collected in pools along its pitted surface, drenching the ever-present piles of wrinkled dollar bills that kept the bounty flowing; dollar after dollar, round after mellow round, lubricating their conversation, strengthening them, unleashing their souls.

"Looka these guys," Tommy muttered to Vince beneath the din. "Can you imagine they got nothing better to do with their lives than get shitfaced in this place every night?"

"What're we doing?" Vince asked.

"That's different. We got good reason."

"Maybe they think they got good reasons too," Vince suggested, draining his glass and signaling Eamon for another straight Scotch.

"Whatta you think?" Tommy asked Shem Weisen, whom they had found drinking at the bar when they got there.

"Philosophy's not my strong suit," Weisen grumped.

"I'm not asking for philosophy," Tommy groaned. "Don't you got an opinion about why guys get shitfaced every night?"

"Guys in general or just me?" Weisen asked.

"You don't get shitfaced every night, do you?" Vince asked.

Weisen shrugged. "I dunno. I don't keep track."

"You think you're an alcoholic?" Tommy asked.

"Who the hell knows?" Weisen tipped his glass.

"I'd probably be an alcoholic if I worked hard enough on it. I just don't have the time to drink enough to get it to kick in," Vince observed.

"If you're serious about drinking, you find the time," Weisen said.

"I had an uncle who went to AA," Tommy volunteered. "Poor son of a bitch went dry just like that. I never seen anybody so miserable as he was."

"They got a tough time coping," Weisen said. "You just try facing what's out there every day without a little something to take the edge off."

"You gotta get blotto every now and then," Tommy agreed. "There's a lotta shit going down that you just don't want to deal with, period."

"Like the police department of the City of New York." Vince raised his glass. "It's times like this I wish I'd become a car-wash attendant or an elevator operator, something really dull and predictable like that."

"You think car-wash attendants don't drink?" Weisen asked him. "Think again. I'll bet I put away a dozen of them every year with livers hard as bowling balls. Drinking doesn't have anything to do with what you do, it's what you're not doing that drives you to the bottle."

Tommy scowled. "You wanta run that one by me one more time?"

Weisen eyed them both speculatively. "What're you guys in here for, because you're rock stars or high-priced company executives?"

Vince shrugged. "I dunno. I guess we needed a little break from all that bullshit going down at the precinct."

"Maybe it's that simple for you, but not for most people," Weisen said. "You ask most of the guys at this bar what it is that makes them drink, and they'll tell you it's because of all the promises they made to themselves that they didn't keep."

"I thought philosophy wasn't your strong suit," Tommy reminded him.

"Nothing philosophical about that," Weisen said. "Just look around you. Most of these yo-yos probably hate their jobs, their families, their wretched little lives. But after three or four rounds in this place, the world starts looking good to them, or at least it becomes tolerable. Sober, most of these guys would tell you they'd wanted to make something of themselves, but drunk they can deal with being shitkickers. You think you'd be in here getting ripped if you were all that happy about what you were doing?"

"I always wanted to be a cop," Tommy said defensively.

"And I always wanted to be a famous heart surgeon."

"So why did you become a coroner?' Tommy challenged him.

"No bedside manner." Weisen polished off his drink. "I don't have to be charming to my patients, but then they don't show me a lot of respect either."

Eamon deposited a fresh round of drinks on the bar in front of them. "Compliments of that guy down at the end."

Vince squinted down the line of revelers until he came to the grinning face of Bob Donofrio. "I'll be dipped. It looks like Sweeney's errand boy is trying to make up to us," he told Tommy and Weisen.

"I can afford my own booze." Tommy pushed Donofrio's offering away and ordered another. "The day I take anything from that cocksucker you can stop being my partner, bro. I got more pride than that."

"I always wanted to be a cop too," Vince continued. "But I gotta admit it turned out a lot different than I thought it would."

"What'd you think it'd be, Dick Tracy all over again?" Tommy grinned.

"Maybe, I dunno." Vince shrugged. "I guess I thought I could really do some good, you know? I thought I had a shot at making this city a better place to live in—"

"Oh, jeez. I think I hear violins playing here," Tommy interrupted him.

"I'm serious, humphead. You telling me you weren't all gung ho when you first joined the department?"

"I guess I was, but it didn't take me long to figure out that an attitude like that would get me diddelyshit," Tommy replied. "You don't have to be no veteran to see that the head honchos are a buncha crumbs, and if you're ever gonna get anyplace in this department, you gotta become just as crummy as they are."

"Such cynicism ill befits you," Weisen remarked. "What ever happened to the idealism of youth?"

"It got fucked over by shitheads like Donofrio." Tommy scowled.

"Whose charity you happen to be accepting at this very moment," Vince reminded Weisen.

Weisen eyed the gift drink and drained his glass. "When the time comes that I start letting principles get in the way of putting on a good bag, you guys can cart me off to the rubber room. This stuff works the same no matter who's money is paying for it."

"And tonight it happens to be mine." Bob Donofrio had pushed his way through the bar crowd and was standing behind them. "What's the matter, you guys got something against taking a free drink from me?"

Vince and Tommy looked at each other. "Go away, Donofrio," Tommy muttered. "You're stinking up the place."

"Hey, is that any way to treat a superior officer, especially one who just bought you a drink?" Donofrio protested. "What's with you mooks? You think just because the department's got the good sense to get rid of that pigsty you call a precinct, that gives you the right to act unsociable?"

"My partner told you to get lost," Vince repeated.

"Your partner insulted me," Donofrio persisted. "I don't like pantywaist rookies to begin with, and when they insult me, I get particularly pissed off." He elbowed Tommy in the side. "How about it, pussy, you gonna apologize to me for that shit you said?"

"You touch me one more time and you're dead," Tommy warned him. "Rank don't count in this place. In here it's just you and me."

"You want a piece of me, be my guest!" Donofrio stepped back and sneered at Tommy.

"He's not worth it, partner." Vince placed a restraining hand on Tommy's forearm. "All your life you're gonna run into assholes like him. You can't punch them all out."

"Listen to you guys." Donofrio guffawed. "A couple of pissy-assed, no-name flatfoots from a pissy-assed, no-name precinct in the middle of the asshole of the world, acting tough when they got a couple of pops in them. Is that what the police department's come down to?"

Vince turned and faced him. "I'll tell you what the police department's come down to, scumbag. It's come down to a bunch of morons like you, who probably never walked a beat or made an arrest, telling me and my partner here what being a cop is supposed to be all about." He edged off his stool and backed Donofrio into the crowd. "Now, Tommy and me don't need to hear that from you because we know what being a cop is about, and it's something you'll never understand."

"I'll take you both on, motherfuckers," Donofrio snarled. "Outside, where we won't get your blood all over the place."

"You think being a cop is sucking up to shitheads like Sweeney," Vince went on, undaunted. "You sit around on your ass all day writing reports and studying for tests and covering your ass so nobody upstairs'll ever find out what an incompetent dick you really are, and then you got the nerve to come up here to The Bronx and tell us what to do? Just who the hell do you think you are, anyway? I was out there in the trenches taking the open shots while you were still pulling your pud back in grammar school. I remember when this department was full of real cops, not ass-wipes like we got today—like you and Sweeney."

Donofrio looped an overhand right, catching Vince by surprise and sending him reeling backward. "I'm waiting for you, motherfucker," he snarled. "Both of you motherfuckers!"

Tommy lunged forward, but Vince held him back.

"Cool it, partner. You get yourself into a fistfight with this ignoramus and you're just sinking to his level."

The split second that Donofrio relaxed following the advice was all the time Vince needed to deliver a well-placed kick to Donofrio's groin. Donofrio doubled over, screaming in pain, as Vince hooked him by his belt and shirt collar, propelling him headfirst into the bar with a sickening crunch.

"Now, what was that about pissy-assed cops in a pissy-assed precinct?" he demanded, lifting Donofrio's blood-spattered face up from the bar by his hair.

Donofrio responded with a barely audible groan. Traces of blood and spittle bubbled at the corners of his mouth.

"You got anything to add to what I already said, partner?" Vince asked Tommy.

"I think you made your point," Tommy said.

"You know it's not going to change anything," Shem Weisen said without looking up from his drink. "They're still going to shut you guys down and he's gonna have the last laugh."

Vince released Donofrio's head and dug a piece of cracked, bloodstained tooth from the wooden railing on the bar. "Maybe so, but he won't look so pretty when he's doing it."

26

"THE BRONX NEEDS *MORE* COPS, NOT LESS"
"NO PRECINCT SHUTDOWN"
"BRONX GETS THE SHAFT AGAIN"
"AT LEAST KISS US FIRST, MR. MAYOR!"

The parade of hand-painted signs flickered across the television screen as the camera panned a jostling crowd of protestors in front of City Hall in Manhattan. It had taken less than twelve hours for C.O. Sweeney's confidential announcement to spread throughout the borough and for the residents of The Bronx to have mounted a massive protest in reply.

"Representatives for various citizens' groups are demanding to meet with the mayor to discuss the reported closing of three precincts in The Bronx," the voice of the on-site newsman reported over the footage. "Spokesmen for several of the protesting groups have told me that they plan on picketing Gracie Mansion twenty-four hours a day until the mayor meets with them and they receive assurances from him that the precincts in question, the Thirty-fifth, Thirty-seventh, and Thirty-ninth, will remain open."

"If that don't beat all," Snuffy Quade commented as he and Vince watched the early-morning broadcast on the precinct TV. "That announcement was supposed to remain strictly inside the department. How do you suppose all those people got wind of it?"

Vince shrugged. "Beats me, Snuffy. I guess the

grapevines musta picked it up somehow. You know how hard it is to keep anything a secret in this city."

Snuffy grinned. "Yeah, some rookie probably got himself shitfaced in a saloon and started shooting his mouth off."

"More'n likely." Vince grinned back. They both knew that it would have been impossible to keep an event like this secret for very long anyway, but they also knew that every member of the Three-Seven had started spreading the report as soon as Sweeney shut his office door. The jungle drums had been beating a steady tattoo ever since the first telephone call to the first snitch in the precinct was completed. Within an hour of the C.O.'s announcement, every malcontent in the borough had been contacted by somebody in the station house, and the mechanisms of protest had been set in motion.

"I'm standing here with Representative Julian Santiago." The camera lens tightened on the newscaster and congressman standing at the edge of the ragged line of protesters. "Congressman Santiago, can you tell me whether or not you were aware of these proposed precinct closings, and if you were, can you tell me how they can be justified in the face of the soaring crime rate in The Bronx?"

"Under no circumstances was I ever consulted about any proposed precinct closings," Santiago protested loudly into the handheld microphone. "And I want to go on record as saying that I applaud and endorse the actions of these people out here today who are trying to reclaim their neighborhoods from the rapists and the drug lords." He stared gravely into the camera. "This proposed action smacks of the type of callous insensitivity the City of New York has consistently shown to the borough of The Bronx and in particular to its black and Hispanic residents. You can be sure that there are no police cutbacks being planned for the mayor's Silk Stocking district in Manhattan. It seems that every time this city experiences any type of fiscal emergency, it's the poor and disenfranchised that have to suffer."

"Are you saying that this action is racially motivated?" the interviewer persisted.

"I'm saying that every time there's a police precinct or a fire station phased out in this city, it just happens to be in the areas with the highest crime rates and the most fires. Now, that doesn't sound like a sensible municipal strategy to me. It sounds to me like the old money-talks politics that have been in effect in this city for a long time," Santiago responded.

"Are you planning to use the influence of your office to do something about this situation?"

Santiago faced the crowd of angry protesters and waited until the cameraman was positioned for a full-frontal shot. "It is my pledge to you today that I will use every power at my disposal to see to it that this outrageous proposal is rescinded," he told the picketers. "Unlike my opponent in the upcoming congressional election, I am not politically tied to this city administration. My loyalties are to the citizens of The Bronx, most particularly to the residents of the Nineteenth Congressional District, whose interests I am sworn to represent. We will not stand for this injustice!"

His pronouncement was met with thunderous applause and shouting.

"That guy's as fulla shit as a Christmas goose," Snuffy commented, turning off the set.

"They're all full of shit," Vince agreed. "But you gotta admit Santiago's on the right side this time."

Snuffy scowled. "He don't care no more for The Bronx than the mayor does. All he's interested in is making political hay out of this thing. Tell me one good thing that scumbag's done good for The Bronx since he's been in office?"

"Tell me one good thing anybody's ever done for

The Bronx," Vince shot back. "They're all scumbags, Snuffy, you know that. There isn't one of them who wouldn't flush the whole borough down the toilet for an extra fifty bucks a week in their pay envelopes."

"At least it's an issue now," Snuffy said. "Maybe now that the bastards see a chance to pick up some political brownie points, they'll let the whole thing drop."

"Don't hold your breath. Everybody'll bitch and moan for a while until they got all the TV exposure out of it they can, then they'll go on to something else. When was the last time you remember a protest got anywhere in this city?"

"Never did," Snuffy allowed. "At least not when it comes to cops. Those motherfuckers down at City Hall get fat at the public's expense and blame the cops every time. I don't see them cutting their salaries because of the budget crunch, do you?"

Vince laughed. "That'll be the day."

"And it ain't never gonna get any better," Snuffy went on. "These people up here don't got no clout. You don't see your average citizen of The Bronx getting busted for illegal campaign contributions, know what I mean? The politicians are gonna keep fucking them over as long as they got no ammunition to fight back. That greaseball Santiago don't give a shit what happens to those people out there; neither does your buddy Quinlan. They get elected and they all turn into greedy sons a bitches."

The telephone interrupted Snuffy's harangue and Vince answered it. "Crowley here, Thirty-seventh Detective Squad."

"Vince, it's Kayo," Kevin O'Grady replied. "I been meaning to get back to you about that Senji Rula guy, but I haven't been able to pin him down yet."

"How about Katie?" Vince asked him.

"I talked to her, as much as she was willing to talk."

"Meaning?"

"She didn't want any part of me, Vince. I don't think she'd listen to anybody who had anything bad to say about Rula at this point."

Vince paused. "What's your gut feeling?"

"I don't like it, bro."

"Thanks, Kayo. Get back to me if you hear anything else." Vince hung up the phone and grabbed his jacket.

The drive to Pratt took almost an hour due to morning rush-hour traffic. Vince arrived at Katie's apartment at 0937 hours and rang the front doorbell. There was no answer. He wound his way through the maze of academic structures on the campus until he found the administration building, where he intimidated a frightened clerk into giving him Rula's class schedule and apprising him of the instructor's current whereabouts. Rula's class was ending just as Vince arrived.

"Mr. Rula?" Vince stopped him as he emerged from the classroom. "I wonder if I could have a few words with you."

"Yes?" Rula seemed at ease, self-confident.

"I'm Detective Crowley, Thirty-seventh Precinct." He flashed his shield. "Is there someplace we can talk in private?"

Rula's left eyebrow twitched involuntarily, but he kept his composure. "I'm due in class in less than fifteen minutes, Detective. Perhaps we can make an appointment to speak about whatever it is on your mind later on in the day when I'll have more time."

Vince eyed him speculatively and instantly disliked what he saw. He'd known guys like Rula before: glib and smart and sneaky, always two points up on the morning line when it came to clever answers but never quite on target. "I'm afraid now's all the time we got, Mr. Rula," Vince responded. "What I have to say won't take up a lot of your valuable time."

Rula shrugged and led Vince to an unoccupied class-room down the hallway. "Now what's this all about, Detective . . . Crowley, was it?"

"Crowley. Same last name as Katie Crowley," Vince said evenly.

There was no response. "I'm afraid I don't know anybody by that name."

"Think again," Vince urged. "She's one of your students."

Rula shook his head emphatically. "I'm afraid you are wrong about that, Detective Crowley. I know all of my students by name and I can assure you there is no Katie Crowley among them."

"Short blond, real pretty?" Vince prodded.

"I have a Katie Sloan in one of my classes . . ."

Vince felt his stomach churning. The thought that Katie was using Jessy's maiden name was hard to take. "That'd be the one," Vince said. "I'd appreciate it if you would tell me what your relationship with her is."

Rula look confused. "I'm sorry, Detective. Is there something going on here that I'm not aware of? Has any sort of crime been committed?"

"That's what I'd like to find out," Vince told him. "I'd be in a better position to know that if you'd just answer my questions."

Rula smiled condescendingly. "Detective Crowley, I'd certainly like to help you in any way I can, but I have no intention of answering any of your questions unless you tell me what this is all about."

Vince hesitated. "What it's about is my daughter. You wanta tell me what the hell somebody like you is doing with a young kid like her?"

Rula bristled. "I'm not sure what you mean by 'somebody like me,' but I can assure you that your daughter is my student, nothing more."

"What I mean by somebody like you, is somebody who's got a reputation for messing around with your female students," Vince clarified. "And somebody who's known to narcotics law-enforcement officers as a drug merchant on this campus. You have anything to say about that?"

Rula headed for the door. "If you have anything further to say to me, you can tell it to my lawyer. His name is Rafninji, he's in the book."

Vince grabbed him by the arm. "Before you go, I think I oughta tell you that I had a long talk with your good buddy Ramón, and from what he tells me you're gonna have a real hard time getting any more product from him. Let's see how popular you are with these young kids once your pipeline dries up."

Rula remained indifferent. "I'm going to ask you once, nicely, to remove your hand from my arm, and if you don't, I'll call for campus security. Just who the hell do you think you are walking in here and making all sorts of unsubstantiated accusations against me anyhow?" His voice had become a snarl. "I don't have to stand here and listen to you tear down my character. If I'm accused of something, arrest me. If not, leave me alone!" He pulled angrily away.

Vince tightened his grip. "Now listen to me, and listen carefully." He measured his words. "I'm not here in any official capacity, not yet at least. I'm here as Katie's father, and as Katie's father I gotta tell you that you are in deep shit with me. Please understand this, I don't wanta have to come back here and hear that you didn't get it straight." He paused, allowing it to sink in. "If you do not immediately cease and desist from seeing my daughter in any capacity whatsoever, I will come to this place and I will make you regret the day you ever set eyes on her. If I receive word from any of my sources that you are anywhere near Katie Crowley at any time—if I hear that you are so much as inhaling the same oxygen that she is—substantiated or not, I will see to it that members of the police department come here and arrest you and put you in a cell where you will become lost inside the penal system of the City of New York and never found again, and where the term 'police brutality' will take on a whole new meaning for you. If you are a religious man, you will end up praying every day for a rope to hang yourself with and end the misery. Am I making myself clear?"

Senji Rula remained resolutely silent, but his Adam's apple was dancing perceptibly.

"Just so long as we understand each other." Vince released his grip and allowed Rula's arm to fall limply at his side. "Have a good day."

27

THE WAXING MOON HUNG LOW IN THE EASTERN SKY, casting muted shadows on the hard-packed earth of the old World's Fair grounds in Flushing Meadows. Leila Turner walked uncertainly among the chanting, sweating assemblage and felt the cold grip of fear clutching her intestines. She was frightened and she was mad: frightened by the horde of frenzied black men and women around her, and angry with herself for ever having agreed to take on this assignment in the first place. What the hell had she been trying to prove? she wondered.

She remembered another warm evening, eight or nine years ago, when she had stood with her high school class in the shadow of the great roller coaster at Coney Island and watched with dread as cars filled with screaming passengers dropped out of the sky and roared past her on the fragile, shuddering tracks. Riding the Cyclone was to be proof of their fearlessness, their determination to meet life head-on, unafraid. Leila remembered the awful sinking feeling in her gut as the car began its slow, shivering ascent. The unallayed panic welling up inside her throat burst forth in a terrified scream as it plummeted toward the spinning earth.

Then, as now, she understood in a moment of clarity that she was a victim of her own bravado. Then, as now, she hated herself for being a fraud. The police department of New York City was overflowing with swaggering macho types who would have been thrilled to land an undercover assignment like this one. There was no need for her to put herself through this kind of ordeal to prove she was tough or determined or worthy of carrying the gold shield. It was just plain dumb . . .

"Detective Turner?"

Stiffening at the sound of the male voice behind her, Leila slid her right hand down the length of the shoulder strap to her canvas purse and felt the reassuring bulk of the .38-caliber revolver inside. She turned cautiously to the disembodied voice. "I beg your pardon?"

"It's all right," the young black man assured her, smiling. "I'm Dred Cooper from Occult Crimes. "Pretend we're old friends striking up a conversation."

"I thought I was supposed to be out here alone on this operation," she said in a semiwhisper.

"Technically, you are," Cooper replied through the fixed smile. "At least you're the only one from NYPD here, as far as I know. They told me to keep an eye out for you and give you an idea how it all lays out."

"What *is* going on out here anyway?" Leila asked, her eyes growing wide.

Cooper began walking and motioned for Leila to follow. "Hard to say exactly what's going on out here tonight," he told her as they walked through the crowd. "Originally it was supposed to be a *fiesta de santo* for Obatala, the father of the gods, but the way those *bata* drums are getting pumped up, it's beginning to look like it can turn into anything."

"I'm afraid you just lost me," Leila admitted.

"That sound you're hearing." Cooper indicated the penetrating rhythm of drums beating just beneath the mingled sounds of chanting and incantations. "I'm not sure what they're getting ready to do, but they're getting themselves worked up for some kind of ceremony."

Leila walked with Cooper to the edge of a large circle of massed celebrants dressed entirely in flowing white robes. Most of them, even the women, were smoking thick black cigars.

"White is Obatala's color," he whispered to her, pointing to the groups of white goats, pigeons, and canaries gathered at the inner fringes of the circle. "The cigar smoke is an offering, rising up to heaven to appease Obatala until they get around to croaking the animals."

"They're going to kill those poor animals?" she asked hoarsely.

"Better them than us," Cooper replied, peering at the sea of white-daubed faces around him. "Sometimes these things can get a little out of hand, you never know what's gonna happen."

Leila heard the ominous sound of drums swelling, felt the gentle rhythms of the swaying bodies around her growing in intensity, their smells of sweat and passion mingling with the circling clouds of cigar smoke in the moist night air. She could see women moving into the center of the circle, their eyes rolled back into their heads in a trance, jerking their bodies convulsively to the heightening drumbeat, tearing away their white robes to reveal their naked hips and loins glistening with sweat. *"Gaulle Gaulle lo mio, Gaulle Gaulle lo mio, Gaulle para meta Gualle . . ."*

Less than a half-mile away, in the parking lot at Shea Stadium, Vince and Tommy sat in a darkened squad car and waited for the dashboard clock to tick away the minutes until they would meet Turner at the rendezvous.

"What the hell do you suppose they're doing in there?" Tommy asked, listening to the faraway tattoo of drums penetrating the night silence. "Sounds like they're getting ready to boil a couple of missionaries for dinner."

"Beats me," Vince replied. "All I know is it's some kind of ceremony and it's supposed to attract characters from all over the East Coast. My guess is that there's gotta be somebody in there that we're looking for."

Tommy took a sip of coffee from a cardboard container. "Any more danish left in that bag over there?"

Vince checked a small paper bag at his feet. "Uh-uh. You musta ate the last one."

Tommy shook his head. "Not me. I hate prune danish."

"So why'd you ask me if there were any more?"

"Gotta do something with your friggin' hands out here." Tommy stared morosely out the window. "If I'da known this was what policework was gonna be all about, I woulda become a computer programmer or something."

"I thought you were gonna become a lawyer," Vince said.

"That's from now on," Tommy pointed out. "But I already put in almost six years of my valuable time in this dead-end profession and I ain't never gonna get that back."

Vince leaned back in the worn vinyl seat and lit a cigarette. "I dunno. I think maybe I'm gonna miss all of this."

"You gotta be shitting me!" Tommy stared at him in disbelief. "You're gonna miss sitting out in some goddamn pitch-black parking lot, drinking cold coffee and eating prune fuckin' danish, listening to a buncha jungle bunnies howling and hooting, and waiting for them to come out and slit your throat?"

"I'll miss the feeling that something might happen," Vince said. "There's a lot of guys who go through their whole lives knowing that nothing is ever gonna happen. Look at Pell. He'd rather hang out all day in some grimy station house than make a lot of money doing a job where nothing ever happens to him. That's sad, know what I mean?"

"Pell's a jerk," Tommy grumped. "Besides, he wouldn't be so all-fired excited about policework if he had to spend half his time on stakeout. There ain't nothing glamorous about this, bro."

"It's not just this." Vince exhaled a cloud of smoke into the blackness. "I guess it's hard to explain. If you don't feel it, it's not working for you."

"Feel what?" Tommy challenged him.

Vince shrugged. "I dunno, what it feels like to be a cop, I guess. For me it was always something special. I remember my first day out of the academy, walking down the sidewalk back in the old Seventy-third Precinct in Brownsville and thinking, holy shit, these people are all looking up to me. I got a uniform and a nightstick and a gun and I can go anyplace in this city and get the same kind of respect I'm getting here. They may not like me, but they sure as hell gotta treat me right."

Tommy scowled. "Maybe it was that way when you came up, but those days are gone forever. Nobody respects cops anymore."

"Maybe not, but once you start thinking about yourself that way, it's hard to shake the feeling." Vince doused the cigarette in his coffeecup and stared out the window toward the World's Fair grounds.

Para me kao Guaye, Guaye lo mio para meke, para meke Guaye para meta . . ."

"Now I don't know what the hell they're doing." Cooper whispered in Leila's ear as a group of men replaced the women in the center of the circle. Almost-naked, they were adorned with a profusion of brightly colored necklaces and copper bracelets, and their faces and upper bodies were covered with hundreds of painted white dots. A bed of coals was arranged on the ground and lit with gasoline, propelling a wall of searing fire upward into the night sky, flames licking the air.

"Chango mani cote, Chango mani cote olle masa . . ."

"Looks like we're making offerings to the god Chango now," Cooper observed as a giant blackened caldron was placed on top of the fire's superheated coals and a variety of birds and livestock was brought into the center of the circle. "I wouldn't suggest you look at the rest of this if you've got a weak stomach."

Leila wanted desperately to close her eyes, but something prevented her. She stood, sickened but transfixed, as men inside the circle ritualistically butchered the birds and livestock, tearing the heads from live chickens and doves, slitting the throats of sheep and goats, gathering the blood in small metal cups and depositing the carcasses of the newly slaughtered animals inside the bubbling caldron.

"Mata sori achebari cote, Arabari cote sori ache Chango . . ."

Another figure appeared at the edge of the fire, dressed only in a loincloth, carrying a double-bladed ceremonial ax, his face shrouded in a black cloth. He was attended by the others, who danced around him to the steady sound of the *batas*, their bare feet striking the ground with a rhythmic, obsessive beat. One by one they brought him offerings—coins, tobacco, gunpowder—which were deposited on the flattened blade of the ax. Liberal doses of rum were poured over the mixture, as well as over the hands, forearms, and upper torso of the shrouded figure. Then a torch was lit from the coals at the base of the caldron.

"My God, they're going to set him on fire!" Leila gasped, reaching instinctively for the revolver in her purse.

"Hold it." Cooper restrained her with a steely grip. "You pull that thing out and we're both dead before you can squeeze off a round."

The burning torch was touched to the ax and the shrouded figure was instantly engulfed in fire, heaving, jerking spastically beneath the wall of flames like a puppet whose strings had become fouled. A wail emerged from inside the inferno. A low moan at first, it grew in intensity until it became a piercing, guttural howl—the cry of banshees in the night, the wordless, sucking gasps of unspeakable pain. Now the dance of death became more frenzied as each of the participants circled the hideous spectacle, swaying to the deafening drumbeat and chanting as the mingled smells of burning flesh and pine pitch from their torches filled the air.

Horrified, Leila watched as the burning figure slumped onto the hard-packed earth and twitched convulsively one final time before it collapsed into a shallow, smoldering mound. Again the dancers surrounded the body, covered it entirely with a black blanket and sprinkled it with the animals' blood they had gathered previously in metal cups. The crowd in the surrounding circle was becoming excited now, moving their bodies in time to the constant pounding of the drums, chanting obsessively as they began to dance in unison around the grisly pyre. Women and men alike seemed to become possessed in the flickering half-light, eyeballs, teeth, necklaces, and copper bracelets writhed and snaked inexorably forward, framed in silhouette against the bizarre illumination of the fiery victim.

"He Kola a deni mani cote, a mani cote mala boti Chango . . ."

Suddenly the smoking hulk upon the ground began to move, slowly at first in response to the even cadence of the chant, then resolutely as the excited rhythms of the dancers became more frenzied. Leila and Cooper stood dumbfounded as the ragged, smoldering entity stood in the center of the circle and lifted his double-edged ax skyward. He emitted an unearthly howl of victory that was echoed by the circling throng.

"He Kola a Chango boti mani a, bari cote oye mani Chango aro gue . . ."

Leila could feel Cooper's fingers tightening reflexively on her upper arm until the nails bit into her soft flesh. "Holy shit," he muttered as the figure removed the shroud from his head and beamed at the crowd with even, unblemished features. "That is one fucking unbelievable trick."

Leila felt the ground sway beneath her, and a clutch of fear grip her intestines as the Cyclone once again plummeted from the sky, hurtling her earthward.

28

POLICE DEPARTMENT
CITY OF NEW YORK

10/4/89

Incident Report Narrative Supplement

Det. L. Capella, 42 PDU, Bronx, N.Y. Incident #81-14715

RE: Investigation, 805 Bedford St., and subsequent arrest of occupants.

At 0930 hours on the above date, acting on information obtained during a routine "buy and bust" operation, the undersigned accompanied a team of special narcotics investigators (TNT) on a raid of the above-mentioned premises. Upon entering the premises we confiscated an amount of bundled marijuana in the amount of approx. 190 lbs., one Walther 9mm semiautomatic pistol (unregistered), thirteen dynamite caps, and two switchblade-type knives. Pursuant to investigation of premises we apprehended three black women and one black male listed as following:

Narcisse, LaGrande, B/M, 37, ht. 5'10", approx 180 lbs.
Narcisse, Rowanda, B/F, 25, ht. 5'3½", approx 135 lbs.

Joubert, Michalea, B/F, 22, ht. 5'5", approx 165 lbs.

Sinegal, Danielle, B/F, 31, ht. 5'7", approx 210 lbs.

Further investigation of the premises disclosed a number of live chickens and two live sheep, along with assorted bones, feathers, ointments, talismans, etc., assumed to be of a ritualistic nature. Subjects were arrested and charged under 230, possession of a controlled substance; 265, possession of an illegal firearm; and admin. code violation 100-3/C, maintaining livestock in a habitable premises.

As part of the ongoing investigation, members of the district attorney's occult crimes unit were contacted and allowed to interrogate the subjects.

The black face glowered through the bars of the holding pen, his eyes penetrating the squad room with fiery beacons of hate.

"We got three women downstairs," Detective Lou Capella of the neighboring South Bronx 42nd Precinct told Vince. "The D.A.'s guys are down there questioning them now, for all the good it's gonna do them."

Vince noted the occupant of the holding pen staring sullenly through the bars. "How about it, does he look like one of the scumbag's we're after?" he asked Leila Turner.

Leila narrowed her eyes and examined the prisoner carefully. "What's your name, mister?" she asked him.

"I don't answer no questions for no cops without my lawyer being here."

"His name's LaGrande Narcisse, a small-time booster and reefer dealer," Capella filled them in, referring to a thin manila arrest record in his hand. "He burst on the scene in a blaze of glory after he found his way up here from some Central American banana republic and he's been making his mark on The Bronx ever since." He handed the folder to Vince.

Vince read Narcisse's rap sheet. "Jeez, you're a regular public enemy number one, aren't you?" he concluded, scanning the list of arrests dating back to 1975. "You wanta tell me about that apartment on 209th Street that you and your scuzzy friends abandoned?"

Narcisse remained resolutely silent.

"You don't have an empty interrogation room by any chance, do you?" Vince asked Capella.

"You know I'm supposed to clear our charges before I give you a crack at them," Capella said. "I got approval to let the D.A.'s ghost busters question them but nobody else."

"Kroll knew how important this is to us. That's why he called me as soon as you notified him," Vince told him. "One of the kids left in that apartment died, and a couple more may never be right because of these bastards."

Capella shrugged. "Sure. Which one do you want to start with?

"How about this sweetheart?" Vince indicated the glowering black man pressed against the bars. "He doesn't look like he's doing anything important right now."

Capella opened the holding pen and cuffed the prisoner's wrists behind his back. "How about it, scumbag? You mind if we interrupt whatever it is you're doing for a little confabulation in the other room?"

Vince raised an eyebrow. "Confabulation?"

"It means a meeting, you dumb shit," Narcisse hissed, scowling as Capella shoved him toward the squadroom door.

"Oh, Jeez, I think you just made your second big mistake," Vince commented as he and Leila followed them toward a small interrogation room off the outside hallway. "I hope that attitude isn't what I can expect from here on in."

"I don't have to talk to you about anything," Narcisse snarled at Vince. "I know my rights."

Vince nodded. "I'm sure you do."

"The only thing I'm saying now is that we will walk away from this phony bust, pig. You have no right to hold this family for anything. We are peaceful, law-abiding people."

"Except for that almost two hundred pounds of reefer we confiscated from your place," Capella reminded him. "In case nobody bothered to tell you before, marijuana just happens to be a controlled substance in this city."

Narcisse scowled. "The *ganga* is our sacrament. Try to railroad us on that and we'll drag you all the way to the Supreme Court for violating our first-amendment rights." His lip curled in a menacing smile. "Freedom of religion, you know."

"Looks like we got ourselves a real constutitional scholar here," Vince observed.

"Did it ever occur to you that those children had rights too?" Leila asked.

Narcisse started indignantly into space.

She shook her head. "If it's okay with you, I think I'll go downstairs and see what Kroll's doing with the others," she told Vince. "I just want to see what kind of women would subject their children to an ordeal like that."

"The sisters are as committed to our family as I am," Narcisse muttered after she had gone. "No amount of police harassment will ever break the bond that exists between us."

Capella removed the handcuffs and shove Narcisse into the room's only chair. "Your PD's on the way, scumbag, but if you want to help yourself, you'll start cooperating right now. The way things are stacking up against you, it'll be a new millennium before you get your ass outa stir. Unless, of course, you see your way clear to tell us what we want."

"I'll tell you shit," Narcisse growled.

"What about Rafael Rosa?" Vince asked.

An almost imperceptible tightening of Narcisse's jaw muscles, but no response.

"It's not gonna do you any good to deny knowing Rosa," Vince told him, rechecking the arrest sheet. "We got it on the record that the two of you were busted together in 1987 and that you both did ninety days out in Riker's. Wanta tell us about that?"

"You're wasting your time, pig!"

"We got plenty of time," Capella responded.

"The fact is, the longer you hump us around here, the more time we got to develop our murder case against you," Vince added.

"Murder? You're outa your fuckin' mind, man—"

"We're talking willfully contributing to the death of a minor here. A child died as a result of abuse and neglect incurred while living with you," Vince reminded him. "At the very least that's manslaughter one—eight to twenty-five years. Plus, it looks like you're turning out to be our number-one suspect in the killing of our friend, Rosa, and that's murder one. Plus, it says here that you and your so-called family were found possessing dynamite caps, and that just might implicate you in a third murder we're investigating; Thomas Falcone. By me, that puts you in deep shit, *comprende*?"

James Kroll knocked lightly on the interrogation-room door and looked inside. "Can I see your for a minute, Detective Crowley?"

Vince joined him outside in the hallway. "What's up? You learn something from those women downstairs?"

"Yeah, but not from anything they told me," Kroll said. "These people are real tight. Ask them a question and they start screaming about their religious liberties. I didn't expect them to tell me anything and they didn't disappoint me, at least not until Detective Turner showed up."

"Leila?"

"It was really something. They were hard as nails until she walked into the room. She just stood there glaring at them. 'I wanted to see what women who would let their children starve looked like,' she told them, and they all just started bawling. You should've seen it. It was like she walked in there and turned on a valve."

"They make a confession?" Vince asked.

"Nothing that drastic, but it was pretty obvious by their reactions that they're the ones you're looking for. I don't think it'll take a lot to get them to open up, they're all pretty shaken," Kroll observed. "I'm not suggesting you give them the third degree or anything like that, but I think a little gentle prodding by Detective Turner might pay off big for you. They seem more inclined to respond to another woman."

"You think she can find out more about this *santería* shit they're involved in?" Vince asked.

"Keep an open mind about that," Kroll warned him. "From what we've been able to learn about them so far, there's no distinct pattern to their beliefs and ceremonies. We may be dealing with something else altogether here, a kind of home-grown synthesis of *santería*, voodoo, Satanism, and God knows what else."

Vince shook his head. "Leila's a good detective, but I'm not sure she's ready to deal with weirdos like this."

"She might have already started," Kroll suggested. "She asked them if they'd been to that big shindig out at Flushing Meadows the other night, and their eyes went wide. I mean, these women were scared to death, Crowley. I don't understand a whole lot of their lingo, but I picked up a word or two when they started whispering among themselves: 'Mayombero' and 'Ikkua,' and a couple of others that got me thinking—"

"About what?" Vince prodded him.

"These are superstitious people, Crowley. They believe in spells and hexes and charms that can do almost anything they want them to do, but most of all they believe in spirits. They believe the dead have magic powers, and if they get pissed off, they can work bad magic."

"Ghosts—" Vince interpreted.

"Not really, and that's the interesting part," Kroll

said. "They don't believe in all that poltergeist crap you see in the movies. To them the dead don't come back to haunt you, but you can make them do your dirty work for you if you know how to go about it. That's what a Mayombero does. He's sort of a witch doctor, a practitioner of Palo Mayombe, the black arts."

"You don't really believe that shit, do you?" Vince asked.

"It doesn't make any difference what I believe," Kroll told him. "The point is that they believe it. They believe they can manipulate the spirits of the dead to obtain wealth or love or power or anything else they want out of life, including getting rid of their enemies."

"So that might just fit right in with a couple of our homicides," Vince suggested.

"Might, but it's not likely you're going to get much out of these characters. They're small-time practitioners. They probably don't get involved with anything much more sinister than arthritis cures and love potions. They could lead you to what you're looking for, though. The way they were acting, something or somebody has them real spooked, and I wouldn't be surprised if it has something to do with that Ikkua they were whispering about."

"What's an Ikkua?"

"I'm not a hundred percent sure, but I think it's the blackest of all the black witches. The word '*ikku*' means death, and unless I miss my guess, Ikkua is the living dead."

"You mean like a zombie?"

"Sort of, but not quite," Kroll said. "A zombie is a Haitian voodoo entity, someone who has been killed and raised from the dead by a malevolent voodoo priest known as a *bocor*. Somehow in this whacko synthesis the Ikkua never really dies. He can live forever, can never really be killed, and his power is practically unlimited. The Ikkua gains strength and power from eating the bodies of his dead enemies, or anyone who has something he wants for himself. It's not entirely clear yet, but we think that's part of the reason we're finding so many bodies with pieces missing."

Vince shivered involuntarily. "You're saying we got one of these living-dead creeps walking around The Bronx?"

"Can you think of a better explanation for what's been happening in the past few months?" Kroll asked. "Bodies turn up with entrails and extremities missing, surrounded by all kinds of ritualistic paraphernalia. Adds up to me."

Vince eyed him skeptically. "You buy the idea that dead men are walking around The Bronx killing people and eating their body parts?"

"Correction. I buy the idea that these people *think* someone like that is walking around. I buy the idea that someone has planted the seed and is nurturing it with these bizarre acts. Don't forget, these are superstitious people and it wouldn't take a lot to convince them. Any good con man with enough knowledge of the rituals could make a pretty convincing show of it."

"For what purpose?" Leila Turner had returned and was standing in the open doorway.

Kroll shrugged. "Who knows? Power, money? There's always a reason. Anyone who can convince people that he has power over his own life and death shouldn't have any trouble convincing them that he has power over theirs. Why do you think they're all scared out of their wits?"

29

"REELECT JULIAN SANTIAGO—A MAN OF THE
PEOPLE—A CONGRESSMAN WHO CARES." Vince and
Tommy read the enormous red-white-and-blue sign in
the storefront window of Julian Santiago's Bronx headquarters before entering the two-story brick building.
Just inside the front door, they encountered an attrac-
tive black receptionist.

"Can I help you?" she asked sweetly.

Vince flashed his shield. "Detectives Crowley and
Ippollito, Thirty-seventh Precinct. We'd appreciate a
few minutes of the congressman's time."

The receptionist scanned an appointment book on
her desk. "Was Congressman Santiago expecting you?"

"We just have one or two questions we'd like to ask
him. It won't take much time at all—"

"I'm afraid it will be a while. The congressman is
running a bit late today. There are so many demands
on his time, you know." She indicated the adjoining
room, which was crammed with a sea of earnest campaign workers manning telephones, stenographers busily
pounding on typewriters, and a file of seated blacks
and Hispanics waiting patiently for an audience with
Santiago. "Everyone wants something from him and
he won't leave tonight until he's seen them all. That's
the kind of man he is."

Vince pretended to be impressed. "If you wouldn't
mind letting the congressman know that we're out
here. We really won't be taking up much of his time."

"Certainly." The smile remained fixed. "If you'll just take a seat inside, the congressman will see you in a short while— "

"Now," Vince urged. "This is police business."

The receptionist irritably punched a button on her desk intercom and waited for a response. "There are two officers from the Thirty-seventh Precinct here," she told Santiago when he came on the line. "They don't have an appointment."

A pause. "Can they come back some other time?" the voice crackled through the desk speaker.

Vince shook his head emphatically.

"I'm afraid they want to see you now," she reported.

A resigned groan. "I'll be out in a minute."

"Worked for the congressman long?" Vince asked her while they waited.

"Only a few months," she replied tersely, returning to a paperback novel she had been reading.

"Like your job?"

"I like working for Congressman Santiago, if that's what you mean," she said. "I think he's a truly caring man."

"Um . . ." Vince eyed the file of ragged people against the wall, waiting to see Julian Santiago. "What sort of things do these people want from the congressman —political appointments, stuff like that?"

"Nothing so glamorous, I'm afraid. Mostly they want their welfare checks delivered on time or the potholes in front of their apartments filled in."

Santiago appeared in the doorway and extended his hand. "I'm Julian Santiago, detectives?"

"I'm Crowley, he's Ippollito, Thirty-seventh Precinct." Vince returned the handshake. "If you wouldn't mind giving us a couple of minutes, we have some questions we'd like to ask you."

There was no outward response. Santiago smiled enigmatically and led them through the adjacent room to his office in the rear. "Now what's this all about?" he asked when he'd shut the door behind them.

Vince removed his notebook from his inside jacket pocket and thumbed through the pages. "Can you tell me how well you knew Thomas Falcone, Congressman Santiago?"

A slight facial twitch. "I can't really say that I knew Mr. Falcone at all. I knew who he was, and of course I heard about his tragic death, but I can't recall ever having met the man in person."

Vince shook his head, puzzled. "If you don't mind my saying so, Congressman, that's really strange. I have page after page of depositions from people who are willing to swear that you and Falcone saw each other on a regular basis. Even his former employers tell us that Thomas Falcone visited your offices two or three times a month."

Santiago nodded impassively. "I think that's probably correct, but I'd have to check my records."

"So how can you say you didn't know the man?" Vince asked.

Santiago went behind his plain metal desk and sat heavily. "Before we go any further, gentlemen, would you mind telling me what this is all about?"

"We're investigating Thomas Falcone's murder," Vince replied. "And we believe you may have information that can aid us in that investigation."

Santiago shook his head. "I can't really imagine what that might be. Like I told you, I didn't know the man personally. Whatever business he had with my office was conducted through my assistant."

"That would be Daniel Keliher," Vince said, checking his notes.

"Correct."

"And at no time were you ever in the presence of the deceased Thomas Falcone?" Vince persisted.

A moist film had begun to form on Santiago's upper lip. "I'm afraid I can't answer any more of your questions until I've had a chance to review my records and speak with my counsel. I'm not under any suspicion here, am I?"

"Would it be possible for us to speak with Mr. Keliher when we're finished here?" Vince asked, ignoring the question.

"Mr. Keliher is out of town, and I'm afraid our business here is over." Santiago stood and headed for the office door. "If you're not willing to be straight with me, I don't see how we can have anything to say to one another. I've built my reputation on straight talk and honest dealings, and I'm not up to playing word games with you. If you have something specific on your mind, let me have it. If you're on some sort of a fishing expedition, you're wasting your time and mine."

Vince shot a sideward glance at Tommy. "Speaking of fishing expeditions, I don't suppose you've ever heard of the *Hanky-Panky*?"

Santiago stopped dead in his tracks. "If you don't mind, gentlemen, I have a roomful of constituents out there who need to see me—"

"Maybe this will jog your memory, Congressman Santiago." Vince handed him a copy of the photograph Tom Quinlan had provided. "Would you mind telling me if you can identify the two persons in that picture?"

The color drained from Santiago's face as he viewed the photo. "Just what is this supposed to mean?"

"You tell me. From where I'm standing it looks like Thomas Falcone and your number one henchman, Daniel Keliher, having a good time aboard the good ship *Hanky-Panky*. Could I possibly be wrong about that?"

Santiago returned the photograph. "I don't know anything about this."

"Do the names Cherry Dressard and Trixie Lee mean anything to you?" Vince asked casually.

"Same answer," Santiago responded.

"Because we have pretty good evidence that the two of them accompanied Keliher and Thomas Falcone on a romantic cruise to nowhere back in August. The captain of the love boat there is willing to swear that the four of them spent the whole time out at sea boozing and grappling with each other, irrespective of gender or time of day. Does any of that square with your recollection?"

"It most certainly does not," Santiago protested. "Just what the hell is this all about, anyway?"

"What it's about, Congressman Santiago, is murder," Vince said evenly. "Four people go out on a cruise, two of them end up dead under weird and suspicious circumstances, and a third remains missing. All the evidence I got points to the fact that Keliher was the fourth party on that cruise and by the looks of it, the only one who made it out in one piece."

Santiago flared at them both. "Are you prepared to make specific charges at this time?"

"Not if you can convince me I'm on the wrong track here," Vince replied.

"I doubt that anything I could tell you right now would make much difference," Santiago observed. "It appears you had your minds made up when you walked in here."

"No sir, that's just not true," Vince corrected him. "We're willing to keep an open mind about all this, as long as you're willing to be straight with us—"

"Don't bullshit me. You come in here with some clumsily retouched piece of garbage and a cock-and-bull story that's obviously designed to make me panic, and you expect me to believe that you're not after anything?" He returned to his desk, sat, and folded his arms in front of him. "Let's have it. What's the real reason you're here, detectives? Is this some sleazy political stunt designed by my opponents to scare me? What did you think this would accomplish? Did you think I'd fold up my banner and drop out of the race because I'm afraid of being smeared by a lot of ruthless swine like Quinlan and his bunch? Well, you can take this back to whoever sent you here: I'm not afraid for my reputation and I'm not afraid for my life. Now get the hell out of here before I call some real cops and have you thrown out."

Vince took a deep breath. "That was some speech, Congressman Santiago. No wonder you got so far so fast."

"I've gotten to where I am today because I've put the people's interests first," Santiago replied coldly. "Those little people out there in my waiting room know they'll get a fair shake from me every time. They trust me to represent their interests because they know I'm not tied to the greedy self-interests that my opponents represent. They know I have the courage of my convictions—"

"Hold it," Vince interrupted him. "You're not running for office in here. You're being asked to cooperate in a police investigation, just like any other citizen. Now, if you don't want to do that, I can go downtown and get a court order requiring you to comply. I wonder how all those 'little people' out there in your waiting room would feel about seeing their congressman dragged into a police precinct on the six-o'clock news?"

Santiago nodded thoughtfully. "The photograph is a fraud," he said finally. "I don't know where you got it and I don't know what you think it will prove. As far as the story about Dan Keliher and those women, it's a total fabrication, an absurd political smear that could easily be disproved if necessary." He looked up at Vince. "The sad part is that it may become necessary, right, Detective Crowley? By smearing my campaign chairman, my opponents have tarnished me with the same brush."

Vince shrugged. "The truth can't hurt you if you're innocent."

Santiago smiled bitterly. "I can see you don't know very much about politics, Detective. If innocent, righteous men got elected all the time, governments would be filled with innocent, righteous men. As it is, they are filled with greedy liars, thieves and scoundrels who have gotten themselves elected by smearing their opponents. It's a strategy as old as politics itself: accuse your opponent of outrageous acts and watch him squirm trying to disprove them. In the end, the voter doesn't remember whether the charges were true or false anyway. In politics, being accused is as good as being convicted."

Vince shook his head. "Congressman Santiago, you got a real way with words. If I had a hat I'd take it off to you."

Santiago suppressed a smile. "You men are from the Thirty-seventh Precinct, isn't that right?"

"Correct."

"And if I'm not mistaken, isn't that one of the precincts that's slated to be phased out?"

"Right again," Vince said.

"I can keep it open," Santiago said. "I'm not telling you I'll do my best here; forget about what I said in front of the television cameras. I'm telling you I can see to it that your precinct is not shut down. I can make that happen. Do you understand what I'm saying?"

Vince looked at Tommy. "You hearing what I'm hearing, partner? If I didn't know I was talking to one of the good guys here, I'd swear I just heard somebody trying to trade political favors." He shook his head. "But I musta heard it wrong. I guess I'm just so used to listening to those politically motivated scumbags the congressman here was just talking about that I can't even recognize a real champion of the little people when I see one."

30

Acting on information furnished by the United States Coast Guard, Substation 61, Sanibel, Fla., a Missing Persons report was issued for Butler, Roger, W/M, 46. Ht. 5'6½", WT. 177 lb. Eyes, brown, Hair, gray and brown (Balding). Most recent photo attached.

SUMMARY OF DISAPPEARANCE:
On 10/7/89, at approx 0730 hrs., a light fishing vessel was reported missing to the coast-guard station at Sanibel. Preliminary information listed on the boat *Hanky-Panky*, a twin screw inboard charter vessel (Fla. Lic. #212-87) as having left Fort Myers Marina at approx 2100 hrs. on 10/6/89 with only the aforementioned Butler aboard. After failing to arrive at its charter destination of Marcos Island on the following morning, a search by coast-guard vessels and helicopters was instigated but was not able to locate the vessel or any trace of debris. As of this date, vessel is presumed sunk and rescue efforts continue.

"I don't fucking believe this!" Tommy read the report that had been facsimiled from the Lee County sheriff's office and slid it across the desk to Vince. "Is this weird or what, man?"

Vince scanned the sheet and the attached photograph, taken from Butler's Florida pilot's license. "There goes the last person who could put Keliher on that boat with Falcone," he groaned. "Sure seems like one helluva coincidence, don't it?"

"If I didn't know better, I'd be thinking somebody, someplace, was sticking pins in dolls," Tommy agreed.

The telephone rang and Vince grabbed for it.

"Crowley here."

"Hold on for District Attorney Quinlan, please." The phone went dead.

"Crowley, I hear you guys paid a call to my esteemed opponent yesterday," Quinlan said when he came on the line. "How'd that work out?"

"Worked out just fine, Tom," Vince replied.

"You know what I mean, for chrissake."

"The man was pleasant, noncommittal, you know—your basic politician."

"What're you busting my balls for?" Quinlan moaned.

"Who's busting whose balls here, Tom?"

An exasperated pause. "Would you mind telling me a little bit about what went on when you went out to Santiago's headquarters?" Quinlan asked evenly.

"The congressman told me and Tommy that he'd use his influence to keep the Three-Seven in business," Vince replied.

"He's blowing smoke, Vince. You know that."

"At least he's blowing the right kind of smoke. I don't remember hearing anything about this precinct from your camp, Counselor. Makes me kinda wonder who's got this city's best interests at heart, know what I'm saying?"

A low groan. "All Santiago can do is get people all riled up, and that's not going to accomplish anything, Vince. The mayor hates his guts, the city council hates his guts; the incompetent bastard's got no political clout at all when it comes to what gets done or doesn't get done in the City of New York, you know that."

"Maybe he doesn't need political clout. Maybe he can just stir up the little people and use them to make the politicos all change their minds," Vince suggested.

"Very fucking funny. Are we gonna get serious here, or what?"

"I'm real serious, Tom. This precinct means a lot to me," Vince reminded him.

"You're not suggesting that you'd allow Santiago's empty promises to influence your investigation into his activities, are you?"

Vince winked at Tommy. "I don't know how you can even suggest such a thing, Counselor. I've got half the precinct checking Santiago out, but you know investigations take time. We're working as fast as the situation allows."

"Meaning?"

"Meaning that we're not getting any help from you or your office, so we gotta go with what we have, and right now that's not a helluva lot."

"You're not by any chance threatening to drag your feet on this thing until after election day?" Quinlan asked.

"What's the matter, Tom, the polls not going your way?"

Stony silence. "The board of estimate is committed to a precinct cutback," Quinlan said finally. "Santiago can't change that, neither can I. The best I can give you is that I'll see what I can do about getting the Three-Seven taken off the list. I can't promise you more than that."

"I can't ask more than that," Vince said.

"And Santiago?"

"We're working on it. At the very least it looks like we're gonna have to haul his ass in here for interrogation."

"Before November?"

"We're both doing our best here, Tom. Right?"

"Right." Quinlan hung up.

Tommy wheeled his chair around on the chipped linoleum floor and faced Vince. "That was slick as bat snot, partner. Does this mean we got a reprieve?"

Vince shrugged. "Don't go putting up any wallpaper yet. You can't trust any of these bastards, you know that."

"Sure, but we got this election playing right into our hands." Tommy grinned. "All Quinlan wants us to do is impeach Santiago's character on prime-time television, and we sure as hell oughta be able to accommodate him on that point. I mean, it's not like we weren't going to drag the congressman's right-hand man in here anyway, right?"

"Don't be so eager," Vince warned him. "Timing is what separates the smart operators from the shmucks. If we bring Keliher in for questioning tomorrow, what's to stop Quinlan from backing off and pretending he never heard of the Three-Seven?"

Tommy grinned conspiratorially. "So we wait for him to make his move before we make ours, right?"

"Well, let's hope that's what Tom Quinlan thinks," Vince said. "We clear our caseload same as always and keep our fingers crossed. If we're lucky, you and me will be sitting at these same desks this time next year."

"I wouldn't count on it, assholes," Bob Donofrio mumbled on his way to the CO's office. His mouth was wired shut, his lower jaw swathed in gauze and adhesive tape. "If I was you, I'd start clearing out my desk right now because this septic tank is gonna be history in a little while."

"Fuck you and the horse you rode in on," Tommy snarled as Donofrio disappeared into the hallway. "The only thing I could think of that'd keep me in this chicken-shit police department would be if I could make inspector without going through all the other bullshit. Then I could transfer that motherfucker to the Holland Tunnel and let him suck bus fumes until he pulls his pension."

"Maybe he'd hang himself before then," Vince joked. "You gotta wonder what it is that makes a guy like that so miserable all the time."

"He could be stuck in a rut." Oxbridge Pell entered the squad room and walked to Vince's desk. "Nobody would know what that's like better than me. I spent most of my adult life doing what it was I thought I was supposed to be doing until I woke up one morning and realized I'd come within an eyelash of boring myself to death."

Vince looked up at him. "You know, Pell, I gotta give you credit, but I also gotta wonder what the hell it is about this place that you find so goddamn exciting. I mean, all we do is sit around the house eating cold takeout and belching and farting and having really stupid conversations. If this is excitement, I sure as hell would hate to see monotony."

"You take chances," Pell said. "I never took a chance in my life up until today."

"Oh, yeah. What'd you do today?" Tommy asked him.

"This—" Pell deposited a heavy manila shopping bag stuffed with papers on Vince's desk.

"What's all this?" Vince asked.

"Copies of ledgers from the Contech Corporation," Pell announced proudly. "I went in there and copied them this afternoon."

"You did *what*?"

"I went to Contech and copied their records. You wanted to see them, right?"

Vince started at him in amazement. "I don't believe this. What the hell did you think you were doing?"

Pell shuffled uncomfortably. "Please don't be angry with me. I know what I did was highly illegal, and I know if I had asked you for permission to do it beforehand you would have flatly refused—"

"Refused? I would've sent you out to Bellevue for a head examination," Vince exploded. "For all we know, those people out there could be murderers, for chrissake. You got any idea what a stupid chance you took?"

"I knew you needed to see their records, and I knew you were getting the runaround from the bureaucracy," Pell explained. "I know all about bureaucracies, Vince. I spent most of my life being a part of one. I wanted to break through and do something brave and reckless for once in my life . . ." He shrugged helplessly.

Vince shot a glance at Tommy, who was grinning broadly behind Pell's back. "Just how the hell did you get in there?" he asked.

"Easy, I'm an accountant, remember? I just walked in there, flashed my credentials, and told them I was from the New York State Department of Audit and that I needed to see their ledgers for the past two years."

"And they just handed them to you?"

"I guess they're so used to being investigated by now that it didn't seem like a big deal to them," Pell said. "I didn't really know what I was looking for, so I just asked for copies of everything."

Vince shook his head. "I gotta tell you right off the bat here that I don't approve of this kind of action in any way. You took a foolish, irresponsible chance that may have placed your own life in jeopardy and may have compromised an ongoing police investigation. Did it ever occur to you that we could've sent somebody from this department in there undercover if we'd felt these records were important enough?"

Pell hung his head. "I guess not . . ."

Vince sifted through the mounds of duplicated ledgers. "Well, I guess it didn't occur to us either. I don't know whether to kiss you or slap you in a cell, asshole."

Pell's face erupted in a webwork of tiny, dancing creases. "That's the first time since I've been here that anybody's called me 'asshole.' Now I really feel like I belong."

31

POLICE DEPARTMENT
CITY OF NEW YORK
Incident Report Narrative Supplement   10/12/89

V. Crowley, 37 PDU, Bronx, N.Y. Incident #24-09303

RE: Investigation 2725 Redfield St., Bklyn, N.Y., and subsequent arrest of occupant.

At 0445 hours, above date, relevant to an incident being investigated by this command, I accompanied Dets. Clancy and Bryce, 67 PDU, on an investigation of a premises suspected of harboring evidence of illegal-drug activities.

Upon arriving at the above-mentioned location, we were met at the front door of apartment 3-C by occupant, Senji Rula, an instructor at Pratt Institute; 36 yrs, Indian male, 5'9", 165 lb., eyes brown, hair black, who freely granted us entry. Observing a firearm (Smith & Wesson .22 revolver) in plain view on a table in the apartment, Det. Clancy inquired as to whether it was a licensed pistol, at which time the subject became noticeably agitated and lunged at the undersigned with a kitchen knife.

A struggle ensued, during which time three clear plastic envelopes of suspected narcotics fell from the subject's pocket and were retrieved by Dets. Clancy and Bryce.

Subject was disarmed, brought under control, and read his rights. After being taken to King's County Hospital, where he received medical attention for wounds received during his arrest, subject was transferred to 67 PDU, where he was further interrogated and charged under 225-10, Possession of a Controlled Substance; 265, Possession of an Illegal Firearm; and 130-5, Resisting Arrest. Additional charges of assault against a female student are pending, subject to further investigation.

The call came at 2:26 on Sunday morning. Connie fumbled for the phone on her nightstand and lifted the receiver. "It's for you," she mumbled groggily, and handed the phone to Vince.

"Vince, it's Kayo. First of all, Katie's going to be all right—"

"What's the matter with Katie?" he demanded.

"She's going to be fine," O'Grady reassured him. "She's just a little beat up right now, but the doctors say it's going to turn out okay."

"Where is she?"

"We're out here at King's County Hospital," O'Grady said. "I brought her in about a half-hour ago."

"What the hell happened?" Vince tried to disguise the panic in his voice.

"We're not sure. She was found staggering around the campus, all bruised and bleeding. Nobody's been able to find out exactly how she got there, but at least she's out of danger. A concussion, a few broken bones, some cuts and lesions—nothing life-threatening, Vince."

Vince took a deep breath. "Thanks, Kayo. Do me a favor and stay with her until I get out there, okay?"

"You bet, pal."

"What is it?" Connie asked Vince as he began hurriedly dressing.

"Katie's been in some sort of accident."

Connie slid from the bed. "I'm coming with you."

They took the elevator to the parking garage, squealed through the basement abyss to the empty street above, and made it to the hospital in less than thirty minutes.

"How's it going?" Vince asked O'Grady at the entrance to the primary-care unit. "Can I see her?"

"The doctors are in with her now," O'Grady told him. "Maybe you better wait out here until they're finished."

"Bullshit!" Vince brushed by him and went to the front desk. "Which room is Katie Crowley in?"

"Are you a relative?" the nurse asked.

"I'm her father."

The nurse handed him a printed form. "Would you mind filling this out?"

Vince stared at the form. "I want to see my daughter, now."

"I'm sorry, but you'll have to wait until the doctors have finished examining her."

"Wanna bet?" Vince strode past the desk to the hallway beyond and began searching the examining rooms until he found the right one.

"I'm sorry," the nurse apologized over Vince's shoulder to the doctor inside. "I told him to wait, but he just pushed his way in here."

"Jeez!" Vince stood over the bed where Katie lay. Her face was bloated and purple, eyes swollen shut, her right arm, shoulder, and upper torso were bound with layers of adhesive dressings. "You okay, baby?"

"Are you her father?" the doctor inquired.

"Yeah. How's she doing?"

"We have sedated her for the time being, so I'm afraid you won't be able to talk to her for a while."

The doctor steered Vince out of the examining room by his shoulder. "Her injuries are serious, but she's not in any immediate danger as long as she remains under observation. For now, it'd be best for everyone if she was allowed to rest."

"Why not let me take you for a cup of coffee?" O'Grady suggested.

"I'm not going anyplace until I find out what happened to Katie," Vince protested. "Now, do I get some straight answers here or do I gotta start busting heads?"

"Calm down, Mr. Crowley," the doctor said. "Your daughter's had a tough time, and screaming isn't going to help her get any better."

Connie grabbed Vince's hand and squeezed it tightly. "If you could just give us some information, it might make everybody feel better," she suggested to the doctor.

The doctor shrugged. "As far as her injuries go, she's sustained a skull fracture, a dislocated shoulder, a badly sprained elbow, several broken ribs, a possible fracture in the third or fourth thoracic vertebra, and possible internal damage. I wish I could tell you more, but we're still studying the results of the X rays and EEG. If they prove inconclusive, we'll schedule her for a full CAT scan."

"She gonna make it?" Vince asked weakly.

"Sure." The doctor smiled reassuringly. "She's not out of the woods yet, but she's getting the best treatment available."

"How did this happen?" he asked O'Grady.

Kayo shook his head. "Like I told you on the phone, she was found outside on the campus, just wandering around. I rode over here in the ambulance with her, but mostly she was just babbling. It was hard to get a coherent statement out of her."

"Was she mugged, beaten up?" Vince persisted.

"From the extent of her injuries, I'd have to say she sustained an extensive beating," the doctor said.

"Kicks, punches—whoever did this wasn't just after her money."

Vince glared at O'Grady. "It was that son of a bitch Rula, wasn't it?"

A pause. "Let's not jump to any conclusions here," O'Grady cautioned. "I asked her if it had been him, and she shook her head no."

"Did you believe her?"

"I don't know what to believe."

"Don't fuck with me, Kayo. Did you believe her?" Vince demanded.

O'Grady looked him in the eye. "I don't want you going out there, Vince. You're liable to do something we'll all be sorry for. We'll call the Six-Seven and have them pick Rula up for questioning. If he did this thing, he'll get what's coming to him."

"Are you out of your goddamn mind?" Vince struggled to get past him in the narrow hallway. "I'm gonna kill that greasy bastard!"

Connie blocked his way. "He's right, Vince. Stop and think about what you're doing."

Vince backed off, his body shaking. "Okay, Kayo, call the Six-Seven, but I want to be out there when they run him in, okay? I wanta see the look on his face when he sees me standing at his front door. I wanta see him squirm when he remembers what I promised to do to him if I ever laid eyes on him again."

It was a look of shock and surprise.

"Inside, motherfucker!" Detective Bill Clancy from the Sixty-seventh Precinct pushed the pajama-clad Rula inside his apartment and entered, followed by his partner, Jack Bryce, Vince, and Kevin O'Grady.

"What the hell is this all about?" Rula demanded.

"Wanta tell me where you got those cuts and bruises?" Clancy grasped one of Rula's hands, swollen and scraped raw with fresh lesions.

Rula pulled away angrily. "What's going on here?"

"Take a look around and let's see what this scumbag's all about," Clancy instructed Bryce, ignoring Rula's question. "This pigpen smells suspiciously like dope to me."

"You can't just barge in here and search my apartment," Rula sputtered.

Clancy grabbed Rula by the shirt front and pulled him forward until their noses were less than an inch apart. "I can do any fucking thing I please, mister, you understand that? I can shoot you right here, drop a gun next to your body, and report you came at me with intent to cause bodily harm."

"Looks like that won't be necessary." Bryce held a small-caliber revolver aloft. "Looka what I just found in his dresser drawer. You got a permit for this thing, scumbag?"

Rula stiffened. "I want my lawyer present, now!"

"And just look here . . ." Bryce removed several glassine packets filled with white powder from the same drawer. "It *do* look like we got ourselves a substance-abuser here, gentlemen."

"You're gonna need a whole battery of lawyers before we're finished with you," Clancy observed.

"How about that?" Bryce pointed to a woman's sweater draped over a chair, its collar stained with blood. "Looks like this is also a substance-abuser who gets it off beating up on women."

"You got nothing," Rula sneered at them. "I know the laws about illegal search and seizure. Nothing you find in this apartment will be admissible in a court of law."

Clancy stared at Vince and O'Grady. "Holy shit, I think he's right! I forgot all about those laws. I just realized what we're doing here is probably illegal."

"Maybe we oughta get out of here before we get ourselves in trouble," O'Grady suggested.

"Good idea." Clancy motioned for Bryce to discontinue his search. "Good thing you reminded us about that, shit," he told Rula as he headed for the door.

"You know, sometimes we just get a little overanxious when we're dealing with guys who beat up little girls."

"You go on ahead," Vince said to them. "I just want to clear up a couple of things with Mr. Rula while I'm here."

"Sure, we'll be waiting out in the hall." Clancy closed the door behind him, leaving Vince and Rula alone in the apartment.

"I'm calling the police if you don't leave right now," Rula said nervously, backing away from Vince, his forehead and upper lip bathed in sweat.

"I am the police, scumbag," Vince reminded him. "And I promised I'd come after you if you ever laid a hand on my daughter, remember?"

"I don't know what you're talking about."

"I'm talking about Katie Crowley, who you just put in a hospital, you greasy prick!"

"That's a lie!" Rula backed into the kitchenette with Vince in walking pursuit. "I haven't seen Katie in days." He reached behind him and retrieved a paring knife from the countertop. "Don't you come any closer to me . . ."

Vince drew up. "Oh, shit! Now look what you went and did. You went and menaced me with a lethal weapon." His left forearm shot forward in a blur, knocking the knife from Rula's grasp. Rula reeled backward, then recovered in time to feel the full force of Vince's right fist hurtling into belly, penetrating the soft flesh almost to his backbone. He doubled over with a groan and saw the room erupt in piercing shafts of white light as the point of Vince's knee exploded full-force into his face, shattering his nose and the bones of both cheeks with a sickening crunch.

"Okay now, pal . . ." O'Grady was standing behind him, his gentle bear hug pinning Vince's arms to his side. "I think you've disarmed this suspect now. What's say you and me go get ourselves a couple of shots and beers and let these policemen do their jobs?"

The room was spinning, a kaleidoscope of color,

planes, and shadows. Vince could feel himself strain-
ing, his muscles tensed and trembling inside O'Grady's
cradling arms as Clancy and Bryce cuffed the huddled
figure on the floor and read him his rights. "I warned
him," he said weakly.

O'Grady looked down at Rula's bleeding, shattered
face. "There's always some dumb shit that never gets
the message."

32

CROSS-CHECK

THOMAS FALCONE . . . CHERRY DRESSARD . . .
TRIXIE LEE . . . AMOS WASHINGTON . . . RAFAEL ROSA
. . . ROGER BUTLER . . . GUY GIULIANI . . . DANIEL
KELIHER . . . JULIAN SANTIAGO.

Vince eyed the hand-printed list tacked to the bulletin board and returned gloomily to the piles of ledgers spread across several makeshift card tables in the squad room. "I just wasn't cut out for this shit," he muttered to Tommy. "I don't know how anybody can spend their lives doing stuff like this."

Tommy looked up from his own stack of Xeroxed records and nodded vigorously. "Amen, brother."

Vince examined another page and discarded it in the wastebasket. "How long've we been at this, anyway?"

Tommy checked his watch. "About two hours."

Vince groaned. "That all?"

"Hey, look at it this way," Tommy said. "Every time you throw a page away, you're one page closer to finding what you're looking for."

"What the hell makes you so goddamn cheery?" Vince growled.

"Hey, man, you gotta look on the bright side." Tommy put the papers aside. "Katie's gonna be okay, Vince. You know that, don't you?"

"I suppose . . ."

"It's always darkest before the storm, partner."

Vince went to his desk and dialed the hospital. "I'd like some word on a patient there, Katie Crowley," he told the female voice that answered.

He was put on hold. Strains of "Tiny Bubbles" filtered through the receiver. "How're you guys doing over there?" he asked Walt Cuzak and Street Crime, who were examining ledgers at another card table.

Cuzak frowned. "I shoulda retired last year."

"Patient information . . ." A voice came on the line.

"Yeah, what's the condition of Katie Crowley?" Vince asked.

"You can dial her room direct. Please make a note of the number: 762-0192."

Vince wrote it on his desk blotter. "I guess that means she's doing okay," he said to the voice.

"You can get that information by dialing direct," the voice said mechanically, and hung up.

"I got a Rose Maintenance Corporation here," Tommy announced from his table. "That's pretty close to Rosa."

"Write it down, you never know," Vince told him.

"Why the fuck do these bastards write so goddamn small, for chrissake?" Cuzak moaned, adjusting his half-glasses on the bridge of his nose and squinting at the page in front of him. "A guy could go blind trying to read this shit."

"It's an efficiency factor," Oxbridge Pell said as he entered the squad room. "Space management is almost as important as profits to big business."

"You here to help us?" Vince grinned at him. "After all, it's your fault we're doing this in the first place."

"No, I've seen enough of ledgers for one lifetime. I'm just here to pick up a few things and say good-bye."

"You leaving us?" Tommy asked.

"Time for me to move on." Pell went to the front desk and began removing items from the drawer. "I guess I've proved whatever I set out to prove to myself. I can't just spend the rest of my life hanging out here making a nuisance of myself. I have a family to think about."

"You were never a nuisance," Vince assured him. "I wish all civilians were as decent as you."

Pell smiled. "That's nice of you to say. I'll remember that, Vince. I'll remember all you guys."

"What do you do now, go back to your old job?" Street Crime asked him.

"No, never that," Pell said. "I don't know what I'm going to do. I've got some money saved up—that's what people like me do, you know; we save money. Anyway, I don't have to make any decisions right away. I think I'll take a vacation with my wife and think about what I could do with the rest of my life that would really mean something. I want a line of work where I can actually see the end product of my labors instead of just being a pit stop for information filtering up through layers of management. Who knows, maybe I'll start writing. I always wanted to write, but I could never find the time . . . or anything interesting in my life to write about."

"You gonna write about us?" Cuzak asked.

"Maybe. Why the hell not?" You're a pretty interesting bunch."

"Jeez, we're about as interesting as bleeding piles," Tommy observed. "Nobody'd ever be interested in reading about this place. Nothing exciting ever goes on around here."

"I guess it all depends on your perspective," Pell said. "Whether I write about you guys or not, I want you to know that you've all been important to me. You've made this part of my life important, and I want to make the rest of it just as important, whatever I end up doing."

"Don't you think this is important?" Cuzak lifted one of the ledger sheets.

Pell shrugged. "None of it's important, unless all

you're interested in is making money," he said. "I know I harp on this, but you won't have to listen to it much longer . . ." He took the sheet from Walt. "You guys see these entries. Do you think anybody understands most of this stuff? If you do, then you're wrong. The people who have to work with these facts and figures are just another level of personnel that's keeping an eye on the level below them. Right on up the ladder; everybody checking on everybody else, covering their asses so the next level can't ambush them and shoot them down; all the time trying to convince themselves that they're making a contribution to society."

"Sounds like the police department," Vince joked.

"You guys matter." Pell said emphatically. "Nothing in big business matters to anyone except the stockholders or the people who are trying to persuade somebody that their jobs are really needed in the first place. Let me give you an example: I spent an entire summer one year visting stores that were carrying one of my company's new products . . . running point-of-purchase checks to see how well our in-store marketing strategy was working. I wrote hundreds of reports and made hundreds of recommendations that were checked and rechecked by eight or nine layers of management above me before they got stuck away in some obscure file and were never seen again."

Pell looked at them thoughtfully. "Do you have any idea what godsend to humanity tied hundreds of people up for an entire summer? The product was a note pad that had been manufactured to look like a ham sandwich. Somebody had taken the time to invent a notepad that looked like a ham sandwich, and my company was spending millions of dollars to market it and thousands of man-hours trying to determine whether or not there was a market for it.

"Think about that, gentlemen," Pell went on. "I know I did, that whole summer. I found myself asking the inevitable question: is mankind really going to be better-off if they can write their messages on a ham sandwich? Am I missing the boat here? Maybe the company knows something that I can't see. Maybe there is some as-yet-untapped primitive emotion in mankind that needs an outlet. Maybe people have an innate urge to write on bread . . ." His voice trailed off.

"Where can I get one of those things?" Tommy asked.

"Sounds like something we could use around this place," Street Crime added.

Pell shook his head, smiling. "I'm really going to miss you guys, you know that?"

Vince reached across his desk and shook Pell's hand. "Stop around from time to time and let us know what you're up to, okay?

"Fuckin' A." Pell grinned broadly. "I hope everything turns out all right with your daughter, Vince."

"Oh, jeez." Vince lifted the telephone and dialed Katie's room.

"Yes?" It was Jessy.

"Hi, Jess. How's Katie?"

"Her condition's been upgraded from 'guarded' to 'stable,' whatever that means." Her voice was cool.

"Can I talk to her?"

"She's downstairs getting more X rays," Jessy said irritably. "I swear, these doctors haven't got the foggiest notion what they're doing. Every time they have to make a decision, they send her out for another test."

"How's she look to you?" Vince asked, ignoring Jessy's outburst.

"She'll survive."

"Have the guys from the Six-Seven asked her any more questions?"

"No, and if they try to, I'll throw them out," Jessy snapped. "I don't want my daughter subjected to any more pain than she's already had."

"Whoa, wait a minute," Vince broke in. "What the hell's eating you?"

"What's eating me is that none of this would have

happened if you'd done what I asked you to in the first place!"

"Oh, Christ." Vince put the receiver to his forehead and took a deep breath. "Now it's all my fault, huh?" he asked finally.

"You allowed Katie to live in this awful place and you can see what happened. Whose fault is it, then? Mine?"

"Maybe it's nobody's fault," Vince replied. "Maybe we just have no power to prevent things like this from happening. Why don't we see what we can do for Katie instead of screaming about who's at fault here?"

Silence. "I want her to come back to Marion when she's released from this hospital," Jessy said.

"Fair enough. Marion's a good place to recuperate."

"I mean, I want her to stay in Marion," Jessy went on. "I don't ever want her to come back to this hellhole again."

Vince rolled his eyes at Tommy. "I guess that's gonna be up to Katie, don't you think?"

"How can you be so goddamned cool about all of this? Your daughter was practically killed," Jessy screamed. "Just because you have to live with this kind of violence every day doesn't mean that Katie does."

"Look, Jess, I don't want to fight with you about this," Vince replied. "I hope she goes back to Marion with you and lives happily ever after. God knows it wasn't my idea for her to come down here. I don't think she had any idea what she was in for."

"Well, at least we agree on that," Jessy said.

"They say when they'll be letting her out of there?"

The doctor said not before the end of the week. I think somebody somewhere just invented a test they haven't given her yet."

"Tell her I called and that I love her. I'll get out to see her in a day or two."

"By the way, your friend was here this morning— that Talbot woman, the newsperson."

"Connie?"

"She seems very nice, very young."

Vince struggled momentarily with the idea of defending Connie's age. "Kiss Katie for me, okay? Gotta go." He hung up.

"Ex-wives, huh?" Walt Cuzak nodded knowingly.

"Why the hell did I feel guilty when she brought up Connie?" Vince wondered aloud.

"Wives got that ability," Cuzak said. "I been divorced from my ex almost thirteen years now, and I still feel like I'm cheating on her when I'm with another woman. Scary shit, man."

"Hey, Vince, take a look at this," Street Crime called him over to the card table. "Giuliani, spelled the same way, only this one's listed as a consultant."

Vince examined the ledger sheet over his shoulder. Among the baffling columns of figures and designations Street Crime had underlined the name G. Giuliani, Consulting, and a corresponding payment of $2,500 posted on August 9, 1989.

"Think it's that pimp of Trixie Lee's?" Street Crime asked him.

"Dunno. How many G. Guilianis can there be in this city? Let's run it down in the directory," he told Street Crime. "Check out all the legitimate consulting firms, chambers of commerce, Jaycees, you know the routine. And the banks, I want a copy of that canceled check to see who endorsed it." Vince looked around the room, where everyone was waiting expectantly. "We gotta keep on checking, folks, you know that. Chances are, this is probably just another dead end."

Vince tried to mask his excitement as they all returned sullenly to the ledgers. Giuliani was the last name he had expected to find in the records, and that was a good thing. It meant that events were starting to happen without his trying to make them happen, and that was an encouraging sign. Good investigations mean lots of legwork and drudgery, he knew, piecing together a bewildering web of seemingly unrelated facts until a pattern began to emerge and the investigation began to take on a life of its own. He could see that happening now, and he went with it.

It smelled right.

33

Guy Giuliani sat impatiently in the interrogation room of the Thirty-seventh Precinct waiting for
Vince to return. He reached into his shirt pocket,
extracted an empty pack of Marlboro filter cigarettes,
crumpled it, and tossed it angrily on the floor.

"Hey, this is my house," Vince said, entering the
room with an armful of files and papers. "You don't
see me throwing shit all over your place, do you?"

"That's the trouble with these rich, young scumbags," Tommy commented, following Vince into the
cramped room. "They never learned no manners growing up."

Giuliani retrieved the crumpled Marlboro pack and
stuffed it into his pocket resentfully. "Would you mind
telling me what the hell this is all about? I told you
guys everything I know the last time you dragged me
in here."

"Well, Mr. Giuliani, that doesn't quite square with
the facts we're getting." Vince deposited the papers
on the room's wooden desk and took a seat while
Tommy remained standing. "It seems that you're involved a lot deeper than you led us to believe."

"Involved in what?"

Vince shrugged. "At this point it's difficult to say."
He shuffled through the papers. "All we know right
now is that you were less than truthful with us the last
time we talked."

"You were lying through your teeth, scumbag,"
Tommy embellished.

"Take the matter of Trixie Lee," Vince went on. "You told us that you hadn't seen Miss Lee since she disappeared somewhere around the middle of August. Do you want to stick with that story?"

Giuliani squirmed in the straight-back wooden chair. "Why not? It's the truth."

Vince nodded thoughtfully. This was the point in an interrogation that he liked the most, the part where his subject began to realize he'd been caught in a barefaced lie and began desperately searching for a way to redeem himself. Most criminals lied as a matter of habit, whether or not the lie was in their best interests, he knew. The lies were as much a part of criminal behavior as the crimes themselves, a pattern that led ultimately to their undoing. Criminal investigations were practical affairs, depending largely on the logical sequence of events and the believability of testimony, like a free-flowing stream. When somebody along the way said or did something that didn't add up, it was like a logjam clogging the flow.

"Why not be straight with us, Mr. Giuliani?" Vince said, thumbing through the array of papers on the desk like a disciplining schoolteacher. "Take some time if you want. We're not in any hurry here."

Giuliani took a deep breath and checked his wristwatch. "Maybe you got nothing better to do than sit around here asking dumb questions, but I got business to attend to."

"You gotta get straight with us first, asshole," Tommy snarled.

"I told you what I knew about Trixie. What the hell more can I do?"

"You can give it some thought," Vince suggested. "You see, we already know about the payment you received from the Contech Corporation just prior to Miss Lee's disappearance. I don't think it'd be too difficult to prove that their check was payment for Miss Lee's participation in that romantic cruise to nowhere." Vince sifted through the papers and extracted a copy of Contech's check. "That is your signature, isn't it?" He displayed the copy with Giuliani's endorsement.

"So what the fuck does that prove?"

"It proves a lot, scumbag," Tommy growled. "It means that you got paid to set up this romantic get-together in the first place; that's lie number one. It proves that you knew all about where Trixie Lee was and who she was with; that's lie number two. And from what we know so far, it makes pretty good sense that you were the last person who saw her alive, and that makes you our number-one suspect in her murder."

"Murder?" Giuliani stiffened in his chair. "Who the hell says she was murdered? Where'd you get the idea that she was even dead?"

"We've got no reason to suspect that she isn't," Vince told him. "Just about everybody else who went out on the love boat ended up dead, and Miss Lee's been missing since it happened. Just what are we supposed to think?"

"My theory is she was holding out on you," Tommy offered. "It wouldn't be the first time a pimp iced his whore for money."

Giuliani searched the ceiling. "She's not dead," he said finally.

"You know that for a fact?" Vince asked.

"She as alive as you or me."

"Are you saying that you know where she is?" Vince asked him.

Giuliani nodded.

"So, why did you tell us you hadn't seen her?" Tommy persisted. "Don't you know it's a crime to impede a police investigation? Harboring a material witness in a homicide case is a punishable offense, scumbag. You can end up doing serious time for that."

"Don't jerk me around, please," Giuliani said. "We can either talk now or we can wait until my lawyer gets here. It's up to you. You're not going to get anything out of me with threats like that."

"We don't want to threaten you, and we know you want to do the right thing here," Vince assured him. "Now, it's to your advantage to tell us where Miss Lee is, and it could save her life. We have reason to believe she's in a lot of danger."

"Why the hell do you think she ran in the first place?" Giuliani asked. "She knew her life was in danger the minute she read about Cherry's murder. She's a whore, but she isn't stupid. She had to figure she was gonna be next."

"Well, she'll be a lot safer under police protection than she is out there alone," Vince observed. "Wanta tell us where we can pick her up?"

"First, I need assurances that I won't be prosecuted," Giuliani said flatly.

"You should've thought about that when you lied to us in the first place," Tommy pointed out.

"I was scared, confused. Trixie made me promise I wouldn't tell anyone where she was hiding."

"That kind of loyalty gets me right here—" Tommy held his heart. "There is honor among scumbags, after all."

"I'm not asking you to like it, I'm just telling you to believe it," Giuliani said.

"I'm listening," Vince told him. "Talk to me."

Giuliani squared his shoulders and exhaled loudly. "Okay, I can tell you she was on that boat with Cherry and a couple of rich old guys. Who they were, she never told me and I wasn't really interested."

"How about telling us something we don't know," Tommy goaded him.

"I'm going as fast as I can, gimme a break here," Giuliani howled.

"Take your time." Vince gave Tommy a cautionary glance.

"She gets back from the trip and tells me she needs a couple of days off before she goes back to work. Fine with me. I got other irons in the fire, if you know what I mean. Anyway, the next time I hear from her, she's calling me from a pay phone in a gas station in upstate New York at three in the morning, pleading with me to come and get her . . ." He paused. "Either of you got a cigarette?"

Vince handed him an unfiltered Camel and lit it. "Where about in upstate New York did this call come from?" he asked.

"Brewster, I think." Giuliani took a deep drag of the cigarette and blew a gray cloud of smoke toward the ceiling. "She told me she was running from some guy who was trying to kill her."

"She happen to mention his name?" Vince asked.

"She probably didn't know it. Someone in Trixie's line of work meets a lot of sickos. She don't stick around to ask their names when they start getting weird, man."

"Was that usual for her, traveling all the way to upstate New York for a trick?" Tommy asked.

Giuliani shrugged. "Who the hell knows? All I know is I humped my ass outa bed and drove all the way up there to get her. She was real scared, man, shaking and crying like a baby all the way back to the city. I took her to my place, scored her some dope, and let her spend the night."

"That where she is now?" Tommy asked.

Giuliani reached into his jacket pocket and removed his wallet. He thumbed through the items inside, extracted a well-worn business card, and handed it to Vince. "That's my lawyer. I've said as much as I'm gonna say until he tells me I'm walking out of this place with immunity."

Outside, Vince checked his telephone messages while Tommy called Giuliani's lawyer: a call from Connie. He lifted the receiver and began to dial when C.O. Sweeney appeared in the squad-room door and signaled to him. "Can I see you in my office for a minute?"

"Yes sir?" Vince asked, shutting the door behind him.

Sweeney handed a typewritten bulletin across his desk. "This is still unofficial, but I thought you'd like to see it anyway."

Vince scanned the sheet; a brief memorandum from the office of the mayor to the police commissioner requesting that the Thirty-seventh Precinct be removed from the list of houses being considered for shutdown. "Does this mean we're still in business?" he asked, barely able to conceal a delighted grin.

"For the time being," Sweeney replied. "I know you probably won't believe this, but I'm happy for you all."

Vince shrugged uncertainly. "I never thought there was anything personal in it, Lieutenant."

"Oh, it's personal, all right," Sweeney corrected him. "I can't think of anything that's much more personal to a policeman than the house he works out of. I know how devastating these things can be to cops, and it always tears me up inside when I'm moved into another precinct that's slated for extinction."

"Begging for lieutenant's pardon, but why not just apply for another job if you hate it so much?"

Sweeney smiled bitterly. "That's a fair question, Crowley, and I wish I could give you an answer that made sense. I guess the best way I can put it is that there are cops who are good cops and there are cops who are good administrators. I found out a long time ago that I was pretty inept out there on the street where you do your best work. Luckily or unluckily, however you choose to look at it, the department found it out at about the same time I did, and they pigeonholed me into jobs with more and more paperwork and less and less policework until I eventually ended up doing this. I suppose there's a certain antiseptic logic to that. I've gotten so accustomed to paper-shuffling that small tragedies like precinct closings become just another set of statistics to deal with."

"I can't say I envy you your job," Vince offered.

"You get used to it," Sweeney said. "It was tough

at first, but I found it got a little easier after Sergeant Donofrio was assigned to help me."

Vince shuffled uncomfortably.

"It's okay, Crowley." Sweeney smiled. "I know all about that fracas the two of you had last week. Believe me, if I'd thought I could've gotten away with it, I would have done the same thing to him a long time ago."

"Sir?"

"Donofrio's an obnoxious son of a bitch," Sweeney said. "Don't you think I know that? I wouldn't waste a good piss on the dumb bastard if I didn't need him so much. As it is, he's about the only thing that keeps this job from becoming completely intolerable."

Vince just shook his head.

"Donofrio's my armor, my bullet-proof vest," Sweeney explained. "Everybody's got one. Some cops take it out on their wives, some kick the dog. Me, I've got Donofrio, a really low, rank individual who inspires loathing everywhere he goes. The way it works out is that the cops I have to give the shaft to end up hating Donofrio so much they practically forget about me. I can get by a lot easier knowing that a lot of cops aren't spending the rest of their careers spitting every time they hear my name."

Vince nodded. "Will you be staying on here, Lieutenant?"

"Probably not. I only hope Donofrio recovers from that pounding you gave him before the next move," Sweeney said. "I'd hate to go into a new house where they felt sorry for the prick. I need my escape valve, Crowley. You know how it is."

"No sir, I don't," Vince replied. "And I'm real glad about that."

34

NYPD FORM DD-5   October 15, 1989
COMPLAINT FOLLOW-UP

Det. V. Crowley   COMPLAINT #8104

HOMICIDE/MUTILATION, CHERRY DRESSARD

INTERVIEW WITH TRIXIE LEE

1. At 1445 hours above date, accompanied by
   Det. Ippollito, 37 PDU, I visited the Prince
   George Hotel, W. 28th St, Manhattan, for the
   purpose of interviewing Trixie Lee, a known
   prostitute and a material witness sought by this
   command for information related to the above-
   mentioned homicide. Also present was Guy
   Giuliani, alleged to be Miss Lee's pimp.
2. Upon arriving at the above location we were
   directed to Room 912, where we found the
   subject unconscious and in apparent distress . . .

Trixie Lee knotted the elastic ligature, secured the
frayed ends in her teeth, and drew it tightly around
her left biceps until the surrounding skin bulged mot-
tled and purple. She probed the scarred flesh carefully
with her right forefinger until she found an uncollapsed
vein below her armpit, where she inserted the point of
a hypodermic syringe and withdrew a small quantity of

blood. Satisfied that the vein was usable, she placed the tip of the syringe into an aluminum bottle cap at her feet and suctioned the melted liquid inside, intently drawing every precious drop into the clear plastic hypodermic tube, where it diluted the crimson specimen of her blood to pale pink.

If there was pain when she inserted the needle deep into her arm, she didn't feel it. She felt only expectancy and a rush of welcoming relief as the heroin coursed upward through her arteries to the pleasure centers of her brain. There was a brief, nervous shudder as the potent liquid teased her sensitive nerve endings, then a heat wave of release as a protective cloud of numbness swept over her and wrapped her in a glow of forgetfulness, of childlike bliss.

"She's been this way for more than a month now . . ." Trixie could hear Guy Giuliani's faraway voice resonating somewhere in the far recesses of her consciousness, a deep, lumbering cadence that punctuated the incessant throbbing in her head.

"I need a drink . . ." She exhaled a foul breath of air.

"Come out of it, Trixie . . ." Another voice, someone gripping her shoulders, shaking, prodding.

She felt a caressing hand at the back of her neck, lifting her head upward, then the touch of a cold glass on her parched lips, water dripping down her chin. "Where the hell am I?"

"You're okay," the voice reassured her. "You're coming down now. Just rest, don't try to say anything for a few minutes."

"Jeezus!" Tommy looked around the tiny room in the Prince George Hotel in Manhattan and winced. "How can anybody live like this?"

"Man, you really went all out furnishing your woman with luxury accommodations," Vince told Giuliani, shielding his nose from the penetrating smells of dope, decay, and stale urine with a handkerchief. "Remind me not to recommend you to any newcomer who's looking to get into the life."

"What the fuck am I supposed to do, get her a suite at the Plaza?" Giuliani moaned. "She's out all the time. It don't make no difference to her what the place looks like, for chrissake."

Tommy eyed the drug paraphernalia on the nightstand near the bed, empty glassine envelopes, a bent, blackened spoon, bottle caps, a Zippo lighter—the hypodermic. "How much of this shit has she been shooting up?"

Giuliani shrugged. "Who the hell knows? A coupla bags a day, maybe more."

"Expensive habit," Vince observed. "Tough to turn tricks when you're passed out most of the time."

Giuliani shrugged. "She had some bread left over from that Atlantic City gig. It must be gone by now."

"Maybe we oughta get her to a hospital instead of trying to question her here," Tommy suggested.

"I'm okay. I don't want to go to no hospital." Trixie pulled herself painfully to a sitting position and looked at them. "Anybody got a cigarette?"

"I'm Detective Crowley from the Thirty-seventh Precinct in The Bronx," Vince told her, shaking the last Camel from his pack. "This is Detective Ippollito, and of course you know this knight in shining armor." He motioned to Giuliani and lit the cigarette. "If you don't mind, we'd like to ask you a couple of questions."

"My bag, where's my bag?" A sudden spasm of awareness drove Trixie to her knees, searching beneath the bed for her missing pocketbook. "Son of a bitch, the cockscukers got everything I had," she groaned.

"Somebody stole your property?" Tommy asked.

Trixie smiled cynically. "Yeah. Can you imagine that? Thieves in a class establishment like this!" She returned to the bed and sat heavily.

"You up to answering some questions?" Vince asked her.

Trixie looked apprehensively at Giuliani. "I feel like shit. Anybody got any Demerol . . . Tuenol?"

"We're investigating the murder of Cherry Dressard," Vince said. "I understand you and she were friends."

She shuddered involuntarily. "God, that was awful what happened to her."

"Well, that's what we're trying to find out, just what really did happen to her," Vince went on. "Now, we know that the two of you spent a week together on the *Hanky-Panky*, we know who you were with, and we know what you did. What we don't know is what happened to Cherry Dressard between August twenty-first, when the boat docked, and August thirtieth when her body was found. We were hoping you could fill us in."

Trixie shook her head and stared into space. "You don't even have any aspirin?"

"We can take you uptown, Trixie. We can hold you as a material witness and let you go cold turkey in the cage," Tommy told her.

"One way or the other you're gonna tell us what we want to hear," Vince added.

"Oh, man . . ." She sucked deeply on the cigarette and held the smoke in her lungs for what seemed an eternity. "How'd I get myself into all this shit?"

"Do you have any idea who might have killed Cherry Dressard?" Vince asked.

She exhaled a column of pale smoke and extinguished the cigarette angrily in a chipped glass ashtray on the nightstand. "I don't know anything for sure." She shook her head strenuously and breathed into her clasped palms.

"Would it have had anything to do with that night you called Mr. Giuliani from Brewster and asked him to come pick you up?" Vince asked.

She raised her head. Tears were streaming down the hollows of her cheeks. "I dunno, man. Cherry was real good people. She didn't deserve to go that way."

"Mr. Giuliani says that you told him you thought

somebody was trying to kill you. Would that some-body have been the same person who killed Cherry Dressard?" Vince persisted.

"I'm so scared, man . . ."

"It's gonna be all right, Trixie. We won't let any-thing happen to you," Vince told her.

She closed her eyes. "We went out there. It wasn't supposed to be no big deal."

"Just where was it you went, and who did you go with?" Vince broke in.

She took a deep breath. "Cherry calls me and says she's got a date with this guy, a friend of the ones we were out on the boat with. She tells me this guy got a summer place on a lake someplace upstate and he wants me to come along and make it a threesome—a grand apiece for both of us for one night's work. I woulda had to be crazy to turn down money like that—"

"This guy, had you ever seen him before?" Vince broke in. Did you recognize his face from anywhere?"

Trixie shrugged. "He looked familiar, but lots of my clients look familiar. I see a lot of people in my line of work, know what I mean?"

Vince nodded. "So you and Cherry went with him?"

"He picked us up at the Port Authority Bus Termi-nal at around eight o'clock and we drove upstate on the West Side. It took about two hours to get there."

"To get where?"

"I dunno for sure, up in the country someplace."

"A summerhouse on a lake, right?"

"Right. It was a big house way back in the woods, on a hill with a path leading down to the water."

"Do you remember the name of the lake?" Vince asked.

She shook her head. "It was just a lake, you know."

"A big lake?"

"I think so. It was dark when we got there so it was hard to tell. Anyway, we get there and we go inside. This motherfucker lights a fire in this fireplace and brings out a bag of coke and we all do some lines, then he pours us drinks and disappears into the bedroom. He's gonna get into something more comfortable, he says." She smiled bitterly. "He got comfortable okay."

"Did he try to hurt you?" Vince asked.

"Not right then. He came out of the bedroom dressed up like . . . I don't know. It woulda been funny if it wasn't so scary, man." Her eyes grew wide. "He had this kinda crown on his head, like he was a king or something . . . and these huge necklaces hanging across his chest. His face and shoulders were painted white— smears like, I think, dots and splotches. I'd had a lot of coke, so I don't really remember it exactly. And he's got a knife, I remember the knife."

Vince shot a glance at Tommy. "Did he menace you with the knife, Trixie? Did you see him stab Cherry with it?"

"He started moaning and groaning, a lotta weird mumbo-jumbo shit like in those old Tarzan movies on TV. And he's dancing all around us, shoving the knife in our faces, pulling it back and laughing like a crazy son of a bitch. I mean, I seen a lot of weird things since I been in this business. I seen guys who are into pain, golden showers, dog collars, even bowel movements. I thought I was ready for anything, but this was something different. Cherry saw it too."

"Was it something he said to you? Did he threaten you in any way?" Vince probed.

"No, it wasn't nothing he said." She shook her head. "It's hard to explain. It's like all of a sudden we both knew that this guy was evil. It was like we knew something terrible was gonna happen if we didn't get outa there quick."

"How did you escape?"

Trixie wrapped her arms around her waist and began shivering. "I'm starting to get strung out, man. Can you give me a little something to tide me over?"

"Just a couple more questions and we'll take you to

a hospital, Trixie. They'll get you fixed up real good in there," Vince promised her.

"You're not going to put me in no cell?"

"Promise, Trixie." Vince nodded.

"I was on the methadone, but this thing really got me all fucked up," she explained. "I can get straight again if I get the chance."

"I promise I'll get you in a program, okay? After that it'll be up to you," Vince told her. "Now, you wanta tell me how you got away from this guy? Did Cherry try to get away too?"

"I dunno about Cherry. I know we both started running, but I lost sight of her after I got out the front door. I just kept on running, through trees, bushes. I got my legs and face all cut up from them." She pointed to recent scars on her forehead and both cheeks. "I don't even know whether he was following me or not. All I know is I've never been that scared before in my life."

"How'd you get to the telephone booth?"

"I made it to a main road and hitched a ride into town," Trixie told him. "I got outa there so fast I didn't even have time to take my purse, so I had to borrow a dime from the owner of the station to make the collect call." She looked around the ramshackle room. "I lost all my shit then and I lost all my shit now. This is one lousy, fucking life, man. I wish to hell I was out of it."

"Keep pushing that stuff into your veins and you will be," Tommy observed.

"Being high's the only time I don't want to die." she responded softly.

"You're gonna live and you're gonna get straight," Vince said. "But first you got to help us get this creep who snuffed Cherry. Now you told us you didn't see her after you left the house. Did you hear anything? Did you have any reason to suspect that he might have been attacking her inside?"

"I was just running. I couldn't hear nothing but my

own heart beating and the noise of my breathing. I never been out in the woods before, man. That was almost as scary as he was."

Vince took her hand and squeezed it reassuringly. "Now I'm gonna want you to look at some pictures when we get you to the hospital so we can get an I.D. We got an idea who this guy is, but we're gonna need you to put a name on him."

She nodded. "He's got a name all right. He told us who he was when he walked out of that bedroom. He said 'Look at me and adore me before you die, women. I am the god Chango!' "

35

CONNIE COULD FEEL VINCE TOSSING IN THE BED NEXT to her, breathing unevenly, grinding his teeth. She eyed the clock on the nightstand: 4:45. "Why don't you just go on in?" she suggested to him through the blackness. "You're not going to sleep until you follow up on this thing."

Vince rolled over and put his arm around her. "I'm sorry, Connie. I guess I'm too involved in this case to do much of anything else right now."

"I noticed," Connie said, recalling their unsuccessful attempt at lovemaking a few hours earlier.

"It's just that I can feel it happening. I can smell it," he told her. "It's hard to explain.

Connie switched on the lamp by the bed. "You don't have to explain it to me. I've chased down a few good stories in my time. I know what it feels like." She walked to the kitchen and placed a kettle of water on the burner. "Just go on up there and get this thing solved once and for all so you and me can get back to having some old-fashioned, down and dirty sex for a change."

"Um, sounds good." Vince pulled on his pants and dialed Tommy at home. "Come on, lazy bones," he said when Tommy answered groggily. "Get dressed and meet me at Mercy Hospital in half an hour. We got a lake in Westchester to find."

Tommy moaned. "It's the middle of the night, Vince. You telling me this can't wait another coupla hours? I was just having a real significant dream."

265

"Yeah, well, this is a real significant case, so get your ass outa bed and meet me there."

"Tommy unhappy?" Connie asked as she handed Vince a steaming cup of black coffee.

"He was having another significant dream," Vince answered. "Tommy's always having significant dreams: snakes, tunnels, bananas, everything's got some deep, hidden meaning to him. One time he dreamed he was a loaf of Wonder Bread. He confided to me that he thought it had to do with fears about his masculinity. You know, waiting for the yeast to rise and all that stuff."

"Maybe he was just hungry."

"That's what I told him." Vince drained his cup and kissed Connie lightly on the lips. "Gotta go."

"Pick up a loaf of bread on your way home," she yelled after him as he exited into the hallway. "Maybe it'll help our sex life."

"Very funny." He took the elevator to the downstairs parking garage and drove to Mercy Hospital.

Tommy was waiting for him when he got there. They retrieved Trixie Lee from the fourth-floor psychiatric unit, signed her out against medical advice and the protestations of the night nurse, and deposited her in the rear seat of the unmarked patrol car.

"This the road you took out of town?" Tommy asked Trixie as he turned onto the Major Deegan Expressway heading north.

"I think so, it was dark," she replied sleepily.

"It's dark now," Tommy pointed out. "Just looka that moon, willya? It's like one of those Turkish sabers, know what I mean?"

Vince observed the waxing crescent moon from the window on the passenger's side of the car: a pale sliver of white in the slowly lightening eastern sky. "Don't worry about trying to identify anything until we get you to Brewster and that gas station. From there on we're gonna be depending on you," he told her.

Trixie slept most of the way. The sky had turned to

a dusky slate blue by the time Vince shook her awake at the outskirts of Brewster. They found the service station at the foot of the Brewster ramp, re-created the telephone call to aid Trixie's recollection, and began to retrace her movements from the night she had called Guy Giuliani. After several false starts they found themselves on a single-lane rural highway that led inland from Route 84.

"This is it, I'm sure," Trixie proclaimed resolutely from the backseat. "We go about ten minutes on this and it becomes a dirt road."

Vince eyed the signs posted along the side of the road listing various access routes to Candlewood Lake. "This is Connecticut, Trixie. You didn't tell me you were in Connecticut."

"How the hell was I supposed to know where we were?" she groaned. "I told you it was dark."

"So how come you remember this particular road?" Tommy challenged her.

"The bumps. Feel them bumps?"

Vince realized that the seams in the road were creating a steady, jarring rhythm of the floorboards of the car. "Not bad." He grinned at her. "You would've made a pretty good detective."

"Try taking those jolts with a stomach full of tequila and Methedrine. You'd remember the rough spots too," she said wryly.

The pavement of the road deteriorated into a painful sequence of potholes, then it disappeared altogether beneath a twisting ribbon of muddy tires tracks and pools of murky water as they drove slowly beneath the thickening forest canopy toward the lake.

"God, this is really beautiful," Tommy said as they bumped along the road, observing the explosion of red and orange foliage around them, spiraling leaves that fell softly to earth and danced in their backwash. "Someday I'm gonna have myself a place up here in the country like this."

"Think about what you're saying," Vince said, shifting his weight uncomfortably in the passenger seat. "Everything out there in those woods and underneath that ground is eating everything else. Are you sure you want to be a part of that?"

Tommy shook his head and continued driving until they emerged onto an open expanse of leaf-strewn lawn that rolled downhill toward a cedar cottage over-looking the water. A gray Mercedes sedan was park-ing unobtrusively in the bushes by the side of the house.

"That's the place," Trixie said excitedly. "And that's the car he drove us up here in."

"Okay, this is as far as we go." Vince raised his hand and Tommy stopped the car at the edge of the forest. "Let's back up and find ourselves a telephone so we can call the local constabulary and get some assistance out here."

Tommy turned the car around and headed back toward the main road. "We gonna have to put up with some local hayseed telling us what we can and can't do?"

Vince shrugged. "We're out of our jursidiction here, partner, you know that. Maybe they'll be so impressed by a couple of big-city detectives they'll forget that what we're doing will probably be technically illegal."

They were in luck. A fresh-faced Connecticut pa-trolman who looked about fourteen years old to Vince arrived at the entrance to the dirt road shortly after Tommy's call from a pay phone they had found along-side the highway. "I'm Officer Reg Halpin." He stepped from a spanking-clean blue-and-white and introduced himself. "What brings you fellows up here to the boonies?"

"Homicide investigation," Vince told him. "We have good reason to feel that a suspect is holed up in that house out there by the lake."

Patrolmen Halpin blinked. "Homicide? Jeez, maybe we should get some help out here."

"I don't think that'll be necessary," Vince assured

him. All he needed was an army of wide-eyed, gung-ho locals charging in with bazookas and screwing up a clean operation. "We don't expect any trouble from this guy. We're just after some information, and we didn't want to step on any jurisdictional toes. For now, I'd appreciate it if you could keep an eye on our material witness while my partner and me ask him a couple of questions."

Halpin looked uncertainly at Trixie, seated in the rear seat of the squad car. "Maybe I should be present when you go in there. I think that's the way it's supposed to work."

"You bet." Vince put a fraternal arm around Halpin's shoulder and steered him to the car. "To be honest with you, though, we're concerned that she'll panic and bolt. You know how skittish these high-toned New York whores can be."

Halpin nodded knowingly. It was apparent to Vince that he'd never seen a New York hooker and was excited at the prospect. "You're not planning on making any arrests, are you?"

"No way." Vince opened the rear door and assisted Trixie out onto the macadam roadway. "This's Patrolman Halpin, Trixie. He's gonna keep an eye on you for the time being."

"I'll have to follow you out," Halpin told him.

"Fair enough." Vince shot a sidelong glance at Tommy. "Just keep on your toes in case we need some backup in there, okay?"

Halpin grinned. "You can count on me." He deposited Trixie in the rear seat, climbed back into his blue-and-white, and followed them through the woods until they reached the entrance to the cottage and parked.

Without saying a word, Vince motioned for Halpin to remain in his car and for Tommy to cover the rear of the cottage, then he walked to the front door and knocked loudly. There was no response. He knocked again, still no answer. He signaled Halpin to keep an eye on the door and walked slowly around the cottage, peering inside through unwashed windowpanes at a series of seemingly unoccupied rooms until he reached the back of the house. "Looks like nobody's home," he said to Tommy, who was standing by the back door.

"Somebody owns that car out there," Tommy said. "What do we do now, wait?"

As Vince surveyed the property, his eyes followed the spacious lawn downward to the water's edge, where a wooden boathouse protruded from the shore out into the lake. "I dunno, partner. I think the son of a bitch is in there and he's just not answering." He tried the latch on the rear door, found it locked, wrapped his arm with his jacket, and broke one of the murky panes of glass with his elbow.

"What about Halpin?" Tommy asked as Vince released the inside latch and opened the door slowly inward.

"He's busy getting to know Trixie." Vince removed his revolver and held it above his right shoulder as he stepped cautiously inside and flattened himself against the wall, directing Tommy to follow with a wave of his hand. He stood momentarily and inspected the room as Tommy shut the door behind them. The living room was spacious: knotty-pine-paneled walls adorned with dusty bookshelves and rusting antique rifles. A moth-eaten moose head and a frozen, laquered trout mounted above the picturesque fieldstone fireplace stared silently out at the carelessly arranged braided rugs and comfortable furniture.

Tommy moved laterally along the periphery of the room until he reached the first of several closed doors along the wall. He flattened himself beside it, released the doorknob with his free hand, and kicked it open. "Clear," he shouted back at Vince, training his revolver on the empty interior.

Vince edged along the wall in the opposite direction, stopping at another closed door. He could feel his heart beginning to race as he fingered the cold brass latch. He shoved the balky door inward and scanned the empty area inside across his trembling gunsight. "Clear," he breathed with relief.

A third door was an empty bathroom and a fourth a darkened stairway leading downstairs. Vince found a light switch on the outside wall, lit the area below, and signaled Tommy to follow him as he carefully descended the creaky wooden steps to the basement landing. The air was thick there, seeping from dark underground crevasses that held the smells of soil and concrete and decaying wood, the oily aroma of diesel fuel, the sick-sweet odor of rotting flesh . . . maybe a dead cat, a trapped squirrel . . .

"It looks empty," Tommy whispered, standing next to him at the bottom of the stairs.

"Be careful." Vince pointed to an open doorway at the rear and began slowly moving toward it, negotiating through random heaps of discarded trash scattered along the floor as he went. A sudden clatter of metal froze him in his tracks, pinning him instinctively against the damp concrete wall. Both he and Tommy leveled their revolvers at the sound as two well-fed rats scurried through a pile of scrap metal on the floor and disappeared into a crack in the wall. Vince let his knotted shoulders sag and smiled nervously across the basement at Tommy, who was pinned to the far wall, sweat glistening on his forehead.

Tommy took a deep breath, stepped over the collected rubbish gingerly, and continued on until he had reached the open door. He motioned for Vince to cover him, crouched, and lunged inside with his gun extended in both hands. "Jesus! Oh, God . . ." He stumbled backward, gagging.

Vince was at his side in an instant, raking the room with his revolver until his eyes became accustomed to the darkness and focused on the grisly scene inside. "Holy shit," he muttered softly. "What the hell is this?"

"Looks like some kinda torture chamber," Tommy said, shivering involuntarily at the sea of dried blood and gore that lined the concrete walls. He held a handkerchief to his face as the smell of putrefaction filled his nostrils. "Just look at that, willya?"

A pair of heavy manacles dangled from chains embedded in the concrete wall, pointing downward to a menacing array of bloodstained leather straps and switches spread across the floor. The headless, rotting carcass of a chicken rested in the corner, covered by swarming flies. A chipped ceramic dish filled with coins, tobacco, seashells, and wispy strands of human hair stood nearby, along with a rectangular black cloth that held a residue of maggot-infested entrails and the shriveled, blackened remains of amputated human fingers and toes.

Vince was shaking in spite of his determination to remain in control of his emotions. "It looks like he was slaughtering more than animals in here," he said to Tommy through clenched teeth.

"Looks like . . ." Tommy spotted something leaning against the wall and pointed it out to Vince. "And it looks like that was what he used to slaughter them."

Vince felt his blood run cold. It was the double-bladed ax of Chango.

36

A STRONG BREEZE GUSTED OFF THE LAKE AND THEY inhaled it gratefully, cleansing themselves. "Better go out front and tell Halpin to call his chief and get us some backup out here," Vince told Tommy. "Tell him to bring dusters, a forensics team, the whole shmear. And somebody who's familiar with the terrain around this place. Chances are we'll probably have to flush the son of a bitch out of these woods."

He eased himself down by the side of the cottage after Tommy had gone and stretched his legs in the tall grass. What time was it? 0826 hours. The day had barely started and he felt like he'd just finished a double shift. The macabre scene in the basement had confirmed his worst suspicions, but it had also left him drained. He felt his age, and that had been happening more and more in recent days. He knew there had been a time back in the early days of his career when something like this would have simply pumped him up, got his adrenaline flowing, and heightened his excitement for the chase ahead. Now all he felt was exhaustion, and an inexplicable sadness.

He stared out over the lake to the shoreline beyond. A panorama of brilliant fall foliage rose from the water's edge to an almost-cloudless sky. What was it about those days that had been different? he wondered. He had been a young man, and young men felt everything more strongly; they were naïve enough to believe that they could really make a difference. Here in the surrounding beauty of the lake, Vince realized that his outrage and his passion were diffused in the immensity of sky and water, the gently rolling hills. He knew that he could no longer love and hate the way he had before. Years of pounding in the streets and alleyways of New York had taken their toll, they had numbed him.

"You okay partner?" Tommy had returned and was standing next to Vince.

"Yeah, just a little tired."

Tommy checked his watch. "Well, you better relax now while you got a chance. It looks like we're in for a long day here."

Vince could hear the sound of wildfowl in the distance. The shriek of a loon echoing from the hillsides . . . The faint hum of an outboard motor. A faraway boat was gliding across the lake like a tiny water bug, returning from an early-morning fishing.

Vince followed the path of the small boat as it skimmed the glassy surface of the water, creating tiny ripples that spread behind its wake in rhythmic swells. He scanned the shoreline. "You see any other boathouses in this part of the lake, Tommy?"

Tommy shielded his eyes against the sun and surveyed the area. "Uh-uh, just the one down at the bottom of the hill there."

"Then, unless I miss my guess, that boat is headed right here."

"Holy shit!" Tommy's eyes grew wide.

"Just stay calm," Vince warned him. "If we can see him, chances are he can see us too, especially if we move around too much. Just ease around to the front of the house and tell whoever shows up what's going down. I'm headed down to that boathouse to meet him when he gets here."

Tommy crouched and moved slowly away, staying low against the wall of the cottage until he was safely out of sight. Vince eased his body down into the tall grass, turned onto his stomach, and began crawling slowly down the hill on his hands and knees, his eyes riveted on the approaching boat, until he was safely inside the boathouse. He lifted his .38 snub-nose revolver from its holster at his hip and released the safety, steadying his elbows on the wooden floor of the landing as the whine of the outboard motor grew in intensity, propelling the boat closer and closer to the shore. He released the safety catch and felt his muscles tense as the engine suddenly died and the boat made a lazy arc into the boathouse.

"Stay right where you are, Santiago!" Vince stood and trained his gunsight on the seated congressmen as a horde of Connecticut police cascaded down the hill behind him.

Santiago was on his feet in an instant, propelling the boat backward into the open water with a wooden oar in an unbelievable display of strength and catlike agility. "That's as far as you go, scumbag," Vince shouted. "Make one more move and I blow your head off!"

Tommy pushed his way through the throng of uniformed policemen. "Hey, I'm sorry, partner," he said breathlessly. "I tried to keep the locals up there, but the dumb bastards just kept on coming." He eyed Santiago, standing motionless in the back of the drifting craft. "Whatta we do now, swim out there and get him?"

An overweight policeman in a captain's uniform arrived. "We can get a police launch here in about fifteen minutes," he puffed.

Vince clenched his teeth. "Fine. Just do me a favor and get your men the hell out of here, okay? There's no telling what this crazy bastard's liable to do if he thinks he's got half the state of Connecticut out here after him."

"Just what is it that you want of me?" Santiago's voice seemed an echo across the span of water separating them.

Vince moved cautiously to the front of the landing as the phalanx of local police began to recede. "We just want to ask you some questions."

"You need pistols, rifles, assault equipment, to ask me questions?" Santiago eyed the heavily armed band to Vince's rear and smiled cynically. "What treatment could I expect if I had committed a crime?"

"Why don't you just paddle that thing in here and we'll talk about it?" Vince urged.

Santiago stood in the boat, seeming taller than Vince remembered him to be. "You have been inside the house, haven't you? You have been down in the basement—"

"It'll go a lot better for you if you just come on in here."

Santiago glowered at him. "Do you think I am unaware of who you are and what you are up to?" he demanded. "Because you are sadly mistaken if you do. I know who you are and what you are. I know your families and I know how to reach them. You would be fools to underestimate my power."

Vince shot a nervous glance at Tommy, who was standing next to him on the landing of the boathouse. "I'm not sure what you mean, Congressman, but if you come on in here, we can work it all out."

"Don't treat me like a fool," Santiago roared across the span of water. "I will not be patronized by the likes of you. Don't you have any idea who it is you're speaking to? Do you think for one minute that you can delude me as to your true purpose?"

Vince cleared his throat and looked uncomfortably behind him at the gaping band of onlooking policemen. "I think I'm speaking to a murderer," he answered softly.

"Murderer?" Santiago threw his head back and laughed, a high-pitched cackle that reverberated off the shimmering surface of the water like a gunshot. "Is that what this is all about—murder?" He placed his hands on his hips and set his jaw. "Just who is it that we are talking about, those who have committed them-selves to the greater glory of the Orisha?" He shook his head. "They are not dead."

"Cherry Dressard, Rafael Rosa: you trying to tell me you never heard of those people?" Vince asked.

Santiago eyed Vince and Tommy with utter disdain. "What consequence are they? What matter is anyone compared with the power of the Palo Mayombe? I could raise them all today if I felt they really mattered."

"Oh, shit, we got a real nut case on our hands," Tommy whispered to Vince.

"Do you think I couldn't hear that?" Santiago de-manded. "Do you think I cannot see into your inner-most thoughts, your most secret fears and desires? That is the power of the Orisha, the all-consuming power of the god Chango. You cannot hide from me any more than you can hide from your own being. I created you and I can destroy you just as easily."

Santiago's voice had become a hollow, discordant clash of cymbals echoing from the caldron of the sur-rounding hills. "You have been given the chance to see, and still you will not see. You cling to the vain, ignorant belief that you have real power over me, that you have dominion over Chango, who created you." He reached into the bottom of the boat, retrieved a five-gallon can of gasoline, and began pouring it over his chest and shoulders. "None is so blind as he who will not see."

"I want to see. Let's not do anything stupid here," Vince interrupted Santiago's incoherent rambling. "Why not put that can down and let us bring you into shore? We'll talk about it and you can show us where we've gone wrong here." He rolled his eyes at Tommy.

Tommy touched his ear, indicating the faint drone of the police launch in the distance. "Keep him talk-ing, man," he whispered through clenched teeth. "They'll be here in a couple of minutes."

Vince studied the path of the drifting boat and noted that it was headed for the shore not far from where they were standing. He signaled the police captain to his rear without averting his gaze from the boat, and he heard the faint rustling of men being deployed along the shoreline. "It's not gonna work, man," he said finally as Santiago emptied the last drops of gasoline on his shirt front and discarded the can in the water. "One way or the other, we have you. At least you've got a chance if you give yourself up to us. Get yourself a good mouthpiece, and who knows what can happen? Do something dumb out there and it's all over, pal. I don't care whether you're Chango or Bonzo or the Holy fucking Ghost. You're dead, man, and when you're dead, you're dead—*finito, muerto*. It's over, know what I'm saying?"

The laugh erupted, deep and guttural. "It's never over, because it never began," he howled. "How can you kill someone who always was—who always will be? What I do, I do because it is convenient, not because I am despairing." He reached into his pocket, extracted a Zippo lighter, and held it aloft.

"Just hold on," Vince pleaded.

"*No!*" Santiago's voice boomed. "Stop your whimpering, you stupid, unimaginative fool! Chango will never die because Chango is not a man; Chango is an idea. Are you so blind that you are incapable of grasping that simple concept? An idea cannot be killed; it grows forever in the minds of men. It becomes a force so powerful that it transcends life and death and the miserable concerns of individual lives. People live only at the whim and sufferance of Chango and they are sacrificed to please him, so that they can become one with him in the body of the Orisha. There is no life, there is no death, there is no good and bad." He lit the lighter and held the flame high above his head, turning momentarily to catch a glimpse of the police launch closing in on him.

"For God's sake . . ." Vince lunged instinctively forward.

His plea was punctuated by the explosion of fumes

and fire as Santiago touched the lighter to his chest. "There is no god but Chango!" His voice resonated through the flames as the entire boat became consumed in a blinding inferno. "And Chango lives forever!"

Vince stood transfixed, his feet anchored to the wooden landing of the boathouse as the dying congressman laughed insanely through the holocaust. The wall of flames parted momentarily, giving him a last horrifying look at Santiago's face. His mouth was twisted into a sneer of pure contempt, his penetrating eyes a blood-red sea of defiance, his tortured death rattle a sneering epithet of hate. Beneath the moans, beneath the sickening crackle of flames and burning flesh, Vince could hear the faraway sound of beating drums.

37

EAMON FLYNN FILLED THE GLASSES TO OVERFLOWING with dark, sudsy beer and slid them in front of Vince and Tommy. "To your health," he toasted them with a glass of his own. "And to absent friends."

"To absent friends." Vince returned the toast and tasted some of the cool, creamy beer.

"To cops," Tommy added resolutely.

"Cops." Everyone drank.

Vince put down the partially filled glass and allowed his gaze to wander down the file of faces lining the bar. Some of the faces were familiar, guys who had been coming to Flynn's for as long as he could remember. Others were a blank to him, faces he had seen but never taken the time to know. Mostly rookies, they were a new breed that wore motorcycle jackets and leather pants, earrings and tattoos and orange hair in spikes and ponytails.

Cops. They were all cops at Flynn's.

Here at Flynn's the old and the new came together in an uneasy collaboration of the spirit, searching for scraps of shared experience to cement the bond between them, however different they appeared. They gathered in the distant hope that someone there would understand and share a glass and pat them on the back and tell them that what they were doing was important; that they were really needed, that they were appreciated.

Cops. None of them would ever be rich.

"None of these guys will ever be rich," he told Tommy.

"No shit?" Tommy smiled wryly.

Vince sipped his drink unenthusiastically. "Quinlan called today and thanked me. Can you imagine that? He thanked me."

"For what?"

"I dunno, doing my job I guess."

"Getting rid of his competition is more like it," Tommy huffed. "Politicians are all a bunch of scumbags."

"The devil to them all!" Eamon hoisted his glass.

"You think they'll find any more bodies when they drag the bottom of that lake?" Tommy asked.

"I wouldn't be surprised, and I wouldn't be surprised if Daniel Keliher was one of them," Vince allowed.

"Fuck all the politicians," Eamon toasted.

"I'll drink to that," Vince toasted back and drained his glass. "But the sons of bitchs always manage to end up on their feet, no matter who else gets hurt."

"Amen, brother," Tommy concurred. "You know who I feel sorriest for in this whole mess? Andrea Falcone, that's who. She had complete trust in that old man of hers and he turned out to be a real scumbag, after all. That fuckin' stinks, man."

"Hey, welcome to the real world, partner. I guess you can't work for a sleazeball outfit like Contech all your life and end up an altar boy," Vince said.

Tommy shook his head. "Too bad we can't tie them into any of this. When you come right down to it, none of those murders would've happened if they hadn't been whoring around Santiago in the first place."

"Don't worry about Contech. They're gonna get everything that's coming to them. Theft, extortion, securities fraud, racketeering . . ." Vince enumerated the charges a federal grand jury had brought against the company.

Tommy placed a fresh twenty on the bar and ordered another round. "What're we gonna do here, get ourselves shitfaced?" Vince asked him.

"You got a better idea?"

Vince shrugged. "Spend your money. You're never gonna be rich anyway."

Cops . . .

Tommy took a slug of the fresh drink and wiped the foam from his lips. "How'd it go out at the hospital today?"

"Okay I guess. Katie was supposed to go home yesterday, but they want to keep her there a day or two more for observation, whatever that means."

"Probably doesn't mean anything. You know these doctors, anything for a buck," Tommy said. "She seem okay to you?"

"I suppose so. She was kind of distantlike, it's hard to explain. It was tough talking to her."

"She's been through a lot. Give her some time, man."

"You're right, " Vince agreed. "Some friends of hers from school went out there and visited her this morning; brought her some presents. That seemed to perk her up a little bit."

Tommy nodded knowingly. "Time . . ."

Across a thousand continents in that fleeting breath of time the Mayombero sniffed the pregnant air with broad black nostrils like glistening caldrons. He prostrated himself on the bare wood floor and folded his arms across the hollow of his chest while unseen hands shrouded his body in a black sheet. Five candles were lit and placed at his head, feet, and shoulders. A doleful chant arose to fill the night sky: *"Chango mani cote, Chango mani cote olle masa . . ."*

The Mayombero felt himself tense as a ritual brew was poured upon the cloth covering him. His eyes rolled back into his head. The muscles of his jaw tightened reflexively behind a froth of spittle. His legs and arms began to jerk convulsively as the spirit of the dead entered his body. He was in a place apart now, a place where the spirits of the sacrifice dwelled: Chango, god of fire and lightning; Oya, his concubine, writhing seductively to the haunting rhythms of *bata* drums, her head enshrouded in a beaded veil of pearls, her open satin gown cascading in her wake, her firm black breasts peaked to erect nipples, spewing the mother's milk of the galaxy across the sky, her naked hips writhing, taunting, tempting her beloved to come lie with her and fill the night with stars, the light of the waxing moon . . .

It streamed through the slats of the venetian blind on Katie's window; shafts of pale-yellow illumination that cut a swath through the semidarkened hospital room and rested like the fingers of a caressing hand across her breasts. The light buoyed her, filled her with excitement that she hadn't experienced in days. She felt her heart beating wildly, blood coursing through her veins and throbbing in her temples like the obsessive beat of the *bata* drums. She stiffened, every muscle, every tendon of her body stretched taut and trembling; her naked arms and shoulders shuddered convulsively to the pulsating rhythms in her head until it seemed she would be torn apart.

She felt the damp kiss of wind on her aroused nipples, and the sweating body of her lover pressed against her, grinding his masculinity into her pliant flesh. She turned toward him and brushed the features of his face with her fingers: eyes that glowed like the Irawo stars in the blackness of his countenance; lips that parted seductively and drew her willingly inside . . . sucking, enveloping, consuming the honey extract of her being in a rush of comets, of penetrating light . . .

Then, as suddenly as it had started, it stopped. Katie took a final convulsive breath, went limp, and sank back into the warmth of the bedsheets, exhausted.

She remained motionless and stared trancelike into the darkness with eyes like live coals, reflecting the cradling fingers of the waxing moon. Her only conscious sensation was the reassuring texture of feather and stone she kneaded lovingly between her thumb and forefinger, the symbol of her beloved, her husband . . . the talisman of Chango.

By the year 2000, 2 out of 3 Americans could be illiterate.

It's true.

Today, 75 million adults...about one American in three, can't read adequately. And by the year 2000, U.S. News & World Report envisions an America with a literacy rate of only 30%.

Before that America comes to be, you can stop it...by joining the fight against illiteracy today.

Call the Coalition for Literacy at toll-free **1-800-228-8813** and volunteer.

Volunteer Against Illiteracy. The only degree you need is a degree of caring.